# Fractured

Gemma Frances

Published by Gemma Frances, 2025.

# Fractured

1st Edition

ISBN: 978-1-7635781-4-2 (paperback)
ISBN: 978-1-7635781-5-9 (e-book)

www.gemmafrances.com[1]
@gemma_frances
Cover design by Musrath Humaira Moon

---

1. http://www.gemmafrances.com

# DEDICATION

*For my husband, who has kept me (just about) sane*
*For the children*

# Fractured

**1.**

## Jenny

Jenny moved her little magnet on the main office board from 'out' to 'in' and grabbed the pile of mail from her pigeonhole before downing a cup of water, stuffing the last couple of bites of her chicken salad sandwich into her mouth, then dashing upstairs to her desk to sift through it all. She was tired, thirsty, and busting for a pee, but she had a mountain of notes to write up before she left for the night and a report that had yet to be written but was due in two days – which left only one day for writing it and another for discussing it with the parents before submitting it to the court. She'd have to text Alex and tell him she wouldn't make it home for dinner. Again. He would be unimpressed.

'Mr Cockburn is on the rampage,' warned Anne, the duty social worker, as she passed by her desk. 'You'd better call him back quickly before he has his solicitor call you.'

Mr Cockburn was fast becoming the bane of Jenny's working life, the one man who could successfully twist her stomach into knots of anxiety at the mere mention of his name, his disdain for womankind evident in his every utterance. There was always one like that on her caseload at any given time.

'Great,' she said. 'Thanks.' She was just about to write 'CALL MR COCKBURN' on a colourful pink post-it and attach it to the edge of her computer screen along with the twenty or so others when she caught sight of another dreaded green file, strategically placed on her keyboard so that she couldn't claim to have missed it. Oh God. Not another one.

'Oh, and Sue said to tell you she's allocated *Season* to you. She would've told you herself only she's got a regional meeting this afternoon and it's got a two-day KPI. I know she agreed in supervision you were at capacity, but she reckons this one's a none-starter anyway - just a visit and a phone call or two and you'll be able to close it off.'

Sure, thought Jenny, like she'd never heard that before. She smiled politely as though she wasn't ready to either have a panic attack, burst into tears, or both. She glanced at the spine of the folder – though their records were all kept predominantly online nowadays, every case still had a paper file to keep originals in like court orders and such.

*Season,* she read. *Summer, Autumn and Winter Season.* Honestly, thought Jenny with a sigh, as she wondered what delightful cocktail of drugs these children's parents had been on when they'd managed to come up with those names, and if she could have some. At least, for once, each of the names were spelled correctly. It could've been worse – it could've been Summa, Ortum and Wynta. Perhaps the mother was still awaiting the coming of Spryng.

'And Belinda Wright called for you before,' Anne continued. 'She's been going on about relinquishing young Kai again. He's broken a window and scratched her car apparently, the little terror, once she found out he'd been lying to her all week about going to school. Sue said you'd better call her too - see if you can persuade her to sustain the placement 'til next week so you have enough time to write that court report and organise a new placement.'

*Sure*, thought Jenny, blinking back tears so that Anne wouldn't get so much as a whiff of weakness - she knew how that had ended for some of the colleagues who had gone before her, and she didn't want to be next in the firing line. 'Sure!' she said aloud, swallowing two paracetamol to stave off the tension headache she could feel building up, before writing out yet another post-it note and powering on her computer. 'I'm onto it.'

*

## Autumn

From the moment Autumn got home from school that afternoon, she knew it was going to be one of those days and her stomach knotted with anxiety. Her mum was on the couch, out for the count, a carelessly discarded bottle of pills beside her, the TV switched onto the cartoon channel in the background playing babysitter. Her stepdad, Kev, was nowhere to be seen and it wasn't hard to hazard a guess as to where he might be or what was likely to be in store for them all once he got back if he'd suffered another loss at the dogs.

Winter's saturated nappy was hanging down to his knees, his toys spread everywhere so that she had to step over them as she carefully negotiated her way towards her little brother, who was conked out on the floor where he'd dropped, fast asleep, a crayon in one hand and a dishevelled Oaty, his comforter in the other. Autumn was just about to lean down and pick him up when her face wrinkled in disgust as her sock landed in something cold, thick, and sticky that had been hidden by one of Winter's soft toys. Vomit.

Autumn retched. She gingerly pulled off her sock and discarded it to be dealt with later, then gently scooped Winter up into her arms and carried him to his cot where she kissed his warm, peachy cheek then placed him down as carefully as she could, nestling Oaty in the crook of his arm. His nappy would have to wait, and besides, she'd looked everywhere and there were no more nappies. She'd have to check her mum's purse and dash to the shop before her sister got home, then get the dinner on before Kev got back from blowing his fortnightly payment on bets and drinking.

She returned to where her mother lay sprawled on the couch and put her cheek as close to her mouth as she could to watch for the rise of her chest and wait for the reassuring exhalation of breath to hit her face. It did. It smelled foul, but Autumn exhaled her relief.

She moved her mum's lighter out of Winter's reach, tipped out the overflowing ash tray, put the safety cap back on her medication and placed the bottle in a high cupboard, then she dampened a towel to scrub the vomit out of the floor before shoving all of Winter's toys into a basket so she could see the carpet once again. She'd found more of his scribbles on the couch and a little at the bottom of the wall, so she used what was left of the baby wipes to attack those, making a mental note to add wipes to her shopping list as well.

At least her mother had had the wherewithal to make sure the front door was locked so Winter hadn't been able to let himself out onto the road again. Last time, Police and Child Protection had come calling not long after he'd been located by a worried bystander who'd found him a couple of streets away dressed in nothing but a saggy nappy, socks and vest on a blowy day, and she knew that both her parents were keen to avoid a repeat visit. She made a mental note to remind her mum yet again to keep her lighter out of reach too before he set the house on fire. She shuddered. She would just bin the lighter - she could always claim Winter had lost it.

The front door opened. Summer was home. Autumn ran to the door to tell her to be quiet in case she woke up their mum or Winter, but the reek of alcohol gave it away before she saw Kev lurch into the porch, his cheeks ruddy, his nose pitted and red. By the looks of him, he'd had another unsuccessful day.

'Look at the fuckin' state of this place! Where's your mother? What the hell's she been doin' all day while I've been out earnin' a livin'?' he demanded.

'Shh, she's sleeping.'

'Sleepin'? At this time? I'll give her bloody sleepin'. *LISA!* Gerrup and sort this place out, you lazy cow!'

'No!' Autumn yelled. 'Just leave her be. Please? I'll tidy up!'

But he lurched unsteadily over to the couch where her mother lay oblivious, picked up the glass of water Autumn had left out for her and threw it over her face and hair. Her mum jumped and spluttered in shock then leapt from the couch. Autumn begged them to stop - prayed for them to stop – as her mum and Kev pushed, shoved and screamed at one other. Soon after, the police arrived.

*

**Jenny**

When Jenny first told people she'd chosen to study for a Social Work degree at university, the reactions of those she knew

5

and loved were not what she might have expected had she chosen any other career, especially when she'd said she wanted to specialise in child protection as opposed to mental health, disability, or older people - which might have been marginally more acceptable in their eyes.

'Don't do it,' Pamela, her mum's social worker friend had warned.

'Why not?'

'Where do I start? The massive caseloads, the stress, the pressure, the lack of support, the deadlines, the paperwork... It's not quite what you'd imagine it might be.'

'But what about making a difference? Keeping children safe?'

Pamela had shaken her head, wearing the sort of sympathetic expression one might reserve for a small child who, despite umpteen warnings, still hadn't fully understood they would get burnt if they touched the hot thing. 'Honestly, save yourself the heartache and run the other way.'

'So, you want to be a child snatcher?' her grandad had asked. 'What on earth for?'

'It's not like that nowadays, Grandad,' Jenny had told him earnestly. 'They're all about keeping families together now.'

'I bloody *hate* social workers,' said the friend she'd gone to school with. 'They ruined my uncle's life. He hadn't even done anything wrong, but he still lost everything! We never see him now.'

Jenny didn't think she could've gotten a less encouraging response if she'd said she'd decided to take up pole-dancing or pursue a life of crime. As if that wasn't discouraging enough, the media was even worse, for never was a social worker referred to in a positive light – they were either branded as incompetent or interfering do-gooders or scapegoated by the press when things went horribly wrong. Nevertheless, Jenny's application had been accepted, and she was about to embark on her dream career.

She'd had all the qualities of youthful optimism in spades. Passionate, motivated, enthusiastic – but most of all she'd cared, and she'd genuinely believed that social work would enable her to make a difference to the lives of children and families in need. This was enough to get her through her studies and placements relatively unscathed. It wasn't until she was about eighteen months in, no longer a sheltered student but well and truly thrust into the thick of her chosen career that she'd realised she'd made a terrible mistake, and that she should have paid greater heed to all those who had tried to warn her.

And now she'd just pulled up outside The Three Seasons. She took a deep breath and picked up her paperwork. *Environmental neglect,* she scribbled, noting the broken living room window and an assortment of household items, empty beer bottles, and rubbish leading from the lawn and obscuring the path to the front door. *Alcohol use.* It was time to go in.

*

### Lisa

Lisa saw the headlights through the living room window and somehow, through the medicated fog of her mind, she just knew it was them. She'd thought she'd done a good enough job convincing the busies that everything was fine, but obviously not given they'd still told the bloody kiddie snatchers to come. Inwardly she cursed Kev. She knew he'd gone too far this time, what with Irina, the old curtain-twitcher next door listening in, but did he take any notice of her? Not anymore.

'Christ, Kev, it's them again! Quick - hide your cans! Autumn, tidy round for me. Summer, you too, love.'

The girls whipped into action, and even Kev was quick enough to get off the couch and do as he was asked without argument for once. Lisa stubbed out her cigarette, stuffed the remnants of their takeaway into the already overflowing bin, nudged the dog into the kitchen and closed the door. Then she flicked on the cartoons to distract Winter and told the girls to get on with their homework – all in the space of a few moments before the dreaded knock on the door. She scanned the living room to make sure she hadn't missed anything. It wasn't great, but it wasn't terrible either, thanks to Autumn's whip around earlier. Either way, it would just have to do.

'Say nothin'!' Kev warned, before answering the door with what was meant to be a smile but looked more like a grimace. 'Come in, pet,' he told the social worker.

Jenny looked to be around mid-thirties, her long hair highlighted and swish, her waist tight. It was obvious she'd never had a baby in her life. Did any of these bloody idiots even have kids? If not, who the hell were they to come in and tell her what to do with hers?

Kev offered her a drink which she politely declined, not that Lisa could blame her judging by the tip of the place. He gestured for her to find a spot on the sofa as she scanned the living room with an eagle eye and smiled. Jenny perched gingerly on the edge of her seat, an ear on the dog they could all hear scratching from the next room, one eye on Kev, and one eye on the nearest exit. For a moment. Lisa realised how important an awareness of the nearest exit must be in Jenny's line of work, especially when dealing with someone like Kev. She hoped he wouldn't kick off.

'Scoot,' he said to the girls. 'Go and play with your brother.' They didn't hesitate to obey, and Autumn ushered an eager Winter along with them. Thank God for Autumn. Lisa didn't know what she'd do without her.

'Hello,' said Jenny. 'You must be Lisa Season? And you must be Kevin Black? I'm Jenny Hurst, a Social Worker from Dunstonborough Child Protection. Do you have any idea why I'm here?'

'Not at all, pet, everything's grand. Enlighten us,' Kev lied.

'Well, there's been a report - two on the same day, actually. While you might be able to hazard a guess as to who the reporters might be, their identity is protected by law so I can't disclose that information to you. One of the reports is that since our last involvement with your family a few months back, the girls still haven't been attending school consistently or are often turning up late, sometimes without lunch. The other is that police were called to an incident here earlier this afternoon, yet the last we heard you two were separated. Can you tell me any more about that?

How much did she know? thought Lisa, wondering how much she could tell without telling, giving just enough information to get children's services off her back.

'Now, I realise this isn't your first rodeo,' Jenny continued, 'and that no-one likes a knock on the door from one of us at the best of times. I realise it can be intrusive and uncomfortable. But just to be transparent, I'm going to take notes of our conversation that will be recorded on your children's files. In a minority of cases these notes get used in the children's court, but they most often simply form the basis of our assessment and record keeping. Shall we start with you, Lisa? Kevin, would you mind stepping out while Lisa and I have a chat?'

Kevin exhaled loudly as though to say he didn't see the point of all this palaver, then gave Lisa a menacing stare that only she could see on his way out. Shit, thought Lisa, sending up a silent prayer to whoever might be listening that she wouldn't lose her kids.

# 2.

**Autumn**

Autumn watched anxiously as Winter tottered over to their mum, and a moment later there was a gentle knock on her bedroom door and in walked the social worker, who smiled at her empathetically. Autumn scowled. She didn't want to like her, her *mum* didn't want her to like her, but it was almost impossible not to. Her smile was warm, her eyes were kind, and she put her in mind of how her mum used to look on one of those rare occasions she had taken the time to do her hair and make-up. The last time was during one of her break-ups from Kev, when she'd gotten their Aunty Kate to look after them all for the night then went for a night out in town with her friends. She wished she could see her mum like that again.

'What do *you* want?' she said.

Jenny perched on a stool in the corner of the room, and after making a bit of small talk about their day and taking an interest in certain items in their bedroom, she fixed Autumn in her steady gaze. 'Why do *you* think I'm here?'

Autumn said nothing.

'Last time,' said Summer, 'you guys came because Winter got out of the house.'

'That's right. Why do you think we're here this time?'

'Because the police came?' Summer ventured.

'Yes. Do you know why the police came?'

'Because mum and Kev had a fight - but I didn't see it because I was at my friend's house, but Autumn was there. Winter was fast asleep - she had to put him to bed because mum was sleeping. She's always sleeping. She takes tablets that help her go to sleep, but sometimes they make her throw up.'

Autumn threw Summer a look as if to say don't go too far, but being three years younger and not really understanding the potential implications, she took no notice.

'Then Autumn said that Kev threw a glass of water at mum because he was drunk, and the house was a tip again. It's not even just mum's fault - *he* makes it a tip too. Actually, Winter's the worst – he gets his toys everywhere, so if you're here about that then you'll just have to blame Winter.'

'I haven't come here to blame anyone for anything,' said Jenny. 'And toddlers *can* be rather messy. Do you girls know what my job is?'

'To take children away from their parents,' Autumn snapped, and Summer's hazel eyes widened with a combination of shock and guilt as she realised she'd probably already said too much.

'Sometimes that does happen,' Jenny nodded, 'but not as often as people might think. Actually, our main job is to make sure kids have a home to grow up in where they feel safe. Our next job is to do our best to support families to keep them together and help make that happen. If ever we *do* have to separate children from their parents, they usually stay with other family members. Foster care is the last choice, and we rarely make those decisions without helping children to understand why and letting them have a say in what they want to happen.'

Yeah, yeah, thought Autumn. 'Why did you make Mum kick Kev out last time, then?'

'Because we couldn't have him in the home and have your mum and you three kids still be safe at the same time.'

'Does that mean you're going to kick him out again?' Summer asked hopefully.

'Maybe.' That was a conversation for Jenny and her manager, and for Jenny and Lisa to have later. 'What do you girls think about that? Do you think your home is a safe place when Kev is in it?'

No, thought Autumn. 'I don't know,' she said.

'What about you, Summer?'

Summer looked to Autumn. 'I don't know either.'

'That's ok,' said Jenny, 'but sometimes, when kids don't know, the grown-ups around them have to figure it out and make that decision. And no-one's saying that if Kev left home, he would have to leave forever - he would just have to show that if he's in the home with you three and your mum, you can all still be safe with him there.'

Huh, thought Autumn. She recalled all the times she'd heard him telling her mum he promised he'd change, and all the times her mum had believed him and given him another chance. Whilst things were always better to start with, in the end, nothing was ever any different. It had been the same story with her dad.

'Autumn, that's why it's important you to try to tell me as much as you can remember about what happened from when you got home from school today until the police came round tonight, so that we can make the best decision to keep you all safe. Do you think you can do that?'

As Autumn looked into Jenny's warm blue eyes, it was on the tip of her tongue to tell her. She was tired of pretending. So tired. But she thought of Kev. She thought of her mum, and her mum's terror that they might be taken away from her. She needed them, and they needed her. Eyes downcast and her mouth set, she shook her head.

'Ok,' Jenny nodded. 'Could you tell me what Summer meant when she said you told her Kev had thrown a glass of water at your mum?'

Autumn opened her mouth to say something, but nothing came out. She couldn't do it. She shook her head.

'*Did* you say that?'

Autumn was silent.

'How has it been for you since Kev came home?' Jenny ventured.

Awful, thought Autumn. Even worse than last time, and last time had been worse than the time before. She could see the concern in Jenny's eyes as she looked at them both, patiently awaiting – hoping - for a response. It was genuine, Autumn realised. Her concern was genuine. But she said nothing, because she was afraid of what would happen next if she did. And, taking her lead from her big sister, Summer said nothing either.

*

**Jenny**

**Initial Assessment - Summarise the protective concerns:**

*Domestic Violence,* Jenny typed, recalling her previous afternoon's visit to Season and providing a detailed context and supporting information for each heading in line with what she'd observed on her visit.

*Marijuana use*

*Parentification*
*Inadequate supervision*
*Parental mental health difficulties*
*Aggression/anger management issues*
*Medication misuse*
*School absenteeism*
*Trauma history (parents).*

**Record your observations of the family's strengths and safety factors:**

Jenny chewed her fingernail. Hmm. That was more difficult.

*A positive, loving connection was observed between mother and children.*

*Police did not identify any criminal offence, breach, or take any criminal action.*

*The situation between the parents had calmed upon arrival.*

*No visible injuries were sighted upon either party.*

*The parents denied problematic alcohol use or current domestic violence.*

*The children generally appeared healthy and well.*

*The parents acknowledged some of the protective concerns.*

*The children made no disclosures of harm.*

*The parents were willing to engage with support services.*

*The parents were open to cleaning up the property...*

'How did you go with Season?' Sue, Jenny's boss asked between meetings. 'I'm guessing there was nothing in it for us and that you're ready to close it off?'

'Actually,' said Jenny, 'I was hoping to catch you about that. I reckon we should stay open a bit longer this time for monitoring and supports. I just don't think Mum is demonstrating enough protective capacity – she's recently taken Kev back, and there's already been another domestic incident between them. He'd obviously been drinking, the kids aren't attending school consistently, and the place was an absolute mess. I also saw a joint they'd forgotten to hide – Kev says he's been using medicinally for a workplace back injury. It makes me wonder what else they're hiding.'

'Everyone's on the happy baccy nowadays, Jenny, you know that. It's not enough. I mean, I get why you're concerned, but where's our evidence? Did the kids make any disclosures?'

Jenny exhaled. 'No,' she said. 'Not as such. Summer said Autumn told her that Kev had thrown a glass of water at Mum, but Autumn wouldn't confirm it.' Jenny didn't doubt there had been more - much more - that been left unsaid by the two girls.

'Well, the police didn't get anything from them either. The DV Prevention Order has expired and Mum doesn't want to get a new one, so all we have is a neighbour who overheard a verbal argument between a couple – not ideal given their history, but it's not a crime. And we know this neighbour doesn't like the family and wants them out, so she's not exactly our most reliable source. And yes, the house is a bit of a tip, but you know what the Magi would say about that – hire a skip.'

Yes, thought Jenny, without addressing the root cause of why they're living like that in the first place, so that within weeks of the skip's removal, the house would be exactly the same all over again.

'Summer said Mum's been sleeping a lot, which I suspect is probably why they haven't been going to school. And I get the impression that unless Autumn is around, Winter is pretty much fending for himself - which is obviously how he got out of the house last time. Anything could happen to him! I'm worried about the mum's mental health too - it's like she's just given up this time and resigned herself to living this life.'

'I know, Jenny,' said Sue sympathetically, 'I know as well as you do that the quality of life for these poor kids is pretty wretched. But is it enough for us to justify taking the matter to the children's court? I don't think so. I mean, Police couldn't identify any offence because Mum kept schtum about the whole thing. Her hair and t-shirt were soaking wet apparently, but she told them she'd just had a wash. There was a broken glass on the floor – she said Winter had knocked it over. They didn't believe her either, but what could they do? Sometimes there's just not much you can do without evidence, and sometimes parenting, even if it isn't to our standards, meets the law's *good enough* standard.'

'I know,' said Jenny, shaking her head. It felt hopeless, and she felt useless. The line between where to intervene and where not to was often more hazy than clear cut.

'Look,' said Sue. 'You know as well as I do that this family is highly likely to bounce back, and who knows, maybe next time the kids might make a disclosure? So why don't you crack on with that court report for Cockburn and let's get a skip hired and get Season closed off. Tell the parents that if we get so much as a whiff of another incident, we'll have no choice but to come down harder on them next time, and tell Kev that if he wants to drink, then he can't be alcohol affected around the children. If Mum wants to sleep all day, she needs to get Winter into childcare. Get them to sign a Voluntary Parenting Agreement, then refer them to Healthy Families, Safe Families. I've got three new cases for our team already, so let's just concentrate on the ones that need us most.'

Let's just hope that by the next time we get involved with Season, we don't we have a dead mum, thought Jenny. She thought of Kai, whom she had visited only that morning to persuade his foster carer to give him another chance, and how traumatised he was by his life experiences and how that was playing out for him now in his adolescent years – with umpteen criminal offences and a stint in remand under his belt at only fifteen years of age. We didn't intervene early enough for Kai, she thought, and look how that's turned out.

But Jenny finished writing her closure assessment, Voluntary Parenting Agreement and Healthy Families, Safe Families referral, then sent out a silent prayer that one of those three new cases Sue had mentioned wouldn't be coming her way. Right, she thought, time to get cracking with that court report. Her fingers ached from all the typing. She stepped outside for a quick breath of fresh air, stuffed a couple of chocolate digestives that would be her dinner into her mouth, then texted Alex to let him know she'd be home late. Again.

\*

**Lisa**

Lisa had set her alarm, and the shriek of it pierced through the thick fog of a medication induced sleep. She needed to get up and chivvy the girls to school. If she didn't, then she knew she wouldn't have seen the last of Jenny. 'Do you even have kids?' Kev had barked at her the previous night when Jenny had hinted he might be asked to leave the home again. She had immediately reddened, and Lisa had felt a small stab of empathy for her, but ultimately she couldn't help but agree with him. Raising kids was hard. Blending families was hard. Relationships were hard. Living off benefits was hard. They were trying their best! What the hell would Jenny know, with her expensive highlights, flat stomach, and posh car?

Beside her, Winter snored, and she snuggled his warm little body into hers and breathed him in deeply. He was so cuddly, and he was sound asleep, just like his father who lay only an arm's reach away from her, yet after their fight the previous evening it might as well have been a mile. What sort of mood would he wake up in today? She wondered, with a shiver. She didn't want to think about it. She just needed ten more minutes, that's all. She hit the snooze button.

'Muuumm? Muuumm!'

Lisa jumped. It was Summer. 'What are you still doing here?' She groaned when she saw the time. Ten to nine.

'You said you'd wake me,' Summer shrugged.

'I did, didn't I? Get yourself off to school, love. If you hurry, you might just make it in time for the bell. Where's Winter?' The bed was empty. Lisa's head hurt. She needed a drink.

'Autumn gave Winter his breakfast then went to school – now he's downstairs watching TV. She did wake me too, but I must've fallen back to sleep. Mum, do I *have* to go to school today? Can't I just stay here with you instead?'

'No, love, not today. You know we've got to keep our heads down after last night. We can't do anything that might draw more attention to ourselves. Where's your dad?'

Summer groaned. 'He's not our dad.'

Lisa rolled her eyes. Kev was the only dad they had. And he *was* Winter's dad. The sooner her girls realised that, the better it would be for all of them. 'Well?' she persisted.

'Gary called him this morning. Gave him a job. Two or three weeks, he reckons.'

Lisa exhaled. Two weeks. That was great news. Two whole weeks of pay, two whole weeks without him on her case twenty-four-seven, and hopefully two weeks of the Kev she remembered – the one she'd fallen in love with five years ago. 'Off you go then,' she said, resisting the pull of slumber and dragging herself out of bed.

'You gonna be ok here, mum?' Summer asked, a little warily. 'I mean, with Winter and everything. You're not going to take any more medicine?'

'No, Sum. No medicine today.' Today was going to be a good day. In fact, Lisa reckoned she'd cook them all a roast – Kev's favourite - for him coming home from work that evening. She was pretty sure there was a joint of meat and some veg in the back of the freezer somewhere. Yes, he'd like that, and so would the kids. She just needed to wake up and get the place into some sort of order first.

# 3.

**Jenny**

One pink line. Jenny's eyes filled with tears. Not pregnant. Again. She looked at the time. She needed to get to work, but now she was going to be upset all day when she had a To Do list a mile long. She knew she should have waited until the weekend, but she'd just needed to know - to have a special secret to hold onto and get her through yet another hectic day at work.

Alex was in the bedroom pulling on his trousers, blissfully oblivious to the significance of that one pink line just as she had been five minutes ago, back when she'd still had hope that this month might be the month. Why did this come so easy for some women? What was wrong with her?

'Don't forget we've got my sister's birthday tonight,' he said. 'If Sue asks you to work late, just tell her to get stuffed, ok? Don't let yourself get pressured into doing more than your fair share. You give enough of yourself to that place as it is.'

Jenny nodded and her eyes blurred with tears. She couldn't cry. She'd just done her make-up, and she was already running late.

'Ok?'

'Mmhmm,' she mumbled, as the first of the tears spilled over and others threatened to follow suit.

'I mean, it's just not healthy. You've got no work-life balance at all. No time to do the stuff you want to do. And you and me – well, we're like passing ships these days, and if we *are* together your laptop is always right there with us – I almost feel as if it deserves its own place setting at our table. I mean, it's just not right. Why can't they understand that? You work in a caring profession, but where's the care?'

Jenny had heard this spiel so many times now, she knew it off by heart.

'Jenny? Are you even listening to me?'

A moment later he was in the doorway. She had her back to him, but he could see her in the mirror over the sink of their ensuite, and the moment he clocked her tear-streaked face and the pregnancy test in her hand, he just knew. In two paces she was in his arms, sobbing into his shoulder until her mascara stained his freshly ironed shirt. He smoothed her hair and she allowed herself to melt into the solid warmth of his chest. It had become their monthly ritual.

'I know,' he said. 'I know. Shh. It's ok, we'll try again. We'll get there, my love. We'll have a family of our own. Remember the doctor said there's nothing wrong with either of us – it's just a matter of time, and it'll be even more wonderful when we do because we'll appreciate it that much more.'

Jenny sniffed. She wished she could believe him – he'd always been the more optimistic one between them, but as one month rolled into another then another, she couldn't help but lose hope. 'I'm sorry I've ruined your shirt.'

'That's ok.' He pulled away from her for a moment to wipe her tears away and hand her a bunch of loo roll to blow her nose with. 'I've got plenty more where that came from.' He looked into her eyes. 'But I only have *one* of you.'

She looked at the time. She really did need to get going. They both did. 'I'll iron you a new one,' she said, but of course he wouldn't hear of it, even if she was going to make him late. He was a good man, Alex, and his considerate nature made her sob all the harder. She loved him *so* much, and she knew he loved her. So why on earth couldn't they extend that love to a child of their own?

*

**Lisa**

Lisa looked at the two pink lines, one a lot weaker than the other but still undeniably there, and hung her head in her hands. 'Shit.'

No wonder she'd been feeling so sickly. She'd thought it was just a side effect of her medication, but things had been a lot better lately so she'd stopped taking it and yet the vomiting had persisted, and now her period – always irregular – was definitely late. What would Kev say? She wondered. She'd have to find the right time to tell him. Now was probably not the best time. They'd enjoyed a great couple of weeks, but whenever he drew close to the end of a stint at work, his attitude tended to plummet with it, and she was already starting to worry what mood he was going to come home in each night, especially tonight – his last day on the job.

Bugger. She'd just have to keep it to herself while she figured out what to do. She knew he didn't want any more kids - he already had two he didn't see - then there was Winter between them, and her two girls, and that was hard enough. That said, he hadn't done much to prevent the arrival of another baby either. Men! He'd probably want her to have an abortion, but if push came to shove, she didn't think she could go through with it. She'd always wanted four, ever since she was a little girl – two of each. The Four Seasons.

'Mama!' said Winter. 'Oos!' He tottered over and shook his empty cup at her, his cheeks beaming red from the teeth that were coming through at the back.

'Juice? I'll get you some, baby.'

She filled his cup with cordial and he sucked away happily on it, laying across her stomach as he played with a toy car in one hand and held his cup with the other, watching some kid's rubbish on YouTube at the same time. Who said males couldn't multitask?

There was a knock on the door and Lisa wondered who the frig it could be, then she remembered – the only way she'd been able to get Child Protection off her back had been to agree to have some other idiot come out and scrutinise her instead. Happy Families or some shit. Well, they could get stuffed. She didn't feel like talking to them today - she didn't feel like talking to them ever. She lay back on the couch with Winter cuddled up in her arms and waited for them to give up. To give her credit, the worker from HFSF persisted, but it wasn't long before Lisa heard something being shoved under her door followed by a car pulling away. Good riddance.

'Shall we go to the park, son?'

The girls were at school, and Lisa had been feeling better in herself over the last two weeks that things with Kev had been relatively uneventful. Not like they used to be, but definitely better. She may as well make the most of it, especially if in a few months' time Winter was no longer going to be her littlest baby and she was going to have to learn to split herself four ways instead of three. She'd get a bit of shopping done too while there was a bit of extra money coming in before Kev blew it all.

'Park!' Winter squealed, his eyes wide with excitement as he leapt off the couch and waved one of his shoes in the air. 'Shoos!'

She didn't have to ask him twice. She was just stepping out the front door when she saw the folded-up piece of paper. *Sorry I missed you this morning, Lisa, please call me to arrange another time that works best for you. Thanks, Sophie.* How about never? She dropped the piece of paper into the bin on her way out. Things were good. She had her man and her kids, money in her purse, a home, and now a tiny new baby growing in her tummy. She didn't need anything else.

She wasn't two steps down the path when she saw old Irina from next door's curtains twitching again. She stuck her tongue out right at her as her grey silhouette disappeared out of view. Nosy cow.

*

**Autumn**

When Autumn got home from school that afternoon, she smiled. Her mum was busy cooking them dinner, Winter was fully dressed, and he kept saying, 'Duck!' excitedly, which could only mean that her mum had taken him to the park to feed the ducks like she used to do with her and Summer when they were little. The toys were in the basket where they belonged, and for once she could see the carpet. The bins had been put out. The benches had been cleared of crumbs and debris and there was food in the fridge, snacks in the cupboard, and enough nappies and wipes to last them at least a week. She'd even bought a pack of double chocolate muffins for them to share after dinner, her favourite, and had brushed her hair and put on a slick of mascara. She was wearing a nice pink top Autumn hadn't seen before.

'Mum! You look nice,' she said, pulling her into a hug. She was making tacos with all the trimmings – salsa, sour cream, cheese and even guacamole.

It wasn't that her mum had gone to any special effort, it was just that, well, it was a relief that was all, to see her up doing the normal mum things, not lying on the couch dead to the world next to a pile of her own vomit leaving Winter to his own devices. Autumn was off the hook – the real parent had returned, so she could look forward to another night off. She hoped Kev would continue to take advantage of the long summer nights and work late again. His boss had a deadline, after all. That way she and Summer and their mum could watch a movie together or something, once Winter was in bed. Maybe even paint each other's nails.

Summer arrived home from school a few minutes later – the primary school was just a few extra minutes-walk away from the secondary school. She searched Autumn's face as though hunting for clues as to how things had been going for her since she got home, then smiled. It was going to be another good night.

They'd eaten dinner, done a bit of homework and cleared the plates while their mum settled Winter. They'd already chosen the colours they were intending to use on each other's nails. Autumn had set out on the coffee table a bowl of popcorn, some drinks, and the packet of chocolate muffins her mum had bought them. They were going to lie on the couch and watch Overboard together, an old favourite of their mum's they had watched a dozen times that never got old, when the front door opened and in lurched Kev. He reeked of the pub - Autumn could smell it from the sofa - and he regarded the cosy scene with disdain, his face red and clammy.

'Where's ya mother?' he snarled.

Summer flinched and looked towards Autumn to answer. 'She's just in putting Winter to sleep.'

'What's the matter, Kev?' Lisa appeared a moment later, her tone flustered and placating. 'Shh in case you wake Winter - he's only just dropped off and it took an age to get him to sleep.'

'What do you call this?' Kev demanded, pointing at the snacks on the table.

'We're just about to watch a movie, why don't you join us?'

'I can see that, I'm not blind. I mean, what the hell do you think you're doing blowing my hard-earned cash on all this crap?'

'It's just a little treat for the girls. We don't do it very often and don't worry, it wasn't expensive. How was your day?'

'I'll tell you how it was. It was bloody long and knackering and my back's killing me, but now the job's done and who knows when there'll be another one? So, it's back to trying to manage on benefits and reigning ourselves in, but there you go splashing the cash like it's going out of fashion. Speaking of fashion, is that a new top?'

Autumn thought that was rich, coming from a man who thought spending money on dog racing and wacky baccy instead of food and nappies wasn't excessive at all, and who had just been fortunate enough to earn cash in hand from two weeks of fiddle-work to supplement his usual benefit payment.

Kev lurched over towards Lisa, and Autumn felt sick at the thought of whatever might happen next. She saw her mum backing slowly away towards the wall, but Kev kept coming at her.

'Well?' he demanded. 'Is it new?'

He grabbed the top and the thin fabric tore in his hand.

'We can afford it, Kev,' said Lisa. 'It was in the sale. It's not like I do this very often - I just wanted to look nice for you.'

'Huh! Look nice for me? I can't remember the last time you looked nice.'

His right hand balled into a fist, and just as he was about to draw it back then plunge it into Lisa's stomach, her arm whipped into action, blocking the blow.

'No, Kev!' she yelled.

He took no notice. If anything, the fact she had blocked him had only made him more determined to meet his target.

'Don't, Kev! You'll hurt the baby!'

There was silence, absolute silence, as the meaning of what Lisa had just said sunk in for three stunned people. Kev's jaw set. He raised his hand again, but this time his palm was flat and he brought it crashing down into Lisa's cheek. She yelped with pain, one hand flying up to cover her red, smarting face. From upstairs, Winter screamed.

Without thinking, in a matter of moments Autumn sprang from the couch, dashed upstairs, grabbed a startled Winter out of his cot, then dashed back downstairs, grabbed Summer's hand and fled. She didn't know where they were going, but almost unconsciously her footsteps took her next door to Irina's house. She hammered on the door with her fist, Winter crying on her hip. It seemed to take a lifetime for Irina to open the front door, her sore knee a perpetual hindrance to her, but she only had to take one look at the two young girls and Winter to reach for her house phone and dial 999.

'She's still in there with him,' Autumn cried as she jostled a screaming Winter on her hip with one hand and Summer clung tightly to the other. 'And she's pregnant.'

'You'd best come in, love,' said Irina, shaking her head at the sorry situation, 'and wait for the police to do their job. She'll be ok, I promise.' Her Bulgarian accent was still thick, though she'd lived in the same street longer than they had.

In the background, Autumn heard sirens.

# 4.

**Jenny**

It was almost six o'clock, and Jenny had been typing like mad with a view to getting out of the office at a reasonable hour to make it to Sarah's birthday with Alex, even if that did mean she'd end up spending most of the weekend working. She was just getting the last of her case notes written up – documenting everything from visits she'd done to conversations she'd had, consultations and meetings, to emails she'd sent and even phone calls she'd attempted (if it's not recorded, it didn't happen), when Sue appeared at her desk with something of an authoritative yet pleading look upon her face. It was an expression Jenny had seen several times before, and she knew immediately what it meant.

'Jenny, it's about Season... I know you have plans tonight and I wouldn't ask, but the case has bounced back to us already and it just makes sense that it goes to you because you know it best, and well, right now there's three kids at a police station, a dad whose gone AWOL, and a mother who needs to be delivered an ultimatum... If it had come in just a few minutes later we could've transferred it through to the After Hours team but it didn't and, well, you know what Friday afternoons are like – everything goes to shit on a Friday, doesn't it?'

Jenny sighed inwardly. If Sue had asked her over email or phone, it would have been a lot easier for her to stand her ground and say no like Alex would encourage her to. But face to face... Well. She swallowed the lump in her throat that had been there since ever since the single pink line that morning, then texted

Alex to tell him she'd just have to meet him at the party. If at all. Her phone vibrated immediately. She stuffed it into her handbag. If she hurried, she might just be able to make it.

\*

**Autumn**

'I know we're at a police station but you're not in any trouble. Your mum's ok,' said Jenny softly, who figured that was likely to be the most pressing question the girls might have. 'She's still in the next room while the police talk to her about what happened tonight. The paramedics came to check her over and there's just a bump and a scratch – she doesn't need to go up to the hospital. She asked me to tell you both that she's alright and she'll see you as soon as she finishes up with Police.'

'Where's Kev?' Autumn asked.

'We're not sure where Kev is, but I suspect Police will want to talk to him about what happened too. Is there anything else you girls would like to know?'

They said nothing as Jenny faced them across a huge brown desk with nothing but a monitor and a black phone on it, a warm smile upon her face, her eyes kind.

'Can you tell me everything that happened from when Kev got home from work tonight up until you went to your neighbour's house?'

Autumn stared at the floor so that the social worker wouldn't see her tears. The 'soft' interview room was stark. The carpet was blue with black speckles and the walls were white and covered with scuff marks. In the corner, Winter was playing happily with some toys that had seen better days and had bits missing. The

31

moment Kev's hand had made contact with her mum's face played on repeat in her mind's eye. It wasn't the act itself that stuck with her so much as the expression on her mum's face when it had happened – that was something she'd never forget. Her shock and fear.

'She's pregnant,' she said. She still couldn't quite believe it. Winter was only one and a half. Winter had been a shock too – she'd never thought her mum would have more children after her and Summer. Now that he was here though, they couldn't imagine life without him.

'Yes,' Jenny nodded, waiting to see if Autumn might be any more forthcoming. She wasn't. 'That's why it's so important we find out what happened tonight.'

'Kev whacked her,' Summer announced. 'He came home drunk and angry. He didn't like the nice new top she was wearing so he ripped it and told her she was ugly when she's not – *he* is, then he hit her, and she told him not to because she's having a baby, but he didn't care so he did it anyway.'

'I see,' said Jenny, as she typed into the laptop resting on her knee. 'And then what happened? I'm just going to write notes as we chat, because what you have to say is really important and I don't want to get it mixed up.'

'We were just trying to have a fun movie night with mum, but he didn't like it. He finished this job he was doing for a friend today, so he was sad, and he wanted us to be sad too, but we weren't – we were really happy until *he* came home! Then Autumn grabbed me and Winter and took us next door where the old lady called the police. Mum hates her – says she's always sticking her nose into everyone's business!'

'When you said Kev hit your mum, what did that look like?'

32

'Like this,' said Summer, whipping out her open right palm and slamming it through the air as hard as she could. Autumn flinched.

'Have you ever seen anything like that happen before?'

'No.'

Autumn shook her head.

'Only when Kev drinks,' Summer added. 'But he's never hit her before. Mum won't be happy either, because he ruined her new top and he woke Winter up - it takes her forever to get him to sleep! And we didn't get to watch Overboard together or eat the chocolate muffins she bought for us. She loves that movie, and we love chocolate muffins...'

Summer was visibly deflated. Her large hazel eyes were downcast, and Autumn felt for her.

'When does Kev drink?' Jenny asked, and Autumn wished she wouldn't. She didn't want to talk about it anymore. She didn't want to hear Summer say the words. She just wished she could rewind time a few hours to before Kev had come home, and that she and her mum and siblings could stay in that moment forever.

'When he gets paid,' said Summer, 'or when he's out of work, or when he loses at the dogs, or when he's sad.'

'What does he drink?'

'Beer mostly. It comes in bottles or cans. Or he goes to the pub.'

'Why do you think he's sad?'

'Because he never looks happy. He's always angry.'

'Can you remember a time he looked happy?'

Summer screwed up her face as though trying to recall. 'When he first met mum, I think. Until she had Winter. And

33

sometimes when he's got work, because then he gets more money for the dogs and his baccy.'

At the mention of his name, Winter tottered over, and Autumn pulled him up onto her lap and squeezed him. She offered him some bits of the jammy toast the police officer had made for them and a sip of cold hot chocolate from a plastic cup, then wiped the excess off his face with her sleeve. His eyes were red. He was exhausted. She cuddled him into her chest. Maybe he'd fall asleep on her knee.

'Is mum's baby going to be ok?' she asked.

'Your mum's baby is going to be just fine,' Jenny reassured her. 'The paramedics said so. Is there anything else you'd like to ask or tell me about what happened tonight, Autumn?' Jenny's voice was soft and encouraging.

Autumn shook her head. She knew her mum wouldn't want them to have said as much as they'd said already, but she knew they couldn't hide it either – Kev had made it too obvious this time.

'I'll have to talk to your mum about making a plan to make sure what happened tonight doesn't happen again,' said Jenny. 'What that'll probably look like, is you three having a sleepover somewhere with your mum for the weekend, but Kev won't be allowed to come see you for a while until he gets some help to work on why he's feeling sad, why he drinks, and why he hurt your mum.'

Summer looked at Autumn worriedly. She was scared. How could this woman ever stop Kev from coming home? And where would they go? Everything they wanted and needed was at home. Why didn't Kev have to go instead of them?

'We don't have anywhere else to go,' she said. 'Mum doesn't speak to my grandma or grandad or anyone.'

'Do you have any aunties or uncles?'

'We've got an aunty,' said Summer. 'But she's got little kids and a little house. She's nice, but there won't be enough room for us at hers.'

'Ok, well, we'll have to come up with some way to make it safe for you all. Maybe she can have a sleepover at your place tonight. I'll have a chat with your mum and my manager then let you know what we've come up with, ok?'

Autumn grimaced.

'Unless you have any other thoughts or ideas you'd like us to explore?'

'I just want to go home,' said Autumn, and Summer nodded. More than anything, she just wanted their lives to be normal - to go back to how things were before Kev had come along and ruined everything. When he'd left after their mum had Winter, she wished he'd never come back.

*

## Lisa

The interview room was nothing short of depressing, and Lisa just wanted to get all this over with so she could pick up her kids and get home and have some time to think and most of all – a fag. She was fed up with all the questions from the police and paramedics, and now she had that bloody social worker in her ear again too. She hadn't been too forthcoming to begin with, but her fear for her unborn child, her shock at what had happened, and her desperation to get out of there had already led her to say more than she should have, and now she was worried about the implications if Kev got wind of it.

She had replayed the evening's events over and over in her mind. If she'd said or done things differently, perhaps the outcome would have been different. What if she hadn't bought that stupid top?

Usually after a stint at work, Kev tended to be in good spirits if the money he'd earned had been good, which she was certain it would have been in this instance – but lately, his good moods seemed to have become fewer and farther between, and his bouts of increased anger seemed to directly correlate with his bouts of increased drinking. She cursed herself. She should have known. She should have anticipated it. She shouldn't have indulged herself and the girls tonight – should have been more sensitive to his needs.

He'd had a hard life, Kev - he'd grown up with a good-for-nothing dad who had harmed him and his mum and brothers, so it was no wonder he was how he was. His mother hadn't been much better. She just needed to be more understanding in future, and far more careful. She wondered where he was now, and if he regretted what he'd done. Did he even care?

'In case no-one's told you yet, Lisa, what happened tonight wasn't your fault,' said Jenny, reaching out a hand and placing it over hers momentarily, but Lisa pulled it away as though burned, glaring at Jenny as she did so. 'Kev made choices tonight to act a certain way – he's an adult and you're not responsible for that, so please try not to take that on your shoulders. We *do* need to work together however, to ensure it doesn't happen again.'

Yes, Lisa nodded. She'd just been thinking the same thing. She needed to be different. Better.

'I've spoken to the girls, and I've had a chat with my manager and Police, and what we've agreed needs to happen is that Kev must stay out of the family home until he gets some help to manage his anger and his drinking. Is there anywhere else you can stay for the weekend until the dust settles, given he's bound to turn up at your place and he might not be in the best frame of mind after police have spoken with him?'

'No,' said Lisa. 'We need to go home. We're going home. And it's fine. He's fine. I can manage him. He's not usually like this.'

Jenny shook her head firmly as though to indicate this wasn't an option, and Lisa cringed. Why was she being treated like a five-year-old girl? She was a grown woman.

'What about staying with your parents for the weekend? Or your sister?'

Was this woman for real? Her dad was an arsehole, and her mum barely remembered she existed. 'I don't have anything to do with my parents, and my sister's place is too small. She's got enough on her plate as it is with her own kids.'

'Well, one alternative we discussed is having your sister come stay with you for the weekend. That way you'll have someone around to support you and call police if Kev turns up or anything else happens.'

'No way!' said Lisa. Did this woman really think she could just walk in and uproot everyone's lives? It was eight-thirty at night for a start, and Kate had never liked Kev - she really didn't need to hear her say *I told you so*.

'I'm afraid I'll have to insist. The alternative would be looking at a refuge, or the kids staying elsewhere for the weekend. We just don't feel confident there's enough safety otherwise. Police have already excluded Kev from the home, so he would be breaching the new DV Prevention Order if he does come back or try to contact you. It's really important we err on the side of caution until we can get measures in place to try to support you all as a family to address these concerns.'

Lisa flinched. 'What bloody concerns? I love my children! I'd do anything for them - they know that.'

'I don't doubt that you love them, but let's not forget what they've seen tonight and how they might be feeling about it all. We need to see you doing the best you can to ensure your kids don't have to witness anything like that happening again, and there's your unborn baby to consider too. Things could be different next time...'

Jenny looked pointedly at Lisa's face. Her left eye was swollen and sore, and she could already feel it was going to bruise nastily. She had a small cut on her cheekbone from the stone on Kev's wedding ring.

'If you can do that, then we won't have an issue with the children being where they want and need to be – and that is with you. But they do have a right to be kept safe.'

'For fuck's sake, you said this isn't even my fault and now you're going on at me like it is!'

Jenny shook her head. 'I'm not blaming you, Lisa. This is a very difficult situation to be in, and all we can do is make the best of the circumstances with the options available to us. It's actually a sign of our confidence in you that we're supporting you to return home with the children after what happened. We want to work with you voluntarily. The alternative would be intervening legally to ensure their safety. So, can you do it, Lisa? Do you understand why we're asking this of you?'

Lisa nodded. She just needed to toe-the-line, get her kids, and get out of there. 'Yes,' she said, picking up the phone with a groan to call her sister and ask her to come over – her brother-in-law would have to look after their kids. They wouldn't be happy. 'Can we get out of here now, please?'

When Jenny acquiesced and Lisa was reunified with her tearful children a few moments later, pressing them into her arms, careful not to wake her sleeping son, she didn't mention that her phone had been vibrating none-stop in her pocket ever since her arrival at the police station, and she had a pretty fair idea of who it was.

# 5.

**Jenny**

Flustered, Jenny waltzed into the party just in time for cake. It was a hired function room with a buffet and dancefloor, festooned with pastel-coloured garlands. She pulled her sister-in-law into a hug and apologised for missing most of what looked as though it had been a great party. Fortunately, she didn't seem to mind. Not as much as her brother did. Stony-faced, Alex had barely acknowledged her presence since she'd arrived. Ravenous and emotionally depleted after the day and evening she'd had, Jenny helped herself to what was left of the buffet before taking a tentative seat beside him.

'I'm really sorry,' she said, laying a hand on his arm. 'I couldn't get out of it.' Besides, in the end, Jenny wasn't sure she had wanted to get out of it. It had been important for those kids to have some continuity after what they'd gone through, and whilst she would have liked to have gone home and gotten on with her weekend, the visit had filled the void of emptiness that single pink line had left her with that morning, and it had felt good to be there for those children, whether they felt that way about her presence or not, in what must have been one of the most difficult moments in their lives to date. *Someone* had to be there, and of her team she was one of few who didn't have the responsibilities of childcare to consider. Besides, either way she was probably going to be allocated one of those new cases so it may as well be one she already knew.

'Has it ever occurred to you,' said Alex through gritted teeth, 'that your job and the stress it puts you under might be the reason for the pink line we see every month? This job isn't healthy. It isn't healthy for you, and it isn't healthy for our relationship.'

'What are you saying?' Jenny asked. Though she'd heard it all before, there was something different in his tone this time, something ominous. It was the first time he'd said that her job could be responsible for their infertility, and it stung. 'These children... It was really important someone was there for them tonight. And I'm still here - I still made it – surely in the grand scheme of things your sister will remember that.'

'I'm saying,' Alex sighed as he searched for the right words, 'that I miss you. That I barely see you anymore! *We* are important too. And now I'm not going to see you all weekend because you'll be glued to your bloody laptop.'

Jenny's eyes clouded with the tears she tried to hold back lest she draw the attention of the in-laws and further sabotage her sister-in-law's party. She knew he was right. Not only was she drained and exhausted, but she was already anxious about the case notes she had yet to complete and the reports she had to write in preparation for the following week. It was one of the ironies of the role that she spent as much time writing about what she did as doing it, if not more. Everything from assessments to case plans to care plans to court reports. And she knew Belinda Wright was teetering on the edge and it would only take one more incident for her to relinquish Kai, which would set off an entire chain of visits, meetings and admin tasks she had no time for. And that was just *one* of her cases. There were always at least two others on her caseload in crisis at any given time. If she didn't continue to keep her head above water, she would surely drown.

'What can I do, Alex? This is my job! It's not like I don't *want* to spend more time with you. Of course, I do. I just don't know how to make changes without falling horribly behind then putting even more stress and pressure on myself.' A single tear strolled down her cheek, but she wiped it away before anyone could see.

Alex sighed and Jenny glanced at him. He looked broken and it hurt her to see it. She hadn't fully recognised their infertility was taking a toll on him too – it was easy to feel that since she was the one getting the period every month, she was the only one it was happening to.

He hadn't missed her tear, and he looked at her with his clear-blue eyes, pale and transparent as water. That's what she loved about him most, his transparency. That he said what he felt, and he was who he was, and that everything he communicated was sincere. If the families she worked with were like that, it would make her job a whole lot easier.

'I'm sorry, Jenny. I'm sorry I said what I said about the pink lines – I shouldn't have said it. It was insensitive and it's *not* your fault. I just miss you, that's all. And after our disappointment this morning, well, I just want to be close to you...'

'Me too,' Jenny sniffed, reaching out a hand and slipping it into his, grateful that he took it and instantly soothed by his touch.

'Maybe we should get away or something? Go somewhere we don't have to think about work or trying to conceive? There's a long weekend coming up. We could spend some time together, even if it's just one night, where it's just you and me, and your laptop stays at home?'

'One night?' A hint of a smile emerged on Jenny's lips.

'One night. A Saturday, obviously, so you can still spend Friday and Monday working.' He winked.

'Ok,' she nodded, whilst secretly hoping she wouldn't end up paying for it the following week. It was the least she could do for them – for their marriage.

*

**Lisa**

Lisa reached an arm out across the empty stretch of bed and felt nothing but cold sheets. She had ignored all Kev's calls and text messages as she'd been instructed, but the truth was, she missed him. Winter was at childcare and the girls were in school and she felt lonely, empty, and overwhelmed. When did things get so bad between them? How could she get things back on track?

He'd turned up of course, on Friday night under the guise of 'picking up some stuff.' She knew he would. But her sister had made sure he didn't see her, and in the end, she'd been grateful because it had been obvious he was still seething after the police had found him at his dad's place and served him his papers. Lisa had given Kate her marching orders the very next day. She'd had no option but to have her there the first night, what with the bloody social worker supervising the phone call to make sure it occurred and greeting her sister at the door before she left, but after that, she and Kate had had a falling out over Kate telling her to ditch Kev once and for all. She barely knew him! What right did she have to an opinion? Lisa thought Kate's husband was a bit of a dick too, but she didn't interfere in their relationship, and she told her as much.

A wave of nausea propelled her out of bed. She knew the drill. She needed to eat something ASAP to stave it off. She supposed she should also make a doctor's appointment, but in the meantime, now that she was pregnant, she just didn't know what to do about it yet. She checked her phone and scrolled through Kev's messages for the umpteenth time whilst eating some dry toast – her go-to for morning sickness and pretty much all she had left in the cupboard.

*You bitch, what have you and your brats been saying to the busies about me?*

*It's your own fault - you shouldn't have triggered me. You're always triggering me!*

*Look, I didn't mean to do what I did, but you pushed me to it.*

*I'm sorry, babe. Maybe I should come round, and we can talk about it?*

*Can we not just forget all this and start over? Be a family – you, me, your girls, Winter, and the baby? Things used to be so good between us.*

*Just remembering that time in Mallorca. It was hot. You were hot. Can you remember?*

*For fuck's sake, Lisa, when are you going to answer your phone so we can talk about this?*

*Lisa! Stop ignoring me! I know you're there!!!*

*This is all your fault! I hate you!*

*That's it. If you don't answer your phone, I'm coming round there.*

*If you don't reply, I'll kill myself.*

*Ok, ok, I get it. You need some space. Look, just reach out when you're ready to talk, yeah?*

And so it went, on and on, round and round in circles until Lisa's head hurt and her heart ached and she didn't know quite what to think or how to feel. She had been distracted since Winter had come along. She'd forgotten how demanding toddlers could be, it had been so long since the girls had been that little. Maybe she hadn't given Kev enough attention? Maybe he'd felt left out? She'd always been so grateful to him for taking on her girls as if they were his own, but maybe since having Winter, she'd pushed him away without even realising it. Then there was the fact that she'd changed. She used to take better care of herself, but she'd put on a bit of weight after Winter had arrived and she didn't have the time to do much about it, or the money to afford a class or gym membership. Maybe he wasn't attracted to her anymore - he'd said as much.

She needed to think, but thinking was too overwhelming. She saw the tablets. She only had one left. She needed to come up with an excuse to get more – maybe she wouldn't tell her GP she was pregnant just yet. Right now, she'd just take one and make the world disappear for a while.

*

### Autumn

Autumn had enjoyed having her aunty over to stay. They didn't see her very often now - her mum didn't like that Kate had maintained contact with her nanna and grandad, and Kate didn't like that she didn't. Also, Kate thought Kev was a waste of space (and Autumn tended to agree), but since her mum (and Kev) didn't appreciate this perspective, it only increased the distance between them.

It was a shame because Kate was fun. She'd cooked for them, then baked and decorated cupcakes with Autumn and Summer the next morning and had even let Winter get involved - despite him getting icing and sprinkles everywhere and sticking his fingers into the mix. Kate had also stopped Kev from trying to come home the moment Police and Child Protection's backs were turned. Her mum had thought she was sleeping when he turned up, but she wasn't – she'd heard him, and she'd been able to tell by the tone of his voice that it wasn't good, even though he'd tried to keep it down in case Irina next door reported him again. Autumn had been really worried about what might happen if he came inside, but her aunty Kate was having none of it. She sent him packing, threatening to call Police or make a scene if he didn't, then Autumn had been able to relax enough to go to sleep once she knew her mum was going to be alright.

Now she was home, and it filled her with dismay that the first thing she needed to do when she found her mother on the couch for the first time in a fortnight, her swollen left eye a blazing purple-blue, was to set aside her school bag to check that she was still breathing then wonder why she hadn't gone to pick up Winter yet. She checked her mum's phone. There were two missed calls. If she didn't get to the childcare centre soon, they'd probably end up sending the social worker out all over again. She could go and get him herself, but that would look too suspicious – she doubted they would hand him over to her anyway, she was just a kid.

'Mum.' Autumn shook her, but she was out for the count. 'Mum, you need to get up and get Winter! Mum!'

The front door opened and in walked Summer. Her shoulders dropped the moment her mind caught up to what was happening.

'Mum!' Autumn tried again, but there was no response. She waved Summer over, and together they both tugged at their mum's arms. She groaned at one point then fell straight back to sleep. The doorbell rang and the two girls froze. Kev.

'Who's that?' Summer whispered, her expression conveying her anxiety. 'Is it him?'

Autumn held her fingers to her lips. 'Shh,' she said, as she crept over to the living room window where she could peak through the slatted blinds without being seen, only to be greeted with the back of a grey bob. 'It's... Nanna!'

'Nanna? What on earth's *she* doing here?'

'Aunty Kate will have sent her, silly. Come on! Mum's gonna go ape when she finds out Nanna's here!'

Autumn rushed to the door and opened it, gesturing to her nanna to come in and keep the noise down, anxious of her mum's reaction. Her nanna gave the girls tearful cuddles, then she walked in, took one look at Lisa, wincing at the sight of her swollen, bruised eye, then stood over the top of her as if she was six-foot-one rather than five-foot-nothing.

'Lisa Jane Woods, get up this instant!'

Autumn didn't know how she did it, but suddenly her mum was stirring. She even pulled herself up to a semi-sitting position, groggy and rubbing her eyes as though to try to rub away this vision of her mum standing in her sitting room.

'Mum?' she said, as though she could scarcely believe it.

'Yes! Get up, I've had the childcare centre on the phone asking why you haven't turned up to collect your child today. I'm first on their list of emergency contacts, apparently. First I knew of it too. I need your car keys so I can get the car-seat and get him for you, then do something about feeding my grandchildren. When I get back, I think, from what I can gather from Kate, you have some explaining to do.'

'Piss off,' said Lisa.

'Watch your mouth around the kids.'

'Huh, you're one to talk! Do you even remember my childhood, or were you too doped up to notice your own potty mouth? I'll go and get my child myself, thank you very much.' But it was obvious even to Autumn that there was no way she should be driving.

'You'll do no such thing. You'll bloody kill someone. And don't even think about dragging up the past in front of these two, Lisa - they're too young to hear it and it isn't fair. Let them make up their own minds about me - a lot can change in twenty years, you know? Just do as I ask for once. I've already covered your arse with the childcare centre, and Winter needs to get home to his mother.'

Lisa said nothing. There was no point. She simply gestured towards her handbag, and Autumn's nanna took that as having her blessing to go. She fished out the car keys from its depths.

'Are you ok, Mum?' Autumn asked wearily when she heard her nanna's car pulling away.

'I'm fine,' she lied. 'Actually, I think I'm gonna throw up. Pass me a bowl, quick!'

Lisa promptly vomited. When she was finished, Autumn got her some tissues and a couple of slices of the dry bread she asked for. She hoped her baby was ok. She didn't know much about pregnancy, but she was fairly certain you weren't meant to take all those pills.

'What did Nanna mean, about the past?' Summer asked, her eyebrows knotted into a frown.

'Never you mind.'

'Well, I'm glad she's here.'

Autumn couldn't help but agree with her. She wondered if their nanna would stay, or if her mum would push her away again, just as she'd pushed away her aunt Kate.

# 6.

**Jenny**

Monday:

> - 9 am: School PEP meeting for Kai Humphries
> - 10 am: Home visit to Nala Omari
> - 11:30 am: Statutory Visit to Novikov siblings
> - 12:45 pm: Supervision with Sue
> - 1:45 pm: Zoom Care Team Meeting for Amir and Rohan Gupta
> - 3:30 – 5 pm: Supervised contact for Bobby and Brooklyn Barnes

Jenny had just gotten back to the office to down a cup of tea and stuff a pasty into her mouth before supervision. As she flicked through her diary, completely overwhelmed by the forthcoming week's commitments, she smirked when she glanced up at her computer and saw a pink post-it note attached, with a picture of a penis in the middle, even if it did represent a most unpleasant task – a phone call to Mr Cockburn. She peered at Fatima, a colleague whose desk adjoined hers, and grinned. Suddenly the day didn't seem quite so bad – they were all in the same sinking ship together, after all, and Fatima's dark sense of humour was part of what helped keep her afloat.

'How's Duty going?' Jenny asked her.

'Shite, as usual,' Fatima sniffed, pushing her wavy black hair back from her face before taking a slurp of fortifying coffee. 'As if I haven't got enough to do on my own bloody cases, now I'm sat here like a mug trying to deal with every bugger else's as well. There's a LAC Review and a contact too – for some kid placed bloody miles away which means driving in peak-hour traffic and getting home at yon time. None of the support workers can do it apparently, and everyone knows I bloody hate supervising contact – especially for *this* family. No wonder Wills pulled a sickie! I've dealt with them before and the mum's a total nightmare - always making false allegations. I'll have to be on my best behaviour before she accuses me of something ridiculous.'

'Ooo, that'll be hard for you, Fati!' Jenny grinned, secretly relieved it wasn't her rostered day on duty. Monday or Friday duty was the short straw – when everything that could go wrong seemed to go wrong. 'Try your best not to sexually assault her.' Everyone knew the mum in question was four-foot-nothing with only stumps for teeth. It was quite sad really. Jenny knew there would be a very good reason why she was the way she was. 'Any visits on there?'

'No, thankfully. At least I'm able to get some of my phone calls out the way and get some case notes done. Might even be able to make a start on that court report for Davies too - it's the final hearing coming up. But the phone hasn't stopped ringing so far, mostly that bloody COCK-burn. He must've called five times already - I don't know how you put up with him!'

'As if I have a choice. He obviously has a bee in his bonnet about something.'

And Jenny knew it wouldn't be long before he projected whatever it was onto her. No doubt he'd had another argument with the mum on the weekend over something *she* had that *he* didn't – his usual trigger for going on the rampage. That, or to make allegations against his children's foster carer to undermine their placement in a misguided attempt to demonstrate how much better at caring for them he would be if, only he was given half a chance – even though he'd had more chances than the proverbial cat.

'How's your day going, anyway?'

'Busy.' Jenny sighed. So busy she felt completely immobilised as she didn't know which task to start on first – they were all as much of a priority as each other, and every meeting she ever attended only seemed to result in an endless list of tasks that were somehow always fell into 'the social worker's' domain.

'Time for a holiday, I think,' said Fatima.

'That's what my hubby reckons.' Alex had been harping on about a holiday a lot lately, but Jenny couldn't foresee a suitable gap to fit one in. They'd settled on a night in a country inn over the long weekend coming up instead – that should leave her just enough time to get caught up with her reports.

'Mine too. Only he works in a job where you don't have to pay with blood before you go and when you get back, by trying to squeeze about two weeks' worth of work into one.'

Jenny laughed. 'And that's just a regular week! More like squeezing four weeks into one.'

'You're not wrong! I'd settle for a night out and a good boogie instead. Anyway, call Cock back, would you, so I don't have to deal with him again today?'

Jenny rolled her eyes. 'You're hardly selling him to me!'

'Ready for supervision, Jenny?' It was Sue.

Fatima arched an eyebrow.

'Sorry,' Jenny smiled, wiping the flakes of pastry off her face, 'But I think you can handle him. You can get me back when it's my turn.'

Jenny had given Sue and update on every case, begging her to hand the Barnes contact over to a support worker, given they were having twice weekly contact which took approximately six precious hours out of her diary each week, when they finally reached Season.

'How did you go with Season?' she asked, as she munched on her Caesar salad. Sue was on a perpetual diet. The Mediterranean one this week. 'I was sorry to spring that one on you, but I'm glad you were still able to make it to your sister-in-law's party.'

Jenny gave her a wry smile. It was hard not to like Sue, even if she was the one who overwhelmed everyone with work until they either went on long-term sick leave or found a job in the charity sector. It wasn't her fault – the cases all had to go somewhere, and she carried a few of them herself. She tried to be considerate - she didn't want to over-burden anyone – but she was accountable up the chain too, and at the end of the day, the work just didn't stop coming in a lot faster than it went out.

'I reckon we should close it off, what do you think?'

Jenny wondered if it really mattered what she thought and felt a stab of panic that the direction of the conversation probably meant Sue had already ear-marked her for another case. 'I still have doubts over mum's protective capacity - it didn't take long for her to breach the Voluntary Parenting Agreement we put in place last time we closed.'

'Mmm,' Sue agreed as she sipped her green tea. 'We always sit with a degree of risk due to our distinct lack of the crystal ball that would make our job a whole lot easier. But at the end of the day, she cooperated with the safety plan we put in place over the weekend, we know there's been an improvement in the kids' school attendance, and she's gotten Winter back into childcare. How about we sit with it until the end of the week? If there's been no further DV incidents and no new concerns have emerged from checking in with school or childcare, we'll have to look at closing it off. I've got another case ear-marked for you, actually – the Bacons - but you needn't worry about that one too much. It's got a five-day KPI, and it looks like there's nothing in it for us.'

Jenny's heart sank, but she tried her best to appear unruffled. She *knew* it. She wished she could call Alex to have a vent and moan, but he would just say what he always said – abandon the sinking ship.

'You need to ensure she engages with Healthy Families, Safe Families and agrees to keep Kev out of the house. Police will have already linked him in with a Men's Insight Program anyway. That should do the trick.'

'Hypothetically speaking, what happens with Bacon if, come Friday, we aren't able to close Season off? I'm just mindful that at our last supervision we agreed I was at capacity.'

'Ooo, I do admire your optimism, Jenny!' Sue winked. 'Well, that was partly because we were expecting everything to go to shit with Kai, weren't we? But it hasn't, thanks to your little pep talk with him and Belinda. And look, if that does happen, well then, I reckon Fatima has capacity to take on one more, at a pinch!'

Shit, thought Jenny. She very much doubted that Fatima would see it the same way.

*

**Lisa**

Lisa didn't want to admit that her mum had actually been rather helpful. Without so much as being asked, she'd tidied round, shopped, prepared a light meal here and there, and picked up Winter from childcare each day, and she hadn't said a word about Kev or the bruising to her face, and she hadn't once mentioned *him*. Her dad. It had been obvious that Winter and the girls loved having her about the place, even if Lisa didn't. She'd tried to contain it, but there was something about her presence that just irked her – like how she'd allowed her dad to bulldoze her and Kate's whole lives as kids, but now suddenly here she was, Mary Poppinsing about the place as if none of that had ever happened. And even worse, bearing an air of superiority as though to say that when it came to her precious grandkids, *Lisa* should know better. Talk about pot calling kettle...

Yes, there was no hiding the elephant in the room, and she was ready to point out that elephant.

'Your sister will be here soon with the kids,' said Tracy, as she pottered about in the kitchen, Winter and the dog both getting under her feet. 'I'm cooking us pasta, salad and garlic bread – the kids'll eat that, won't they?'

Lisa gave her a wry smile – she'd like to see anyone successfully get something green down Winter. 'Then we'll all be one big *happy* family, won't we, Mum?'

Lisa was groggy and nauseous. She'd managed to blag more pills from her GP and slept almost all day every day. But at night her thoughts tormented her, and she longed for Kev to come home and hold her and for everything to be ok between them again, the way it used to be when they'd been a family - before everything had gone to shit.

Tracy said nothing. Either because she was too absorbed by what she was doing, or because she knew no good could come from engaging in the conversation. The front door opened and in walked Kate with her two little girls, Lily and Mia, aged two and three. They'd grown so much. Lily was so like her dad, and Mia was Kate's double. It didn't seem like five minutes since Autumn and Summer were that age. The girls immediately kicked off their shoes and made themselves at home playing with Winter's toys. Fortunately, Winter was so excited to have become the centre of their attention that he didn't seem to mind.

Kate's eyes narrowed when she noted Lisa sprawled on the couch so late in the afternoon, her thick, dark hair something of a bird's nest. Even though she tried to hide it, Lisa didn't miss her disapproval, and it both pricked at her conscience and annoyed her in equal measure. 'What are *you* looking at?' She gestured across her general person wearing what could best be described as loungewear. 'This is the Dunston look. Too good for Dunston, now though, aren't ya? Moved up in the world? Forgotten where you come from?'

Kate rolled her eyes. 'Don't *you* start. Mum!' she yelled through to the kitchen. 'She's already going off on one. I told you this was a bad idea - I don't want my kids around her when she's like this.'

'Come on, Lisa.' Tracy walked through from the galley kitchen into the little living room, tea towel in one hand, plate in the other as she rubbed at it vigorously. 'Let's try and be civilised for one night. Think of the kids, eh? They've been looking forward to seeing their cousins all day.'

The door opened and in walked Autumn, followed moments later by Summer, who'd been extra keen to get home quickly to spend the night with her aunt, nanna, and cousins as promised.

'Think of the kids?' Lisa spat. 'Like you did, eh?'

Tracy flushed, a flash of hurt crossing her face.

'Enough, Lisa,' said Kate, with a glance at the children who were now either sat or stood quietly in their respective corners of the room as they absorbed the tension emanating from the adults. 'This isn't the right time or place to have this conversation.'

'Except there never is a right time or place, is there? You two just want to sit back and play happy families and pretend like the first twenty years of our lives never happened.'

'Things change, Lisa,' said Tracy. '*People* change.'

Kate nodded. 'They do. *He* has.'

'Do they? Well, I'm very happy for you, Mother. It's just a shame that change was too little-too late to have any bearing whatsoever on my upbringing or how I turned out. And please forgive me if I'm still holding a grudge from watching my drunk father beat us all black-and-blue while you stood by and did nothing. NOTHING! I'm so bloody sorry if my feelings about all that somehow hurt both of yours!'

'How did you turn black and blue, Mummy?' Mia tugged on Kate's stylish knee-length cardigan. 'Did Grandad paint you?'

'YES!' Lisa answered for her. 'He painted us all kinds of colours – yellow, green and red, too. You can ask your mum or nanna all about it.'

'Honestly!' Kate tutted.

'What would you know?' Lisa turned on her sister. 'You weren't even there for half of it. I made sure you weren't. Just get out of my house, right now! I didn't ask you to come here, and I don't want you here. The kids don't want you here either – why would they? They barely know you and it's your own bloody fault.'

Tracy shook her head sadly. 'I'm going,' she said, a film of tears over her eyes. 'But mind you don't make the same mistake I did, Lisa, or one day this might be you standing here with one of *your* kids.'

Lisa shook her head. 'At least I'll know who to thank for it, Mum. Goodbye.'

'I'm going too,' said Kate, grabbing Tracy's arm and turning her and her children in the direction of the door. 'I'll drive you. We can grab something for dinner together on the way home. I told you she was a lost cause – I don't know why you bothered wasting your time.'

When it dawned on Mia and Lily that the outing their mum had planned would no longer be happening and the shoes they had taken off were swiftly pressed back onto two sets of uncooperative feet, Winter's toys prised from their reluctant hands, they began to sob inconsolably. Winter watched them, and even though he didn't really understand, he cried too. Only Autumn and Summer were silent, their faces impassive, their eyes the only feature to hint at the tumult of emotions beneath. Lisa knew they were hurting but chose to ignore it. They would understand one day, when they were older.

*

**Autumn**

Autumn awoke with a start. It took a few moments to register what sound had disturbed her, but as the haze of sleep dissolved, she was conscious of knocking followed by hushed voices downstairs. Kev. She felt her heartbeat accelerate rapidly. As quietly as she could, she crept out of the lower bunk then stood on the bottom rung of the ladder to stretch up and check on Summer at the top. Thankfully, she was sound asleep, her blonde hair spread across the pillow like a halo as she breathed deeply.

Avoiding the creakiest floorboards of the old, terraced house, she walked into her mum's room and plucked a sleeping Winter from his cot, popping his discarded dummy back into his mouth when he showed signs of stirring, before slipping back into bed with him at the foot of hers, the ladder to the top bunk acting as a railing, Oaty the comforter by his side.

Autumn tossed and turned but she couldn't sleep. She wondered what was happening downstairs and if her mum was ok. *Why* had she let him in? Why hadn't she sent him away yet? If only her nanna was there. She thought about texting her, but it would only cause World War Three if she came round, and she didn't want to do anything that might set Kev off again. Minutes later, to her dismay she heard two sets of footsteps coming up to bed, one tread light and familiar and the other heavy and foreboding, and when Autumn did eventually drop back off to sleep, she had the first of a recurring nightmare that would haunt her nights for years to come.

# 7.

**Jenny**

A dreaded green file lay in wait on Jenny's keyboard when she arrived in the office on the morning after the long weekend. *Bacon,* it said. The upbeat mood that her lovely night at the country inn with Alex had left her with instantly dissipated in the face of this sharp new reality check. There was a post-it note from Sue, apologising that she was in meetings all day but could Jenny please 'just look at' the file with a view to closing it off. Already dubious, it only took a couple of phone calls for Jenny to determine that closing it off was nothing more than a pipe dream, after layer upon layer of concern was revealed from her follow-up with the Bacon children's school, childcare centre, and health visitor.

She sighed. At least she'd been able to close off Season, and thankfully Kai Humphries was settled for the time being. She still had a couple of cases bubbling away with the potential to boil over, but they were mostly just simmering at the moment.

'How's it going?' Fatima asked her, reading her expression over the top of their cojoined desks. 'I'm just grabbing a cuppa before I have to head out, do you want one?'

Jenny momentarily brightened. 'If it's your homemade masala chai, then I'm definitely up for some before everyone else gets in there.' Everybody knew Fatima made the best masala chai. It was very popular in the office.

'It is - we're running low but there's just enough left for us, so don't go telling anyone.'

'I won't. How's your day going?'

'Shitful, Jenny. Too much to do, too little time, and Sue wants to talk to me later about an allegation that crazy mother made about me last week on the contact I covered for duty. Said I was aggressive or something, apparently.'

Jenny arched an eyebrow. Fatima had the warmest, sweetest face. 'You? Aggressive? Mother Theresa must have been more aggressive than you!'

'Ridiculous, isn't it?'

'What did she accuse you of?' Wills was in the kitchen avoiding work whilst eyeing up the remains of Fatima's masala chai at the bottom of the tin, and a dubious looking wedge of cake from someone's birthday that had been there for several days. 'Knocking her teeth out? Bahaha!' He cackled at his own joke, and Fatima and Jenny couldn't help but grin. It was below the belt – everything Wills said was below the belt, but his dark sense of humour and pure entertainment value helped make up for the fact he pulled more sickies than he did days' work.

When Jenny got back to her desk, she had a missed call from Belinda Wright and knew instinctively it wasn't going to be good. Oh Kai. Her heart ached as she pictured his freckled face, hazel eyes and auburn hair carried off by that lovable Jack-the-lad charm. As she sipped on Fatima's calming concoction of cloves, cinnamon and cardamom, she psyched herself up to make the call.

'Hi Belinda! It's just Jenny, returning your call.'

'Hi Jenny, thank you. Sorry to do this to you, love, but you'll have to get Kai out of here. He punched me in the shoulder last night, and I've got a bruise. If it was only up to me, I'd probably give him one last chance, but my husband is pulling the plug, I'm afraid. He's just not willing to open our home only to have either one of us get assaulted, especially not on top of Kai having damaged our car - when he knows how much Gary loves the car - and lying to us all the time about what he's been getting up to... He's taken off - I think he knows he's gone too far this time. He's gone to a friend's place.'

Jenny knew from Belinda's tone that she was resolute, even though she also knew Sue would ask her to see if she and Gary could be persuaded to give it just *one more* last try to prevent further disruption to Kai's care arrangements and minimise his sense of rejection, whilst on a practical level also avoiding the inevitable avalanche of tasks that would follow. Oh well, at least the worst had happened on a Tuesday and not a Friday – that gave her a few days to play with to get something organised.

'Gary's already packed his stuff,' said Belinda, as though anticipating Jenny's next sentence. 'He's not welcome back tonight, sorry. And I think we're going to have a break before we take someone else in - it's been a bit hectic dealing with Kai and his additional needs on top of all those behavioural issues too. I really didn't want him to have to move on again, the poor lad - I know it's not his fault. Not really.'

'It's ok, Belinda,' said Jenny, 'I understand. You don't have to explain it to me. I know you haven't made this decision lightly and you've both given it a really good go. Kai's been with you and Gary longer than he's been with any other carer.' Fifteen months to be precise.

'Yes, well, I'm not sure how the next person is going to manage him, but hopefully they're made of stronger stuff than we are. I hope he's ok. Tell him we're sorry...'

Jenny knew that the next 'person' to care for Kai wouldn't be a person at all, but a whole team of staff in a residential unit full of other young people as challenging and hard to place as he was, now that he'd burned his bridges with foster care. She'd have to tee-up with Belinda's fostering social worker to make it official, then put in a referral to Placements to get the ball moving on finding a new one. In the meantime, she'd be expected to pull a mountain of paperwork out of her butt and initiate the Looked After Children processes, which would no doubt lead to an endless list of meetings and additional tasks for her to complete.

First though, she needed to call Kai to make sure he was ok and deliver him the bad news. Then, she needed to figure out how to fit Bacon into all of this, given that based on what she'd learned so far, it needed actioned ASAP. The mum was obviously spiralling into psychosis due to non-compliance with her medication, and an inpatient admission looked imminent.

As she sipped on her chai tea, it was hard for Jenny to believe that a mere forty-eight hours ago she and Alex had been lounging in a free-standing bubble bath, legs entwined as they drank prosecco, ate chocolate strawberries, and talked the night away before finally enjoying some intimacy without the pressure to conceive. Now here she was, chasing her tail as if the whole thing had been nothing more than a dream.

*

## Autumn

The school bell rang. Home time. Autumn didn't want to go home any more now that Kev was back – whilst there'd been no more incidents, she couldn't fight the sense that everyone in the house was simply waiting for something bad to happen, and in the meantime, trying their best to fly under Kev's radar to make sure it didn't. Things had been so much better when her nanna had been there, but her mum had made it clear that neither her aunt Kate nor her nanna were welcome. She didn't understand why - they'd only been trying to help, and from what she remembered of her grandad, he wasn't so bad.

She lingered getting her bag ready, stuffing her books and pencil case into it one by one. Mrs O'Neil eyed her from her vantage point behind her desk.

'Come on, Autumn,' said Starr, her best friend. 'If you don't hurry, we'll never run into Blayze on our way home.'

'I'll just be a sec.'

Mrs O'Neil got up and walked towards her. 'Is everything going ok, Autumn?' she asked, peering at her over her thick-rimmed glasses.

Autumn forced a bright smile. 'Sure! See ya!' And she was out of there before any more questions could be asked.

'What was all that about? Anyone would think you wanted to stay at school.'

'Never mind.' Autumn knew that Starr wouldn't understand. Her parents had been married since before she was born. They were nice to each other. They even seemed to still quite like each other after all these years.

'Oh my God, there he is! Isn't he gorgeous?' Starr adopted a dreamy expression, her sapphire eyes shining with adoration. 'Just look at him!'

Blayze was gorgeous. He was only in the year above but was already a head taller and far wider across the shoulders than most of the boys in their year, and he'd just dumped Chantelle Leigh, which made him seem all the more attainable to every other year nine girl who fancied him – including these two.

'Oh my God, he's looking this way!' Starr's grip on Autumn's forearm tightened and Autumn smiled awkwardly. 'Quick, act normal!'

Blayze was a few metres ahead of them with a group of his mates, but they'd stopped to chat to a couple of the guys who were about to turn off down the street. Most of them were vaping, and Autumn could smell their sickly-sweet exhalations carried towards her on the breeze. Starr adopted her most confident expression and fixed him in her gaze, smiling coquettishly. Embarrassed by how obvious she was being, Autumn had kept her eyes down to the ground, but at the last moment she glanced up and his eyes met hers and stayed, trailing her as she walked, a confident smirk on his lips. He *was* gorgeous.

'Oh my God!' said Starr. 'Did you see that? He's *totally* into you! That's ok, I'll have his friend, Coby - he's nice too.' She grinned.

Autumn rolled her eyes. 'See ya tomorrow,' she said, as their paths veered off in two very different directions – Starr's towards a lovely estate of new houses that had just been built a couple of years ago, and Autumn towards the council estate that just happened to be located at the very edge of the school's catchment zone.

As Autumn approached the metal railings surrounding the paved driveway that their small patch of grass had been ripped out by the council to replace, she didn't feel quite so lucky. As much as she wanted to be there for Summer and Winter and her mum, she veered off at the last moment and took the cut that led towards her nanna's house instead. To hell with the consequences, she thought. It had to be better than being at home with that intolerable wait for the worst to happen.

Five minutes later, her nanna opened the door and enveloped her in her soft arms. Autumn couldn't help it - she sobbed.

'Is everything alright, love?' Tracy asked.

Autumn nodded. 'It is, but... he's back.'

Tracy was concerned but not at all surprised. 'You'd best come in. You'll be alright here, though your mum'll kill me if she finds out!'

Autumn smiled and allowed her to be led inside the lounge room she hadn't been in to see the grandad she hadn't seen for several years. The house was almost identical to theirs, but it didn't feel the same – there were knickknacks everywhere and framed photographs of her mum and Kate when they were children, pictures of Autumn and Summer as toddlers and Winter as a baby, as well as of her cousins. It was clean, cosy and warm – nothing like their dingy terrace made damp and cold when Kev spent their money on betting and alcohol instead of heating.

From what she'd heard her mum say, Autumn expected her grandad to be some sort of ogre, but the unassuming man in the armchair by the fireplace reading his newspaper was slight, frail and friendly.

'By,' he said, 'you're a double of your mother.' And when he pressed her into his arms, Autumn couldn't understand what her mum's problem with him was at all.

*

**Lisa**

Now that Kev was home, Lisa was determined things would be different. She'd made more of an effort to keep the house clean, more of an effort to get the kids up and out to school and childcare in the mornings – not that she needed to tell Autumn twice these days - it was Summer who would take advantage of any opportunity she could to stay off. She'd even started to make a bit of an effort with her hair and adding a slick of tinted moisturiser to her skin and mascara to her eyes each day. She didn't look great - she was still carrying the weight she'd never quite lost after having Winter - but it was certainly an improvement.

Kev had secured another stint of work, so he was ticking along ok. He'd been loving and apologetic when he'd first come back – buying her flowers and keeping the cupboard stocked with her favourite chocolates and wine, but the long days of physical work were starting to take their toll, and she'd noticed he was starting to get a little grouchy. So long as she remained understanding and attentive, she reassured herself it would all be ok.

*Stopping at Starr's for tea x* said the text message that came through from Autumn moments after Summer had gotten home. Oh well, thought Lisa, piling Spag. Bol. onto Kev's plate – his favourite.

Summer minded Winter and the dog for her while she cooked, then Kev came home and she gestured for him to sit down and poured him a glass of coke. He flicked the TV off Winter's favourite cartoon channel, which immediately caused a tantrum, and Summer tried her best to distract him.

'How was your day?' Lisa asked.

67

'Shite,' said Kev, as she handed him his dinner and he took a mouthful then grimaced in distaste. 'But what would you know? Loungin' around here all day like lady muck.'

Lisa said nothing. There'd been nothing leisurely about her day, but she knew better than to argue back.

'How long's this muck been lying out for?' he asked. 'It's bloody freezin'. Trying to poison me, are ya? That'd be right.'

Lisa winced at his tone. The dinner was fine - she'd only just cooked it, but maybe the pasta had gotten cold while she'd been waiting for the sauce to heat up. She'd have to time it right next time. Summer's eyes darted to hers, and Lisa gave her a reassuring smile.

'And what's that crap on your face?' Kev continued. 'Been out somewhere nice, have ya?'

'No!' said Lisa. 'I've been home all day, apart from taking Winter to childcare and back.'

Her phone beeped.

'Who's that then?'

'It's Autumn,' said Lisa. Honestly, who else did he think it could be?

'Give me your phone.'

Lisa frowned, then handed it over to him. 'I've got nothing to hide, Kev, you know that. I'm carrying your child, for crying out loud!'

'Dunno about that,' he said, 'why else would you be done up like a dog's dinner? Probably isn't even mine.'

He flicked threw her messages then hurled the phone back to her, narrowly missing her shoulder. It landed face down on the floor and the screen cracked. He cackled.

'Serves you right,' he said. 'Slapper!'

Lisa mentally retraced her steps of the evening, wondering how she had managed to get it so wrong.

# 8.

**Jenny**

Two pink lines. Jenny could hardly believe it. Alex came in to brush his teeth, took one look at her face and the white stick in her hand and beamed, pulling her in close.

'Don't get too excited,' she warned. 'Not until I'm at least twelve weeks!' But even Jenny had already mentally calculated the due date, placing her at approximately five weeks. Twelve weeks seemed so far away – not one of her three babies had made it to twelve weeks. As she assessed her reflection in the mirror, she wondered what she would look like if she ever got far along enough to produce a baby bump. She couldn't imagine it. It didn't seem possible. She mentally examined her body – did she *feel* pregnant? Yep, her boobs were a little bit sore. That had to be a good sign.

'I can't help it,' he said. 'That's our baby in there. I knew a night away would do us the world of good!' He knelt down and parted her dressing gown, lifting up her pyjama top to plant a kiss beneath her belly button. 'Whatever happens next, little bean, we love you.' He stood. 'Though I have to say, I have a good feeling about this one...'

Jenny's eyes misted over. She wished she could so confidently say the same. 'I need to get going.'

'Remember to take it *easy,*' said Alex. 'Even if you have to tell that old battle-axe who piles on all the work. I insist.'

'I know,' said Jenny. 'And she's not a battle-axe, you know. Or old.'

'You know what I mean. Just protect yourself. And protect our bean, because *they* won't.'

Jenny nodded and kissed him. She could see how happy he was and hoped it wasn't too premature. His eyes were bright and there was a spring in his step that she hadn't seen for some time. Oh Alex, she prayed, let there be no more disappointments.

*

## Lisa

Lisa awoke to Winter in her face. 'Mama,' he said, over and over until she could no longer pretend to ignore him. He'd climbed out of his cot, the rascal, then climbed up onto her bed and proceeded to roll all over it until she was seasick. She'd optimistically tried cuddling him back to sleep but it hadn't worked, and he'd stayed awake while she dozed, but now he was getting restless, and yet she still couldn't bring herself to leave her bed. Kev was at work, which was one small comfort, and the girls had gotten better at getting themselves to school, so they were otherwise alone.

'Ok, Winter,' she groaned. 'Coming.'

She dragged herself up. It was gone ten. There was no point taking him to childcare now. She felt a momentary stab of guilt – he was far better off there with his little playmates than he was bored at home with her, and in all honesty, she was better off with him there too. It would give her some time to think.

She ate a handful of crackers and promptly threw them up because she'd left it too late to eat something. She cleaned herself up, then shook out some biscuits for the dog. They were running low on dog food, but she was reluctant to ask Kev for some money even though it was pay day. Her head ached. She knew she should have known better than to think things could be different this time round. She could almost hear her mother and sister saying, *I told you so.* She was exhausted, physically and mentally – physically from the toll of the first trimester, and mentally from the toll of walking on eggshells in her own home all the time. The only thing that helped was oblivion.

She saw the pills. Noted she was running low again. She took them anyway. She left some toast and a drink out for Winter, flicked on the cartoons, then curled up on the couch and waited for the world to disappear.

*

**Autumn**

'Oh my gosh, Blayze actually spoke to you!' said Starr on their walk home.

'He said 'hey',' said Autumn. 'I'm not exactly sure that qualifies as a conversation.' 'He doesn't even *need* to acknowledge you exist, but he did. That's definitely something.'

Autumn shrugged. She didn't have the space in her mind to care about Blayze. All she could think about was whether to go to her nanna's, which is where she really wanted to go, or home because it was a Friday, which meant payday, and Kev coming home in either a good mood or a bad mood. If it was the latter, she needed to be there for Winter, Summer and their mum. She opted for the latter.

'Bye Starr,' she said.

'Bye Autumn,' said Starr. 'Hey, do you want to catch up tomorrow night down the wasteland? I heard Blayze and his mates always hang out there trying to get someone to buy their drink for them. Some of the others are going...'

Autumn couldn't see beyond tonight. 'Maybe,' she said, as they veered off in two very different directions. For Starr it would be drama and dance classes over the weekend followed by shopping with her mum and maybe a meal out and a trip to the cinema or bowling. For Autumn, weekends were spent at home, helping out with Winter and wondering what mood Kev was going to be in, and if her mum would ever get round to kicking him out for good. For a moment she wondered what it might be like to swap lives.

When Autumn got home, her mum was on the couch out for the count, and a trail of devastation lay all around her courtesy of Winter. She shook her head in dismay. There were toys, crumbs, a packet of crisps he must have dropped, a cup of milk he'd spilled... He'd been drawing on the walls again, this time with the blue biro Kev normally used to do his crossword. In the background, the cartoons played on. She couldn't see Winter though, and her heartbeat quickened.

'Winter?' she yelled. 'Where are you, baba?' Then she saw it. Little red drops on the carpet. Blood? 'Winter!' she cried.

'Oaty!' Oblivious to her concern, Winter tootled into the living room from the kitchen, a big grin on his face when he saw Autumn. He'd always called her Oaty - could never pronounce her name - and he adored her so much he had named his little comforter after her. Right now, he had food all about his mouth, and a trail of dried blood coming from what looked like a gash at the top of his forehead. His cheeks were tear-stained, and Autumn gasped.

'Winter!' she yelled. She was with him in seconds and scooped him up into her arms. 'What happened, baba? What happened to your head? Is it sore?'

'Fall down,' he said, as though it was nothing. Autumn looked towards the dining table, on top of which was Winter's favourite musical toy that their mum would often put up there out of reach when she got fed up with hearing it. There was a dining chair that looked as though it had toppled over onto the floor, and Autumn assumed he must've tried climbing onto it to get to the toy, then fell to the ground after losing his balance. 'Ow,' he said.

Autumn was no doctor, but even she could see that the cut looked nasty. She thought he might need stitches – or glue at least. The front door opened and in walked Summer, who was horrified when she caught sight of Winter's injury.

'What happened?' she asked.

'We have to wake Mum,' said Autumn. 'I think he needs to see a doctor.'

But though Lisa groaned, they couldn't fully wake her. There was a bang at the door, as though Kev's entire body weight had laid into it. As usual, they could smell him before they saw him as he stumbled in through the door.

'What the-' he said when his brain eventually processed the sight before him. 'Lisa!' he yelled. 'Wake the fuck up! What have you done to my son?'

Lisa groaned and tried to wrestle herself from the clutches of sleep. Kev covered the small room in two paces, grabbing her by the shoulder in an attempt to shake her awake. Autumn froze. Winter wailed. She turned him away in her arms so that his face was towards her shoulder facing away from their mum, but he craned his neck anyway and cried for her.

Autumn was unable to stop him from seeing Kev's fist make contact with their mum's jaw, as she and Summer looked on, rooted to the spot and begging her to get up while begging him to leave her alone. Summer was crying, and Autumn realised her own face was wet. She wanted to cover her ears to block out her mum's pain and Kev's words, as he rained his abuse on her, accusing her of all sorts of terrible things that she knew weren't true.

Fight him, Autumn willed. Fight him, Mum! Kev was different this time. Out of control. She had to do something. She thrust Winter, who was screaming now, into Summer's arms.

'Go to Irina's.'

'But what about you? I can't leave-'

'Now!' Autumn's tone was firm. Desperate.

Summer went. They were out of the door in seconds. The police would be there soon -Autumn only hoped they'd make it in time.

'Stop!' she screamed. 'GET OFF HER!'

She pulled at Kev's arm as he rained blows on her mum's body, but he grabbed Autumn by the arm and pushed her to the floor. She fell awkwardly, landing on her elbow. She wondered if might be broken.

Her mum was alert now, fully awake. She guarded her stomach with one arm and her head and face with the other and screamed back at Kev. She was eventually able to get herself up off the couch where they engaged in some pushing and shoving until they heard the sirens, and the physical to-ing and fro-ing subdued into a to-ing and fro-ing of words. Horrible words.

A couple of minutes later, Kev was led away in handcuffs, arguing with Police about why he was the one getting arrested when *she* had injured his son, and that if anyone deserved to get arrested, it was Lisa. Thankfully, they didn't listen. Autumn crawled over from where she still sat on the floor and, sobbing, she wrapped her mum in her arms. Not long after that, the ambulance arrived, and all the while, all Autumn could think about was her brother and sister. She hoped they were both ok.

Autumn was certain her mum would now agree that Kev was no longer welcome back home. From here on, things could only get better.

*

## Lisa

Lisa knew she was stuffed. Not because of Kev. Not because of her broken jaw or the bruising to her aching body, but because from the moment the police had been called and the paramedics had arrived and the probing questions had been asked, she knew it wouldn't be long before the social workers came knocking too, and this time there was nothing she could say or do to stop whatever would come next.

'We'd still like to work with you voluntarily,' said Jenny, against a backdrop of a blue cubicle curtain that afforded them little privacy. Lisa had visions of the patient in the next bed eavesdropping intently, as she would in their position. 'So, I'll need your consent to place the children elsewhere. I've got some forms for you to sign.'

'My kids are coming home with me,' said Lisa through gritted teeth, though she knew in her heart of hearts it was futile.

The decision had already been made, so it didn't matter what she said or did next. She was powerless.

Jenny shook her head. 'You know that can't happen and I've explained why. We've had three reports in almost as many months. Things at home have gotten worse, not better. You weren't supervising Winter today and he got hurt, needing stitches, and you've let Kev come home and now Autumn's arm is in a sling, and your jaw is broken. It's lucky your baby wasn't hurt. You've been taking Valium and sleeping when you should be caring for Winter...'

Lisa bridled. 'I didn't *let* him come home!' she retorted, her voice rising as this list of her failures was rattled off. 'I didn't have a choice!'

'If you felt you didn't have a choice,' Jenny continued, 'then there are places you could've have gone – people you could have called who would have helped you. We talked about that at length previously, and you agreed. I know it sounds like I'm judging you – but my job is to assess whether I think you can keep your children safe, and right now I would have a very hard time convincing my manager, or a court, that you can keep yourself safe, let alone your children.'

Lisa glared at Jenny. 'I'm not signing my children away.'

'We're trying to give you an opportunity to work with us voluntarily. If you can't do that, given what's happened, I've already spoken to my manager and I'm afraid we'd be left with no option but to go down the legal route. I know you love your children, Lisa. I know you do. And I think you can do it, I honestly think you can, with the right support, but right now it's too early. I don't think you're able to put the children first yet. To make safe decisions for them. Part of that is because you're the victim of domestic violence, which isn't your fault – you can't be blamed for what Kev has done or for the poor choices he has made - but we do need you to develop the insight to be able to act protectively on behalf of your children when you deal with Kev, or men like him, in the future.'

Lisa sighed.

'I know it's a lot. I know you're hurting. Your kids are hurting too. They love you, but they don't want to go home right now because they're scared Kev will come back, and we can't be certain you would tell us if he did, can we?'

Lisa said nothing. What could she say? It was the truth.

'Autumn's suggested staying at your mum's...'

Lisa recoiled. 'No way. Absolutely not. My dad's a violent alcoholic.'

Jenny frowned. 'I've spoken to him. I understand there's a past, but from what I can gather those are no longer current concerns, and they haven't been for many years. He plays an active role in his other daughter and grandchildren's lives.'

'My kids can stay with my sister. They'll be safe there.'

Jenny shook her head. 'We considered that, but your sister's living in a two-bedroom property, so we wouldn't be able to place your three children with her just yet. Because Winter's still in a cot he could share a room with your sister and brother-in-law, but it would mean separating him from the girls, and I think Autumn in particular would really struggle with that.'

Lisa's heart ached at the thought of her babies getting separated. She knew how much that would hurt them, especially Autumn. 'I'm not going to sign my kids over to my parents, and they're not going into foster care.'

'Well, I'm afraid it's got to be one or the other unless you can put forward someone else, but from what I've read about your girls' dad and the paternal family, we couldn't go down that route.'

'They're all arseholes,' Lisa agreed. 'Bunch of junkies, and their dad's been in and out of jail for years - we have nothing to do with them. The girls don't even know that lot! But they barely know my mum either.'

'Really?' said Jenny. 'Autumn said she goes round there most days after school.'

Lisa spluttered. 'You're kidding me!' All those nights she'd supposedly been having dinner with Starr - she'd been such an idiot.

'Look, we don't disagree that the very best place for kids to thrive is at home with their parents, but research shows that if that can't happen, the next best place is with their family. No-one wants children to enter the care system, so we always work hard to avoid that if we can. That means taking the next best option available to us, and whilst we all know the absolute best is with you, that's just not possible at the moment.'

Lisa said nothing.

'Your mum and dad present as appropriate and they meet our assessment criteria. Lisa, we really wouldn't send them there if we were concerned they might not be safe...'

Appropriate. The word stung. It didn't tally with Lisa's memories of her dad beating the crap out of her mum. And now she was expected to just forget. To let her own children be cared for by him as if it had never happened, as if not that long ago the shoe wasn't on the other foot! Everyone expected her to forget – her mum, her sister, Autumn and now Jenny...

It was a joke. The whole system was a fucking joke. She wouldn't sign the papers. No way. But in the end, it didn't matter, because the court placed all three of her children with their grandparents anyway, and Lisa would never forget Winter's cries or Summer and Autumn's grave faces as they left the hospital without her, with a plan for her to begin having supervised contact with them the very next week. Supervised by her parents - the same two people Lisa held responsible for her getting her into all this mess in the first place. Well, there was no way she was going to go along with that. After discharge, she couldn't wait to get home where oblivion awaited her.

# 9.

**Jenny**

'Hello there, my name's Jenny from Dunstonborough Child Protection. I'm just calling to seek an update regarding a family I believe you've been involved with over the last couple of months. *Season*. Lisa Season is the mother?'

Jenny could hear the clacking of computer keys in the background as the Healthy Families, Safe Families worker looked the family up for her.

'Ah yes, I'm afraid we're closed,' said the receptionist, 'about a month ago, due to non-engagement.'

Damn it. *Non-engagement,* Jenny scribbled. *Re-referral required.* 'Can you give me the dates?'

'Sure, give me a sec.' Moments later, Jenny had a list of dates of their attempted phone calls, attempted visits, and finally details of a text message from Lisa essentially telling the HFSF worker to get stuffed and go hassle another family.

Next on the list, a phone call to Winter's childcare.

'He was going well there for a little while, especially when Nanna was bringing him in,' said the childcare worker. 'He was getting dropped off on time, collected on time and had good hygiene, appropriate clothing and was provided with a good lunch.'

'But?' There was always a but.

'Well, it's obvious he's got some delays – language and motor skills mainly. And he's actually become quite aggressive towards the other kids. It's created some issues for us with the parents, as you can imagine. He bit one of them... The mum was not impressed!'

*Developmental assessment required,* Jenny scribbled. He was only twenty months old.

She contacted Summer's primary school.

'There's been a definite improvement in her attendance,' said the headteacher, 'but from what I can gather that's more to do with her sister than her mother. She's quite open with her teacher, not a closed book like Autumn was when we used to have her at our school. The thing is, she's disorganised and struggles to concentrate. Can be hard to engage in lessons and fairly cheeky, bordering on rude at times. Not especially academic. Seems quite anxious. I wouldn't be surprised if she had ADHD. Hard to say though – as you know it can be harder to diagnose in girls and could be more to do with whatever's been going on for her at home. Her friendships are all over the place – best of friends one moment, worst enemies the next. Very emotional girl.'

*Emotional support required, developmental assessment required,* Jenny scribbled. Next, she contacted Autumn's school.

'Ah, Autumn,' said Mrs O'Neil, her form tutor. 'A deep one, that one. Lovely girl. Bright. Responsible. A lot of potential. Never been a bother really. But I'm aware she's recently become interested in a year ten boy called Blayze, and his crowd are not a good crowd. From what I can gather, there were some issues between him and another year nine girl last term. There's talk he pressured her into doing things she wasn't comfortable with. Sexual things. We spoke to her about it, but she wouldn't say anything, of course. He's heavily into vaping and who knows what else. Bit of a troublemaker. Troubled background – lived with an uncle for a while. I'm hoping Autumn sees sense and moves on before she starts her GCSEs next year...'

Bugger, thought Jenny, as she dialled the number of the family's GP and hoped he'd be free for a quick chat.

'Pregnant? No, I had no idea,' said the GP. 'If I'd known, I'd have been far more hesitant in prescribing her with any more Valium. Been going through a rough patch, she said. Down, depressed, anxious. Trouble sleeping. The usual things. But nothing about a pregnancy. Thanks for letting me know, I'll document it. We're going to have to wean her off the medication - it sounds like she's developed a dependency... We'll give her a call and send her a letter encouraging her to make an urgent appointment.'

Jenny shook her head. That poor baby. And there *she* was, unsure if, or for how long, she'd be able to keep her own baby inside her. Next, she called Police to clarify the conditions of the Domestic Violence Prevention Order.

'The order we put into place after the second last DV incident was later varied by a Ms Season to allow contact with a Mr Black, however it has since reverted back to a full order following the last incident, prohibiting contact for Mr Black with Ms Season and her three children,' the police officer verified. 'Obviously he can have contact with the children if it's supervised by Child Protection, but Ms Season can't be present when this occurs, and any contact must take place according to the elder children's wishes...'

Yes, thought Jenny. Kevin would only be having contact with Winter from now on anyway, because the girls didn't want to see him and Winter was unfortunately still too young to be able to articulate his wishes on the subject.

'I'm not sure if you're aware, but it looks as though a previous partner must've had a DVPO against Mr Black too – almost four years ago. A Miss Smith. It's expired now though.'

Jenny raised her eyebrows. Why was she not surprised? Turned out she didn't know about it because there hadn't been any children involved at the time, so there'd been no need for Child Protection to be informed. Last of all, she called the Men's Insight Program.

'Woods? Kevin Dean Black?'

'Yes,' said Jenny.

'Closed due to non-engagement. He attended two of the ten sessions before basically stating that the program was a waste of his time because he's, quote, not like the other blokes.'

Yeah right, thought Jenny, taking a sip of her cold coffee. Decaf of course, which made it even worse. 'How was his engagement when he did attend?'

'Superficial at best. No meaningful engagement. No sense of accountability. No sense of remorse.'

Jenny scribbled all that down in her notes then put the phone down and sighed. *Denial. Re-referral required.* It didn't paint a good picture.

She collated a list of contacts and sent out a group email inviting them all to be part of the Season's care team and setting up the first of what would be monthly meetings, before typing up the referrals to HFSF and MIP while she had a little bit of time on her hands before having to do the Barnes contact, which had still yet to be allocated to a support worker. Last time, the contact had had to be curtailed when the mum turned up to the office emotional and drunk, meaning she'd had a thirty-mile round-trip in school-hour traffic for nothing but two very disappointed little boys and a mum who had been furious at her for cancelling after she'd gone to the trouble of getting there on public transport.

'How's it going?' Fatima asked.

'You know,' said Jenny. Shit, she thought.

'Yeah,' said Fatima, sipping masala chai out of her 'PISS OFF!' mug, 'I know.' She grinned.

But then Jenny called Tracy, the Season children's grandmother for an update, who said they'd settled into their new placement remarkably well, and suddenly all the long hours and the tumult of emotions that came with it felt that little bit more worthwhile.

*

**Lisa**

The house felt empty. It was still and silent. There was no Kev in bed beside her - no warm little Winter to snuggle into. The only comfort was the baby growing in her tummy. It made Lisa feel less alone, and no-one could take that away from her. Not yet anyway. Another day stretched before her, an empty chasm that nothing could fill. She had no idea what to do. Didn't know who was when she wasn't being what she'd been for the last fourteen years. A mum. She could barely remember a life before that.

Her school days had been little more than a yarn - skiving most days, getting into trouble others, a far bigger interest in boys than her schoolwork, and a baby by twenty. She hadn't travelled, hadn't studied - hadn't done much of anything or gone far beyond the boundaries of the British Isles except for a trip to Spain once with her grandma. She had no formal qualifications.

She'd had a flair for hair, she remembered that. Her friends all thought she'd go on to become a hairdresser. She'd started a course at college, but then she'd met Autumn's dad and that had been far more exciting - to begin with - than anything else. The rest, as they say, was history.

She checked her phone. There were the usual text messages from Kev, text messages that spun round in circles from blaming, to argumentative, to sorry and back again. Messages that hurt and muddled her head and her heart in equal measure. She wondered what he was doing right now. Did he have any regrets? He'd lost Winter too. Should she text him? See if he was ok? No, best not go down that road again...

She wondered how the girls were and how Winter was doing. If her mum and dad were celebrating their victory over her - their *I told you so*. She thought about calling Kate, but she couldn't bring herself to do it. She wouldn't understand, so what was the point?

It was all too painful. She stubbed out her cigarette. Saw the pills. She was just about to take them when the doorbell rang.

'Now what do they want?' Lisa muttered, expecting to see Jenny or some other do-gooder from Happy Families on the other side of the front door. But it wasn't them, it was Irina. She immediately went to close the door in her face, but Irina whipped out her wrinkled hand just in the nick of time.

'For fuck's sake,' said Lisa, thinking of the pills, of the relief she knew they would offer her. 'What do *you* want? Haven't you already done enough damage?'

'It was either that or stand by and let you get beaten to a pulp, dear. I don't think I had much choice, do you? And neither did your kids. Now, hear me out,' Irina persisted, her wizened old face serious, her eyes brooking no argument. 'I've *been* there. It wasn't quite the same – it was emotional not physical. But I do know what I'm talking about.'

Lisa sighed. She realised she must be desperate for company if she was letting *Irina* in of all people. 'I'll put the kettle on,' she said reluctantly. 'Careful where you sit, though - the dog's been pissing all over the place. Ever since the kids were taken, he doesn't know which way is up, and I must say neither do I.' And over a pot of tea in the kitchen, the only part of the downstairs living area that didn't reek thanks to the fact the floor was moppable, an unlikely truce began between the pair.

*

## Autumn

It was nice at her nanna's, but it wasn't the same. Autumn missed her mum. She wondered how she was doing. She was only a few streets away, and if she really wanted to, she supposed she could call round any time, but if her nanna found out there'd be hell on, and if Kev was there, it would be even worse. She'd see her tomorrow after school, anyway. They were going to the park, and she couldn't wait. She hoped she was ok. Not for the first time, she wondered when she might be able to go home. Her nanna didn't seem to know - told her she'd have to ask Jenny the next time she visited, but whenever she asked an adult something, she seemed to be left with more questions than answers.

She was walking to school with Starr, but the thought of all those classes ahead of her felt overwhelming. She wished she could turn round and go straight back to bed. Was that what her mum had felt like? Was that why she took all those pills?

Up ahead, Autumn recognised Blayze with a group of his mates. There were about ten of them. He'd taken to saying hello whenever she passed him, and right now he was smiling at her.

'Y'alright, Autumn?'

Her cheeks burned. 'Fine.'

'You don't look fine to me,' he said, gesturing at her arm that was still wrapped in a sling. 'Where you goin'?'

Honestly, where did he *think* she was going dressed in her uniform and carrying her school bag on her back. 'School. You?'

'Nah! Can't stand the place. There's an empty house on Stowell Street near the wasteland - a few of us like to hang out there. Wanna tag along with us? It'll be fun. More fun than school anyway.'

Autumn looked to Starr, and Starr looked back wide-eyed. They were both uncertain. 'But we'll get caught!'

'I'll write you a note.' Blayze grinned and his mates laughed. Coby was there too, along with a few kids they didn't know from the next year up. He shrugged. 'Ok, suit yourself.'

'Let's do it,' Starr whispered. 'It can't hurt just this once. Let's just see what happens?'

'Ok,' said Autumn. Sod it. What did she have to lose?

Blayze held his vape in one hand and threw a careless arm about her shoulders with the other as they walked along the wet concrete path, avoiding the puddles dotted here and there, heading in the opposite direction to all those other kids who passed them in their uniforms on their way to the school. Autumn's could smell the strong scent of some sort of spray-on deodorant. It was too much, almost enough to make her gag, but somehow she found that she didn't mind. It felt weird being in a boy's arms. It felt... exciting. Grown up. She couldn't help but smile. Starr walked a couple of paces ahead of her with Coby. She was flirting outrageously, and when he reached out a hand towards hers, Autumn noticed that she gripped it tight.

'Whose place is this?' she asked when they got there.

It was a downstairs flat at the edge of an estate bordered by fields that had a tendency to flood, hence why they'd called it the wasteland, so their comings and goings were less likely to draw the attention of the neighbours. According to Blayze, it had the added bonus of being in close proximity to their local supermarket where they would dare each other to shoplift whatever they could get away with, then share the proceeds between them in some sort of fallen honour system.

'It's Coby's uncle's place,' said Blayze. 'He stays with his girlfriend most of the time, and he doesn't mind what we do so long as we don't wreck the joint or piss off the neighbours. The bloke upstairs works during the day anyway, so he's none the wiser.'

'Speaking of joints,' said Coby, producing a spliff from his back pocket. 'Shall we?'

'Do you girls smoke?' Blayze asked.

Autumn felt flustered and she could see that Starr was shocked. 'Sure we do,' said Starr, trying her best to appear completely unruffled.

Coby laughed. '*Sure* you do.' He produced a lighter, took two deep draws, then handed the spliff to Starr as the rest of the party arranged themselves in a circle on the living room floor and watched her eagerly. She coughed and grimaced and the others laughed, then she handed it to Blayze who made it look easy.

'Wanna couple off?' he asked, handing the spliff to Autumn.

Autumn wasn't sure. Kev and her mum both used it, and her mum had always warned her off ever trying anything like that herself. But now... Well, what did it matter? It was just a couple off. She drew deeply of the sickly-sweet smoke, and Blayze gave her an encouraging slap on the back. There. She'd done it. She felt no different. Someone produced a bottle of vodka and handed it around. It burned Autumn's throat when she took a sip. She started to feel relaxed, and to her surprise, found she was quite enjoying herself. By the looks of it, so was Starr. Blayze was right - it was certainly more interesting than school.

# 10.

**Jenny**

As Jenny lay on the bed staring at the blank screen in anticipation, she gripped Alex's hand so tightly the skin had turned white. He looked deep into her eyes. *It's going to be ok,* his expression told her. But really, he was no more certain of that than she was, and she could feel his uncertainty in the way he squeezed her right back. Tightly. The sonographer rubbed the cool jelly onto her lower belly and Jenny closed her eyes. In the past, these appointments had never ended well.

'This is the yolk sac, and this...' Jenny held her breath. 'This is the heartbeat.' She played it out loud to them, and it was the sweetest rhythm they'd ever heard.

Jenny opened her eyes. She was crying. They both were. Alex kissed her. The baby looked just like a jellybean, it's subtle movements a mere flicker.

'Hello Flick,' said Jenny. 'I'm your mummy.'

They exited the hospital hand in hand. Alex couldn't stop smiling. The pored over the grainy ultrasound image, determined to figure out which bit was which, even though at only eight weeks there was so little to see. Still, there was a part of Jenny's heart that she kept strictly under lock and key, and it was the part she was most desperate to throw wide open. Just four more weeks, she told herself. Four more weeks and then maybe, just maybe, she could.

*

**Lisa**

More than anything, Lisa wanted to take the pills to combat the intoxicating combination of loneliness, isolation, guilt and regret – her only true companions nowadays - but she didn't. She was required to attend their very first care team meeting at social services within the next twenty minutes, and if she didn't, she knew how that would be perceived and how damaging it might be to her chances of ever getting her kids back into her care. So, she spent her last tenner on petrol and parked outside the depressing old council building set in the most notorious estate of Dunstonborough, fenced off with tall iron railings, and took a deep breath. She couldn't help but notice that the building itself looked as defeated as she felt.

In the short walk from the street to the reception, she felt exposed. As if anyone who happened to glance out of their living room window would know why she was there and judge her accordingly. As if some of them weren't in similar positions themselves – they just hadn't had the misfortune of getting caught. She felt inadequate in her black tracksuit – about the only thing in her wardrobe that still fitted her since she'd had Winter - her greasy hair scraped back into a ponytail as she took a seat next to a bunch of smartly dressed professional men and women who hid behind piles of paperwork and false smiles. She reminded herself that no matter how pleasant they were, how polite, they were absolutely not on her side.

Her mum was there, and though Lisa was secretly glad of it, she ignored her anyway. She checked her phone. Kev would be joining the meeting, but Jenny had arranged it so they wouldn't both have to be present at the same time. That meant she had about half an hour in the meeting, then a fifteen-minute window to clear off before he turned up. She hoped they wouldn't cross paths. She hadn't psyched herself up to deal with him yet, and wasn't confident she wouldn't take him back just to fill the void of emptiness he and the children had left her with.

Jenny cleared her throat and explained that they had basically gathered to discuss bottom lines. Specifically, what needed to change, and what Lisa and Kev needed to do if they were serious about stopping the snowball that could lead to a final care order granted by the children's court, and the children being removed from their care for good.

'I think we're all agreed that the case plan for the children is for their safe reunification back into parental care. That means, Lisa,' said Jenny, 'that we would like to support you and Kevin to address the protective concerns we've already discussed, with a view to the children potentially being able to return to your care. We have six months to demonstrate to the court that this would be in your children's best interests.'

Six months! Half a year. Winter would be over two by then. Autumn would have started her GCSEs. It was too long. Way too long. She wasn't sure she could survive it. All those milestones missed! She told them so.

'I've already submitted referrals to Healthy Families, Safe Families and the Men's Insight Program,' Jenny reassured her. 'They should be in touch with yourself and Kev soon. Basically, what we need to see is *meaningful* engagement from both parties. We need to evidence that you can both implement whatever strategies those services provide you with, and that you can sustain those positive changes long-term to benefit your children. We find that anything less than six months is not usually enough time to demonstrate this, but anything longer means that children are waiting too long to achieve stability in their care arrangements. Basically, they need to know, as soon as possible, what their future is going to look like.'

Everyone stared at Lisa. 'But I'm not seeing Kev anymore,' she said. 'That's one of your concerns taken care of. And I haven't taken any more medication.' A white lie. 'And I've booked in to see my GP to let him know about my pregnancy.' Also a lie. She'd booked in to ask him for some more Valium - just one last lot couldn't hurt, then she'd stop. 'I've cleaned up the place as well – you can come see it if you like.' Partly true – there was far less mess with only her and the dog in the house.

'That's great!' said Jenny. 'But it's just the beginning, Lisa. Like I said, what we need to see is that you can sustain these changes longer term. I'm aware there've been instances in the past for example, in which you have reunited with Kev - and as you're aware there's an order in place that prevents contact between you, so we need to evidence that both of you can adhere to it. That means we should be receiving no further reports of domestic violence within the next six months, and there should be no reports of you two having breached the order.'

'There'll be no chance of that,' said Lisa. 'We're done.'

She could tell by the expressions of those seated around her however, that they weren't convinced. Not for the first time, Lisa wondered if what she had to say meant anything to these people – they were just going to do whatever they wanted anyway. Child snatchers, her grandad had called them. She told them as much.

'Lisa,' said Jenny, 'if that were true, we wouldn't be pursuing a plan for reunification. You're a victim-survivor of domestic violence. That's bound to have been negatively impacting upon your mental health, your use of medication to manage it, and your motivation to get the kids to school and childcare and keep the home in order. We believe that with support, you stand a good chance of achieving the outcome you hope for. We must inform you however, that Kev is seeking to be considered as an independent carer for Winter, and we are obligated to conduct that assessment.'

Lisa laughed a bitter laugh. 'Are you for real? He whacked me right in front of Winter and almost broke my daughter's arm!'

'I understand your concern.'

'Hang on... If he wants Winter, does that mean he wants...'

Jenny nodded. 'The new baby? Yes.'

'But he does bugger all with the kids!' she said. 'Ask the girls! He's only saying it to get at me – he knows that taking the kids from me is the one way he can truly hurt me. He's got no bloody interest in looking after either of them. He doesn't even *want* this one.' She gestured at her expanding stomach.

Jenny nodded. 'If he does what we're asking of him and makes the necessary changes, then he also has the right to be given a fair chance. Do you think he can do that?'

No, thought Lisa. *Not unless he does it to get to me.* In which case she knew he would go to whatever lengths possible.

'He won't be able to do it, love,' said Tracy. 'Don't worry.'

But Lisa's hunch was proven right when she walked to her car, and moments later she observed Kev pull up in his dad's car, deliberately early, a smirk on his lips when he glanced her way. It was obvious he wanted her to see him. When he stepped out of the car, he was wearing a smart suit she'd never seen before – obviously borrowed – and with his tattoos covered and his face shaven, he wouldn't look too far removed from the other people seated at the table. Which was the whole point. She shook her head. There was no way she could win this. He was too clever for her. Too strong. And he knew it.

*

**Autumn**

It was different being at Nanna's to being at home, and Autumn alternately either appreciated or resented it. There were rules - lots of them. And in that one day she and Blayze had spent together, she'd already broken several – for most of which she fortunately had yet to be found out. Her nanna had been both surprised and disappointed in her for bunking off school, as had Mrs O'Neil (only Summer had been impressed), and she'd earned herself a week of detention and being cut off from the internet. Blayze was bad news, Mrs O'Neil had warned her, and whilst they wouldn't hold her 'slip up' against her, they did want to deter her from doing it again. Starr was in the same boat with her own parents.

Still, there was something about Blayze and his attraction towards her that Autumn found magnetising. She couldn't quite imagine what a year ten boy might see in her, and she found it flattering that he had given her so much as a second glance. It had been incredibly exciting for her to be held in his arms – the first time she'd ever really had that experience. Given how things had been for her at home lately, she'd never felt like she'd had much in common with Starr or the other kids, but with Blayze and his crowd, she somehow felt less alone. She couldn't help but imagine what it might be like when they were next able to spend time together, and she hoped he wouldn't forget about her in the meantime.

Otherwise, things were going ok. Her nanna's house was always clean and tidy – everything in its place, but the knick-knacks that filled every nook and cranny kept it homely. Autumn and Summer had their own bedrooms that their nanna had allowed them to decorate when they'd first moved in, and Autumn no longer had to get up for Winter in the night because he now slept with her grandparents in a cot in their room – so she always had her bed to herself.

Her nanna was a wonderful cook – she made a roast every weekend and baked endlessly, everything from sausage rolls to jam tarts, fudges, cakes, crumbles, toffee apples and gingerbread. Autumn could see where her Aunt Kate must have gotten it from, and she'd started imparting her culinary wisdom on to her. She would come round every weekend with their uncle and the kids, and they'd bake together and chat. Then their grandad would initiate a game of cards or Ludo, as the three little ones got under their feet and generally wreaked havoc.

As usual, Summer resisted the early morning wake-up calls for school, until her nanna made it clear that for every morning she got herself to school on time she would earn herself two quid. She hadn't looked back. Winter was thriving on his new routine, and his behaviour had improved from all the extra sleep and stimulation. He was even coming out with one or two new words. Autumn though, felt restless. It didn't matter how much they were enjoying the time with their nanna and grandad, one thing was still missing. Mum.

They called it 'contact', but it wasn't an exercise in alien communication, simply a catch up with her mum and siblings at the local park. It wasn't really park weather, but her mum was determined to avoid seeing her grandad, so they'd had no option but to find low-cost things to do in the community, and the park had the bonus of being free. Winter was in his element, and Summer was still at an age where she could enjoy the equipment on offer, but whilst there wasn't a great deal there to occupy Autumn, she didn't care, she was just overjoyed to see her mum again and anxious to see for herself that she was ok.

Lisa was on time, pacing the pavement beside the tall park gates as she waited for them wearing her usual tracksuit pants with a long-sleeved top that showed the hint of a baby bump. As soon as she saw them her face exploded into a wide grin.

'My babies!' she yelled, covering the ground between them to squeeze them into her arms. Winter was quite stand-offish to begin with, which Autumn could see hurt her mother, but it was all forgotten once the oats she had brought to feed the ducks with came out, then they set about hunting for sticks, a favourite activity of his, actively discouraging him to resist the temptation to pop them in his mouth. Any awkwardness between them all simply dissipated.

Autumn was relieved that her mum was safe and well, and though she wondered what had become of her and Kev, she could sense her mum didn't want her to go there with her nanna in the background looking on.

'Is he gone?' she asked quietly, when they happened to find themselves side by side hurling oats into the water, to the great delight of Winter and a flock of hungry ducks skimming across the water from every nook and cranny of the small lake.

'He's gone, love,' said Lisa.

'For good?'

'Yep.'

'Does that mean we can come home?'

Lisa shook her head, and Autumn fended off the tears that sprang to her eyes. 'Not yet,' she said. 'But soon. I promise. Whatever it takes, I'll do it.'

'Everything ok, Autumn?' her nanna asked, concern etched into the corners of her crinkly eyes.

'Fine!' she replied. She fervently hoped that was true. No matter how many things were different for them at their nanna's, most of all she hoped they could soon go home and be a family again – without Kev. And when that awful time came for them to go their separate ways, she knew her mum and siblings hoped so too.

# 11.

**Lisa**

Lisa hadn't been able to get any more pills from her GP because it turned out that he and the bloody social worker were in cahoots and she'd told him she was pregnant, therefore she'd had no option but to assure him she could take it or leave it lest he tell the social worker she was addicted. Which she wasn't. Obviously. She just couldn't tolerate the intrusion. Her life had become a goldfish bowl, and if she hadn't struggled with anxiety before, she certainly did now. To make matters worse, the idiot from Happy Families was coming out to see her again in a few minutes, so she did the best she could to Febreze the crap out of the piss smell on the carpets and the weed smell in the air – the next best thing to pills - then she tidied round and shoved the dog into the kitchen.

The doorbell rang. As much as she wanted to wait until the woman went away, Irina had urged her to give her a chance because unfortunately, social services weren't going to disappear any time soon, and if she didn't meet with this woman, they'd be even less likely to leave her alone. She was in a catch-22.

'Hi Lisa, I'm Sophie from Healthy Families, Safe Families.' She had a neat bob, practical clothing and warm manner. 'I'm so glad we finally get to meet. Can I come in?'

Ok, thought Lisa. At least she looked old enough to have kids. With some reluctance, she held the door open wider and allowed Sophie to come in.

'Watch where you're sitting, the dog's had a bit of an accident.'

'Is that Febreze I can smell? Lavender? I use that one myself.'

Lisa nodded. It irritated her when these people tried to find common ground with her, as if she could ever truly connect with anyone who held the power to keep her kids away from her.

'What kind of dog is he?' They could hear him whining and scratching at the door. 'Mine's a Cocker Spaniel.'

'Bull Terrier.'

'What's his name?'

'Rocky.'

'Mine's Teddy.'

Lisa nodded. 'Have you got kids?'

'Three boys,' said Sophie, the pride evident in her eyes. 'They're all grown up now, but they're not too keen on moving out. Hubby says they've got it too good at home. Saying that, I reckon one of them is going to pop the question soon, so watch this space. You've got three as well, haven't you?'

'I did,' said Lisa. It hurt so bad.

'You *do*. You're still their mother. Nothing will ever change that.'

Lisa arched her eyebrows. 'They're certainly trying to.'

Sophie put her bag down on the floor beside her feet, a brave move in this house, Lisa thought, and pulled out her notebook. 'Let's have a quick look at the case plan your social worker will have sent you.'

Lisa rolled her eyes. She'd received the case plan in the post the previous morning and had found it as upsetting as it was overwhelming. She had no idea how she was ever going to achieve everything on the list in the narrow timeframe she'd been given. They had a look through it together:

**Goal 1:** The children are protected from the risk of physical harm
   **What it looks like:**
   - The children are not exposed to Domestic Violence
   - There are no further reported incidents of Domestic Violence
   - There are no breaches of the Prevention Order
   - The perpetrator takes accountability for his actions
   - The perpetrator takes the necessary steps to meaningfully and sustainably address his harmful behaviours
   - The victim-survivor takes the necessary steps to protect themselves and their children from the perpetrator
   **How we achieve it:**
   - Both parents abide by all conditions of the Prevention Order at all times
   - The Prevention Order is not varied to permit contact between the parents before the Father's harmful behaviours have been addressed or without CP approval
   - The Father engages with the Men's Insight Program
   - The Mother engages with a DV victim-survivor program to develop her insight into DV and complete safety planning
   - The Mother follows her agreed DV safety plan

**Goal 2:** The children are protected from emotional harm
   **What it looks like:**
   - The children are not exposed to Domestic Violence

- The children are not exposed to alcohol or substance use (including addictive medications)
- The children are not exposed to their parents' mental health difficulties
- The children have stability in their care arrangements
- The children are kept safe by a protective parent

**How we achieve it:**
- The children are referred to and supported to engage with relevant emotional/mental health supports
- The parents complete Supervised Urine D&A screens which evidence reducing levels of alcohol/substance/medication use
- The parents access treatment and support to address their alcohol/substance/medication use
- The parents support the children to remain in an alternative safe placement pending the matter being resolved in court
- The parents seek relevant emotional/mental health assessment and treatment
- The parents consistently attend planned contact with the children and abide by supervision requirements
- The children are referred for relevant developmental assessments as required

**Goal 3:** The children's basic care needs are met
**What it looks like:**
- The children have enough to eat and drink
- The children have access to necessities such as heating/cooling, bedding and appropriate clothing

- The family home environment is maintained to a 'good enough' standard
- The children are kept safe from harm
- The children attend school or childcare regularly
- The elder children are not relied upon to take on adult responsibilities

**How we achieve it:**

- The children are taken to school/childcare daily and are dropped off and collected on time
- The parents obtain a medical certificate for any school/childcare absence
- The parents undertake the primary care role for each of the children and do not delegate this responsibility to either of the children
- The home environment is maintained to a clean and hygienic standard with safe entry/exit points and working smoke alarms
- Essential provisions for the children are financially prioritised with the parents seeking benefit and budgeting supports and advice as required

**Goal 4:** Family Reunification

**What it looks like:**

- There protective concerns have been addressed
- The protective parent is able to sustain meaningful, positive change
- The protective parent is able to offer the children safe, stable, consistent care

- The children are able to reside safely in the care of a protective parent

**How we achieve it:**

- The parents comply with all aspects of the reunification plan

- Reunification plan commences when commitment to achieving these goals can be evidenced by the parents' engagement with services, decreasing urine screen results, absence of breaches of the Prevention Order or new reports of DV, absence of any further disclosures of concern from the children, improved school/childcare attendance record, and the Care Team observe accountability and consistent meaningful engagement by the parents

- The reunification plan of increasing contact with the children and decreasing levels of supervision will then commence, including eventual overnight contact

'This all looks a bit overwhelming, hey?' Sophie voiced Lisa's thoughts as they read through the paperwork together. 'Do you want to know the secret to getting them back?'

Lisa shrugged.

'Those professionals throw so much jargon around, it can be hard to understand exactly what it is they're expecting from you. I've done this job for a long time, and I've realised it all boils down to just one thing. In every decision you make from now on, show the social workers that you're *putting the kids first*. If you get that bit right, everything else will just fall into place.'

'It's that simple, is it?'

'I think so.'

'I thought I was doing that already - my kids are everything to me.'

'Well then, how about we explore what that looks like for you a little more in your day-to-day parenting?'

Lisa shook her head. She didn't want to go there. It was too raw. Too painful. Sophie seemed to sense this.

'Let's start with your husband, Kev, then. If I said this to him, what do you think he would tell me?'

'The exact same thing I said.'

'And do you think that in his case it's true?'

Huh! 'No way.'

'Why not?'

Where did she start. She could write a book on the subject. He showed barely any interest in either of the kids – not even Winter, his own flesh and blood.

'And what do you think he would say about you?'

'He would say that I'm useless - as a wife *and* as a mother.'

'Do you think that's a fair assessment?' Sophie raised her eyebrows. 'It doesn't sound very fair.'

Lisa hesitated. 'He doesn't see anything good in me anymore. But I do think there's some truth in what he says because I know I could do better. But our intentions are different. I love my kids and I *want* to be a good parent to them, I just don't often get it right because I've got too much going on myself. I'm not sure Kev would honestly be able to say the same thing.'

'Great. That does sound fair. We can build a lot on insight and good intentions, Lisa, and I would really like to help you do that.'

'Can I just ask you one thing?'

'Sure.'

'In your experience, is it a done deal with social services, or do I really stand a chance of getting them back?'

'Honestly,' said Sophie, 'that all depends on you. But the answer to your question is yes – you do stand a chance.'

Lisa exhaled. As much as she resented Sophie's presence, that's what she wanted - needed – to hear. Otherwise, there was no point to anything but oblivion.

*

**Jenny**

Jenny had spent the morning with Kai getting him settled into his new placement with his best mate from school. Not the best move, in her opinion, given teenage friendships could be as changeable as the weather, but as Sue had pointed out during supervision they had little choice, and at least it wasn't with – God forbid – a girlfriend, which would be liable to change even faster, resulting in yet another placement breakdown and another round of deadlines, meetings and paperwork. They knew they were clutching at straws given the amount of bridges Kai had already burnt, but Cole's mum was a salt of the earth type with a big heart, and with the sweetener of carer payments thrown in, Jenny hoped she would be able to sustain things until a better alternative presented itself.

'Remember what I said, Kai – we're at the end of the road now on the placement front, and I just want you to have somewhere secure to stay until you can start your joinery apprenticeship - I know how much that means to you.'

'I know, Jenny. I'll be a good lad this time – promise.' He grinned. It was hard to take him seriously, especially given Jenny had heard it all before.

'Keep out of trouble.'

'I'll try.'

Jenny could have hugged him, but she didn't – she didn't want to overstep the professional boundaries or make him feel uncomfortable. He looked so vulnerable at times – beneath his bluster, there was still the occasional hint of a small boy alone in a big world. How she wished that world would just envelope him, protect him, care for him, and keep him safe until he could learn to do those things for himself.

Next in her diary was a visit to the Season children to obtain their views for her preliminary assessment for court that would occur after three months of child protection support and intervention, by which time she could better assess the likelihood of a successful reunification based on the parents' degree of commitment to enacting the case plan. Tracy greeted her warmly with Winter in her arms and welcomed her in.

'Hi!' he said with a grin as he squirmed in Tracy's grasp, clearly wanting to be let down.

Winter looked well, Jenny noted, and she was pleased he had greeted her with words instead of unintelligible noises as he had done previously – when only his sisters had seemed to understand him. She suspected that rather than some inherent developmental delay or impairment, his delays were most likely due to a lack of stimulation, and if she was right, then with the right care he would most likely come on in leaps and bounds.

Tracy already had the kettle on and offered Jenny a cup of tea and a couple of ginger snaps. Usually, Jenny would say no, but in this case she felt it would be rude not to, so she acquiesced gratefully, relieved that for once it was a home environment in which she could relax and let down her guard.

The ginger snaps and the cramped terraced council house itself put her in mind of her own nanna – even down to the dynamic between the grandparents. Her own grandparents had had a tense relationship, and her mum had repeated that pattern with her father, until she'd eventually left. Her grandad had mellowed over the years and her mum was now happily remarried, but if it wasn't for those painful experiences Jenny had growing up, she would never have become a social worker hoping to help others in similar situations. It was similar for Fatima, who had a history of childhood emotional abuse, and no doubt several of the others she worked with, though it would never be appropriate for them to share that information with their clients, even if it offered a source of connection.

'So,' said Jenny, jotting down her notes and observations as they talked, 'how have things been going for you all?'

*

**Autumn**

Autumn could hear the adults talking. It felt weird, hearing her name come up every now and then and hearing them talk about her parents and how they weren't going too well. She wanted to tell them it was all Kev's fault, but the reality was that it was her mum too. She knew that in her heart of hearts - each time she'd come home and found her mum sleeping on the couch, Winter left to his own devices where anything could happen to him - but every fibre of her being still wanted to defend her. If Kev hadn't treated her the way he did, then Autumn was certain she would never have behaved that way.

'When can we go home?' Summer asked Jenny when it was their turn to meet with her, her hazel eyes earnest. 'I miss Mum.'

Jenny had brought a huge box full of art materials, and Summer was engrossed in making a card for their mum to give to her at the next contact, whilst Winter scribbled happily on a piece of paper and thought nothing of encroaching onto the table, which Jenny was swift to clean up with a baby wipe.

'I know you do, Summer. That's what I'm here to talk to you both about today – what you want to happen. We take that very seriously, and so does the judge at the children's court. He's the one who makes very important decisions around where children should live until they grow up - where the adults around them are best able to keep them safe.'

'But we just want to go home. Mum can keep us safe! We don't want Kev to be there though - not ever. And we want mum to stop sleeping on the couch, don't we, Autumn? Because when mum's asleep, Autumn has to do everything for all of us even though she's got homework.'

'Is that right, Autumn?'

Autumn shrugged.

'What would *you* like to happen?' Jenny asked her.

'What Summer said.'

'Nanna said that Kev wants to take Winter away from us,' said Summer. 'He can't have him though, can he?'

Autumn paled. She'd felt sick when she'd heard it. Winter had been with them from the very beginning, so surely a judge wouldn't split them up? Surely there was no way Jenny would allow that to happen? Kev didn't even do anything for Winter –

Autumn knew that even *she* could look after him better than he could.

Jenny fixed both girls in her gaze. 'I won't be recommending that Winter goes to Kev, because of how he has been to your mum and yourselves, and also because it would be very upsetting for all three of you not to be living together. The judge would have to look at any good changes Kev might make to his behaviour, but he would also have to take our worries seriously. It's a bit like your nanna's kitchen scales just there!'

Jenny pointed at her nanna's vintage metal scales, a keepsake from their great grandma. She looked towards Tracy for her permission to use them, and she nodded.

'The judge's job is to look at our worries about you three children on one side.' She put three coloured pens on one side of the scales, and they tipped. 'And the things that can help keep you safe on the other.' She added three pens on the other side until the scales were balanced. 'Then he must make the best choice. But with Kev, there are too many things on the worries side.' She added three more pens on that side, and the scales tipped again. 'That means that right now, a judge would be unlikely to consider him caring for Winter full-time, unless he could balance out those worries. And even if he did, they would still have to be thinking about what you two want to happen, and what is best for Winter.'

'Why does Kev even want Winter?' Autumn asked. 'It's just to get at mum. I know it is! He doesn't even do anything for him - Mum and I do it all.'

Jenny nodded. 'Those are the sorts of reasons that would tip the scales against Kev being allowed to look after Winter. A judge would always want kids to have contact with both parents as far as possible, but not necessarily to live with them full time if that can't happen safely.'

Autumn said nothing. She sat sullenly in her chair at the dining table. She wasn't sure what it was about Jenny that brought out that response in her – she seemed nice enough, but it seemed to Autumn that she had all the power, and they had none, their mum included, and she didn't like the direction she could sense the conversation was heading in.

'The other thing we need to keep in mind is that there are also changes we need your mum to make. Summer, you mentioned one of them just before – about your mum's sleeping. If she can't make those changes, I know it's painful to think about, but a judge would then need to consider what you two would want to happen if you couldn't go back to living with her. I know that might be hard for you to answer or even think about right now, but I don't want to keep secrets from you, and I want you to know we will be doing everything we can to help your mum. Your nanna says she will always be able to offer a place for you to stay if for whatever reason, it's decided that it's not safe for you to go home.'

'But that's bollocks!' Autumn yelled. She knew it. She'd known all along. They'd never let her go back home.

'Watch your mouth,' said her grandad, but Autumn didn't listen. She sprang from her chair and was out of the front door in a matter of moments.

'Autumn, wait!' Summer yelled.

'Autumn, I'm sorry-!' said Jenny.

But Autumn didn't care what they said - nothing could stop her from seeing her mum. Within a couple of minutes, she was at the cut leading into her mum's street. She was just rounding the corner when she saw Kev pulling up in his car, careful to park at the bend across the road just out of view of Irina. He wore his hood up over his cap and kept his eyes down, but Autumn would know him anywhere and she felt her heartbeat quicken. He looked from left to right then knocked, and to Autumn's dismay as she stood out of sight hard up against the brick wall shielded only by a neighbouring plant, she heard her mum let him in. Minutes later, she was at the wasteland near her school and in the arms of Blayze, who kissed her hard, then took one look at her face and passed her a spliff.

# 12.

**Lisa**

Sophie from Happy Families had told Lisa that to start putting the children first, she also needed to learn how and when to put herself first. She was talking about self-care, specifically of healthy ways to practice self-care that didn't involve her usual crutches of sleep, weed and pills. Lisa didn't know if she had it in her, but she was about to find out. The theory was that if she was in a good headspace herself, she should somehow be better prepared to manage the demands and challenges of parenting.

It had been years since she'd stepped inside any kind of educational facility and yet there she was, at Dunstonborough College, surrounded by teenagers and feeling positively past it as she leafed through the prospectus with the career's woman about twenty years too late. She was pretty sure she'd been skiving the day the career's woman had paid a visit to her school as a youngster, but it was better late than never, she supposed.

'We've got heaps of courses that should fit the bill,' she enthused. 'We have a subsidised nursery on site too that you could put your little ones into if you don't have childcare. I recommend you start with the combined level one in hair and beauty before starting on level two the following year - if it's specifically the wedding industry you're hoping to break into. There's also the option of studying part-time, though you did mention you're in a bit of a hurry to get it done before your baby makes an appearance. They're both one-year courses. Around your due date you might be able to negotiate doing coursework from home for a few weeks or defer for a year if you need to.

The best thing about our course is that we offer real on-the-job experience within our onsite salon offering discount services to students and members of the public.'

Lisa left the appointment with a stack of leaflets, an application form, and a feeling she barely recognised it had been so long since she'd felt it – anticipation and excitement for what the future might hold if she did something she really wanted to do. For her. Kev had never encouraged her to do anything for herself before. Neither had the girls' father, who had told her she was too stupid. According to Sophie, the kids would also benefit in the long run too, not just financially, but from Lisa getting an education and a job, enabling her to role-model her independence and commitment to them.

After the college visit, she'd made an appointment with her GP to get the ball rolling on her maternity care, then had a brief telehealth to discuss her therapy goals with a DV service Sophie had referred her to. Finally, she'd had to drop into the clinic to do a supervised urine test for Jenny. She already knew it would show up positive, but she also knew it didn't have to stay that way, and as humiliating as it was to have someone stand there and watch her pee, she was quite looking forward to showing her doubters she could and would do better.

She grabbed a whole heap of cleaning products from the supermarket on her way home and decided to do a thorough clean-out, starting with eliminating the piss smell from the carpet once and for all.

She couldn't remember the last time she'd felt so motivated. It was almost as if the more she did, the more she wanted to do. It felt so good, she was too distracted to think about weed or pills. So good that, when Kev sent her another text message asking if he could 'just pop round', this time she didn't hesitate to delete it. Not like the last time, when in a weak moment she'd let him come over to pick up some of his stuff both against her better judgement and the conditions of the Prevention Order. She'd been feeling lonely. She'd hoped he might have realised what he was missing out on and missed her too. That he still thought about the good times. But he didn't.

Rather than setting her back however, if anything his visit had propelled her forward. He'd turned up no different at all, completely full of himself and all the things he was doing to get Winter back into his care like the whole thing was some sort of competition between them. A game he was certain he would win. Well, she could play that game too and do it better. Only it wasn't a game to her at all. It was her family. Her life.

Lisa paused to have a cup of tea, trying to be mindful to savour the taste and the moment of rest, like the App on her phone that Sophie had recommended told her to do. Whereas the hours of the day would usually stretch out before her like some awful empty chasm, by the time she'd scrubbed the floors, suddenly it didn't feel like long at all until she'd be heading to contact with the kids. This time, she couldn't wait to see them and tell them all about her progress. These were her very first steps towards bringing them back home where they belonged.

*

**Jenny**

Jenny sat at her desk and breathed a sigh of relief as she crumpled up the last post-it note attached to her monitor and threw it in the bin. Thanks to a slog of long evenings, she was up to date with her case notes for the first time in what felt like years, and whilst she knew it was just a matter of time, at that very moment, not one of her cases was in crisis and she was looking at a bona fide miracle – a whole weekend of freedom. She and Alex might even get out to dinner! He would love that. They both needed it. Especially if there was a chance they really could become parents soon.

'You look happy,' said Fatima. 'Are you sure you're in the right workplace? Or is my masala chai really that good? I did add a secret ingredient this time, you know. Don't tell Will though or he'll drink it all.'

'You called?' said Will.

'Oh, you're here, I thought you were off sick.' Fatima grinned.

'Not today, love, maybe tomorrow - I think I feel a migraine coming on.'

'That's not a migraine,' said Fatima, 'that's work-itis.'

'Nothing your masala chai wouldn't cure!' Will winked. 'Tastes extra special today too. When are you going to bring some more of your pistachio burfi in? Or your gulab jamun? That was delicious.'

'If you turn up for work two weeks in a row, I'll think about it. I'm on duty next Tuesday and I don't want to be picking up your slack again.'

Jenny smiled. She loved working alongside Fatima. She wished she could tell her her news, but she'd stopped telling people after her first pregnancy – it had made for too many awkward conversations when the baby she'd told her closest family and friends she'd been expecting had failed to materialise. But now she was the furthest into a pregnancy she'd ever been.

She even had symptoms, and one of them, unfortunately, was that the very thought of Fatima's ordinarily delicious tea was suddenly repellent to her. Her boobs ached, and she constantly felt just that little bit sick. It was the most wonderful thing. Just three more weeks, then she would tell Sue during supervision, and maybe even Fatima too.

'Team meeting, folks,' announced Sue as she marched through the office rounding up the troops. 'Meeting room two in five minutes. Brenda's got some news for us.'

'Oh, do you think they've finally agreed to halve our caseloads? Get more staff? Fix the leaking roof? Turn the heating on?' Will winked at Jenny and Fatima on their way down the stairs.

'In our dreams,' said Fatima.

If only, thought Jenny. Turned out, it was quite the opposite. Some sort of new agreement between education providers and child protection services designed to identify at-risk children sooner to encourage early intervention and improve outcomes, that essentially meant a massive increase in workload due to all the man-hours and paperwork required.

'This assessment isn't too different to the initial assessments you already complete,' said Brenda. 'You'll just have a few more of them.'

'Do you mean our twenty-six-page initial assessment?' said Nicholas, a true dinosaur who still remembered the good old days, when social work had meant spending more time talking to people than writing about them.

Brenda's eyes narrowed. 'Yes. That's the one. Only the aim of the game here is brief intervention so that we can effectively identify the areas of need and refer the case on to relevant services before it reaches crisis point, then in the meantime close them off.'

'How does this meet the criteria of significant risk?' Will asked. He was referring to the Child Welfare Act, which defined the threshold for child protection involvement – that a child must be at risk of *significant* harm in order for children's services to intervene.

'Well,' said Brenda, 'it's designed to meet the needs of children before things get that far. Basically, if we do it effectively, whilst it may result in a slight increase in workload initially, ultimately over time, it should eventually reduce it.'

'Sounds like a complete load of bollocks to me,' Fatima whispered, and Jenny couldn't help but agree. 'I wonder which pen-pusher came up with that idea?'

'By the time it's become effective, we'll be retired,' Will snickered.

'The notifications have already started rolling in since this was introduced,' Brenda continued, 'and we have built up quite the backlog, so you'll each be getting allocated a couple of these assessments with a KPI of two weeks.'

Two weeks! There was a collective gasp, as everyone in the room tried to calculate how to juggle their already crammed calendars to squeeze in two (if indeed it was two) separate assessments within the next fortnight – which they'd been told involved meeting with the children, their parents, their school, and contacting any other relevant professionals - and still find time to write up the lengthy report and make the necessary referrals alongside all their other responsibilities.

'What about those of us who are already at capacity?' said Jenny. 'The traffic light system doesn't seem to be working.'

In an attempt to better manage caseloads, each case had been given a traffic light system in which green meant a case was stable, orange meant it was dicey, and red meant it was in crisis or the workload was at the intense end of the scale. The colours were to be reviewed at each supervision, and if you had three red lights on your caseload at any given time, you weren't meant to be allocated any more cases. Given supervision was hard to prioritise and the cases never stopped rolling in however, it had been all too easy to lose track.

'Yes,' said Will. 'And what about those of us still managing a lot of our own contacts – will Case Support be expanding their capacity to support us with this new initiative?'

Jenny sighed. Will had been trying to palm off the Cook contact for weeks. Knowing her luck, to prevent him from going on long-term sick leave they'd take it off his hands, even though she'd been waiting a lot longer for someone to pick up the Barnes contact which still consumed so much of her weekly availability.

'I'm afraid Case Support are at capacity,' said Brenda, 'but a few of you have some contact reductions coming up once the final orders come through, so that should free up some spots. We also have Shay, our newly qualified social worker starting next week. We can ease her in with some of your contacts and a couple of these assessments, so I suggest you speak to your individual team managers about that.'

Sue seemed to be taking a remarkable interest in her notebook, as did the other three team managers who were sitting in on the meeting with them.

'I give them six months,' Fatima whispered.

'Who? Will?' said Jenny.

'No - Shay. Not sure if that's a male or a female, are you? Could be anything, these days.'

Jenny nodded. She suspected that Fatima wasn't far wrong. Six months, eh? Even though she was an experienced worker who had seen enough of these harebrained schemes come and go in her time to know that this one surely couldn't last, six more months of working at this pace suddenly seemed intolerable. She was sure Alex would agree. She sent a text telling him to choose the restaurant because she was taking him out tonight. They'd better savour that dinner, because it was probably the last meal they were going to get to eat together in a long while.

*

**Autumn**

At contact that afternoon, Autumn's mum had been full of all the things she was doing to get them back, but Autumn was angry. She couldn't believe her mum could just lie to her face like that when she knew she was obviously seeing Kev again. She'd taken off straight from contact to the wasteland to meet up with Blayze, Starr, Coby and the others. It was initiation night, and she was equal parts excited and terrified.

'Ok,' said Blayze, 'here's what you kids have to do. To be one of us, you either have to buy something you're too young for, or steal something useful to the group. Either way, the most important thing is not to get caught and to share your haul with the rest of us. Understand?' Autumn nodded. She noticed that Starr looked as scared as she felt. They walked across the wasteland together and ducked under the underpass towards the square, comprising of a little L-shaped row of shops with a carpark at one end and a small branch of a major supermarket at the other. Autumn thought she could pass for older than she was, so she was going to try her luck buying a bottle of fizz with the pocket money her nanna had given her. Just as she was about to go in, Blayze grabbed her and kissed her hard on the lips, his pungent, cheap deodorant filling her nostrils.

'You can do it, babe,' he said, lending her his jacket more to cover up her school uniform than to protect her from the bite of a spring chill. 'Just go in there lookin' boss, like you own the place. Make sure you pick the youngest one to get served by – they're less likely to ask you questions, ok?'

Autumn took a deep breath. 'Ok,' she said.

'We'll wait for you down at the wasteland.'

'Do we really want to do this?' Starr ventured when they were out of earshot of the others.

Autumn shrugged. She didn't know what she wanted any more. Wasn't sure she even cared. '*You* don't have to.'

'If I don't, Coby will dump me.'

Same, thought Autumn. 'Good luck then!'

'You too,' said Starr.

They went in separately, and Autumn picked up a family-sized packet of crisps and did her best to affect a nonchalant expression as she perused the alcohol aisle, confidently ignoring the sideways glances of the other shoppers around her. She forced herself to compare prices and varieties as though she had every right to, when what she really wanted to do was to just grab and go. Maybe she should do that instead? No, she reasoned, she'd only end up in way more trouble if she got caught.

She selected a cheap bottle of sparkling from the bottom shelf then hid it beneath the crisps in her basket. She chose the youngest checkout assistant she could find and held her breath as she served her. She couldn't believe it. She was getting away with it. She was just a few feet from the door when she heard an older shop assistant yelling at the one who had just served her if she'd asked to see her ID. When the girl shook her head, the woman yelled, 'STOP!'

Autumn paled and her heart began thumping in her chest. There was nothing for it but to run. Without a backwards glance she paced towards the exit, picking up speed, then the moment she was through the barriers she ran flat out towards the cut through the bushes leading into the wasteland, as wet puddles splashed mud up the legs of her school pants. She didn't once stop to look behind her to see if she was being followed. When she got there Blayze grinned and hugged her. She knew she couldn't show her face at that supermarket for a while.

'You get first dibs,' he said proudly, twisting off the cap and holding the bottle out for her to take a sip. 'I knew you could do it!'

As she did so the others cheered, and Autumn suddenly felt as though she belonged and as if the whole ordeal had been worthwhile.

No doubt Starr would have seen the whole thing – maybe Autumn had even become something of a distraction to help her out. She crossed her fingers and hoped Starr would fare better than she had. If so, at least there'd be a celebratory sip of wine waiting for her when she got back – if the others hadn't downed it all first.

# 13.

**Lisa**

Lisa had been unable to scrub away the piss smell, so she'd lifted the living room carpet to find the ninety-year-old original floorboards underneath in relatively good nick – or they would be once she'd varnished them. Inspired by this new blank canvas, over the course of the next few hours she'd even painted a feature wall in the living room. It was a soft shade of sage over the breast of the fireplace that Kev would have said was far too girly, but she liked it. It looked so much better. She had a vision for the whole living room which had been looking tired, grubby and outdated for years, but her budget unfortunately didn't match that vision. She was accustomed to the limitations of a budget however and had already begun scrolling through marketplace to find some bargains, aided by Irina from next door whose own little house was neat as a pin.

Keeping busy and making plans helped Lisa keep the cravings at bay. She longed for pills, and her body was crying out for her to get it, but she wouldn't listen. Keeping busy was the only thing that worked. Then an idea came to her – she could decorate the kids' bedrooms for them coming home. It would give her a sense of hope and purpose, and she knew they would love getting involved in picking out their colour schemes without Kev's interference. There were only two other bedrooms aside from her own – with a bit of luck the baby would be a boy then she could have him and Winter in one room and the two girls in the other – otherwise three girls in the one room might be a bit of a crowd, and she'd have to re-think the name Spring.

She looked forward to discussing it all with them at their next contact. It might even cheer up Autumn, who'd been particularly distant with her lately.

'What about this love? This is nice,' said Irina. 'It's the sort of thing we had in my day. Just goes to show, if you keep something long enough it'll make a come-back sooner or later!'

It was a gilt mirror with an elaborately carved frame, and it was going for a song. Lisa could just imagine it painted a nice, shabby-chic shade of off-white. It would make a lovely contrast with her black fireplace. She already had plans to paint the top of her pine and glass coffee table the same shade. 'Yeah, I'll have that, but I'll see if I can knock him down a bit on the price first.'

'You're a sharp one, you are, Lisa. I can't get over the difference you've made to the place already. That woman from social services will be amazed!'

Lisa very much doubted it. 'I think it'll take more than a lick of paint to impress her, but thanks. And it's not much, really. All I've done is taken away a rotten carpet and painted one wall. The rest is all just a bunch of grand ideas in my head.'

'If anyone can do it, you can,' said Irina, who knew all too well how much a few words of encouragement might mean to someone in her position.

'Thanks, Irina. Keeping busy helps.' Tears sprang to Lisa's eyes before she could stop them.

'I know, love, I know.'

It was still very much a council house, but it was her council house. Lisa had managed to get Kev's name taken off the paperwork thanks to the Prevention Order, and as a single parent, her benefits had been changed. There was no denying the extra cash Kev had brought in during periods he'd been working had come in useful, but it wasn't as though she'd seen much of the fruits of his labour which had quite literally gone to the dogs, so she doubted she was going to miss it too much.

That afternoon she had her first appointment with the Domestic Violence psychologist, and the first question she asked her once she'd been made aware of what had been happening with her kids was what her own experience of parenting had been like and if she could draw any parallels from that. For the first time in her life, Lisa began sharing with a professional what it had been like to witness the violence playing out between her own parents as a child, and once the tap had been turned on it all poured out in a torrent. For an hour or so afterwards she felt truly shitty as she struggled to process all they had discussed, and a hundred-and-one other things came to mind that she would have to try to keep a lid on until next time, so she rolled a joint and very nearly caved to calm her racing thoughts. But she didn't. She took the dog out for a walk instead, and for that she was truly proud of herself.

*

**Autumn**

Autumn and Blayze were officially an item, and Starr was still mad for Coby. They spent their days at school and their nights at the wasteland together with the others, smoking spliffs and drinking cheap fizz, laughing, kissing and generally just having a good time. Mrs O'Neil had warned her that if she returned one more bit of homework late or not at all, she'd be given a week's worth of detentions and her nanna would be informed, but Blayze had just laughed and said that Mrs O'Neil

126

could do whatever she wanted to Autumn, it didn't need to change anything between them. Autumn had never thought of it like that before. Even though part of her still baulked at the idea of getting into trouble – it was the only thing stopping her from skiving school again - she supposed he was probably right.

The only thing that niggled at her was that when they were kissing, he was constantly pressuring her to go further than she wanted, and if he wasn't hassling her in person, then he was texting her for nudes all the time. She didn't really want to send him any because she didn't fully trust what he might do with them, but Starr had sent some to Coby and she didn't seem to think it was such a big deal, so Autumn decided she was probably making a big fuss over nothing. Everyone did it, and part of Autumn did want to know if he thought she looked alright underneath her school uniform.

'Autumn, are you still in there?' It was Summer, wanting to use the bathroom. Autumn had been in there for ages shaving her legs, applying moisturiser and a layer of fake tan to her skin then standing in front of the mirror trying to find the most flattering angles and the best light.

'Yes!' Autumn yelled. 'Give me five minutes!'

'That's what you said ten minutes ago!'

'Sorry!'

She'd been scrolling through social media for inspiration and had decided to copy a woman who was bent forward in a side pose so that her bottom and breasts poked out and the angle slimmed her stomach and stretched out any extra padding to her thighs and butt whilst also making it look like she had more of a cleavage than she really did. Autumn pouted for good measure, chose the best of the images then added a filter and before she could think better of it, sent it straight to Blayze. She was gratified when a succession of positive emojis came through moments after followed by a text message saying: *'Damn, you're on fire! I'm so hot for you right now. Send more!'* Autumn smiled. That was just the sort of reaction she'd been hoping for.

She exited the bathroom moments later to find Summer with her legs crossed at the top of the stairs, trying not to pee. 'You took ages!'

'Sorry!'

'Nanna said she'd give you some money to take us to the cinema tonight, can we go?'

'Oh, Sum, I can't tonight - I'm seeing Starr.'

Summer scowled. 'But you're always seeing Starr! I never get to do anything fun or spend time with you anymore. Winter doesn't either. And Nanna isn't happy with you being out all the time. Says she's going to talk to you about it later.'

Autumn felt a tug of guilt for both her siblings. She'd been like a second mother to Winter when they'd still lived at home, and now she hardly saw him. She did feel bad. She would make it up to both of them, just not tonight – tonight she was seeing Blayze, and when she got a moment, she was going to use it to find out from Starr just how far she should be prepared to let him go. The thought of it made her anxious and excited all at the same time.

'I feel like I've lost mum *and* you since we came here,' said Summer, tears springing to her eyes.

'But you've gained two grandparents, as well as your aunt and cousins!' said Autumn dismissively. 'Look, I'm sorry.' She sighed as she slicked on one more coat of mascara and some glittery lip gloss before pressing Summer into a hug. 'I'll make it up to you. I promise.'

It didn't take long though, for the alcohol to go down and for her promises to be forgotten. Maybe this is what it's like for mum, thought Autumn, as she felt her mind start to distance itself from reality and from all the pain, confusion and hurt it brought with it. And this time, it was that distance from reality that stopped her from pushing Blayze's hands away when they found their way into her bra and underwear as they hid behind the bushes just feet away from the others, wondering where it would all lead and if she still wanted him to stop.

*

**Jenny**

Jenny was overwhelmed. On top of her usual cases, which she struggled to keep up with at the best of times, she had come into work that morning, logged onto the system where they kept every detail of every case, and found she had been allocated not two, but FIVE of those initial assessments they'd been told about at the last team meeting. Five - to complete in a fortnight!

She'd immediately emailed Sue, who was obviously laying low, to ask if there'd been some sort of mistake. She received a response about an hour later saying that nope, there'd been no mistake, and as all five cases were interlinked and relating to the same concerns, there was no point in divvying them out to the rest of the team when Jenny could probably just cut and paste chunks or her assessment across each case. Jenny knew that was a cop out, because every report she ever completed had a massive section covering every area of each individual child's lives, and she couldn't even cut and paste that sort of information across a sibling group let alone across five separate young people.

'Y'alright, Jenny?' Fatima asked. 'Is it those bloody initial assessments? I've been allocated three - the bastards said only two! As if I haven't got enough on my plate! I was telling Rohan about it last night, and he told me that's enough of this stupid place and to hand my notice in. If only it were that simple.'

Jenny sighed. 'I've been allocated *five*!'

'Five! Dhhatt! I think you'll be needing to borrow my PISS OFF! mug today. Your husband will go spare!'

Jenny nodded. It didn't bear thinking about how she was going to get through the next couple of weeks, or if she and her relationship would survive the pace, which had basically gone from frantic to... well, what came after frantic?

'I think we need a night out, but how on earth could we fit it in?'

'We couldn't!' Jenny was glum.

'Just do what I do, ladies,' said Will with a wink. 'Make use of your sick leave 'til it all blows over and they introduce some other ridiculous scheme to replace this one.'

'How many assessments have *you* been allocated?'

'Three, but they can get fucked - I won't be breaking my neck to get them done in two weeks. It's impossible. We know that and they know that. It'll just be like any other KPI we don't meet - we'll have to record a rationale as to why. Obviously, the rationale is because demand seriously outstrips resources, as usual. Or because the assessment asks you to answer the same freaking question in twenty-six different ways. My advice is not to worry about it - you'll only drive yourself crazy if you do.'

It was unfortunate that Jenny didn't share Will's work ethic. She suspected that if she worked her absolute arse off to get them done in time, Sue might take pity on her and give her a little reprieve before allocating her anymore. She glanced through the notification notes:

The reporter provided the following information (Jenny noted that the reporter in this instance was a member of the local police force, but by law their details had been redacted from the notes and withheld from the children and their families to maintain the reporter's confidentiality):

- The children concerned are Coby Curran, Blayze Burns, Starr Knight, Nevaeh Martin and Keira Cross. They each attend Dunston Springs Secondary but are split across different year levels.

- The children are known to congregate at the property of a Mr Harry Curran, aged 38 years, of 1 Prosper Street, Feather Glade, Dunston, who is the paternal uncle of Coby Curran.

- In exchange for alcohol, marijuana and other substances, it has been reported to Dunstonborough Police that Mr Curran has been provided without their knowledge or consent, intimate images of several young females, including the three females named above, some of whom are yet to be identified due to lack of identifying details in the photographs.

Mr Curran's phone has been seized and the images taken as evidence.

- This information has come to light from Mr Curran's ex-partner, recently separated, who has reported the matter to Police along with a Domestic Violence complaint. Investigation ongoing. Criminal charges likely.

- A protective assessment is recommended to ensure that safety planning occurs with the victims and their families.

- Please note that Coby Curran and Blayze Burns are potentially facing charges relating to the acquisition and distribution of these images, which are effectively child pornography.

Jenny sighed. At least it now made sense why she'd been lumbered with all five cases. *Blayze.* Where had she heard that name before? Then she remembered. He went to the same school as Autumn Season. Wasn't that the boy her teacher had said she was interested in? If so, she hoped that by now, his appeal had well and truly worn thin for her, otherwise who knew what sort of trouble she might be inviting into her life - the poor girl had quite enough to deal with already.

She generated the assessment document for each child, so that she had five tabs open at once, and hoped the system wouldn't crash. She picked up the phone and scrolled down to the 'education' section of each report. That an easy one. She'd start by calling the school to get an update on each child's attendance, attainment, and general presentation. With a bit of luck, the information gleaned should help fill in some gaps in the health, culture, development, behaviour, self-care and social skills sections. She couldn't pretend she wasn't a little anxious as she dialled the number and asked to be put through to the assistant head. With every phone call made, new concerns would often emerge, closely followed by a heap of tasks that usually ended up as the social worker's responsibility. Oh well, at least after that she'd be one section down – then there'd only be forty-three left per child to go.

She opened another tab and typed in 'social care jobs.' She didn't mean it, obviously. She loved working with children and young people – they were what kept her coming into work each day no matter what was thrown at her, just as *they* continued to live day after day despite all that had been thrown at them. But she could still dream.

# 14.

**Lisa**

'Wow!' said Jenny, as she entered Lisa's refreshed living room. It was clean and tidy, the smell was gone, the dog was calmer from more regular attention and walks, and though simple, the makeover was a vast improvement on how things had been before. 'Lisa, this is great!'

She shrugged. 'Keeping busy helps.' It had helped keep her mind off Kev. The pills. The loneliness of missing her kids.

'Evidently.' Jenny perched less precariously than she usually would on the couch. 'You've done a wonderful job! You should be proud of yourself. There aren't many who could do all this while going through what you're going through.'

Lisa smiled. Whilst she didn't altogether trust Jenny, she had to admit she wasn't too bad either. Neither was Sophie from Happy Families, really, nor her psychologist. Like Irina said, they were all just doing their job. In their own way, they were all trying to help. Irina had pointed out there were no end of other jobs these people could be doing, but they had chosen to do what they did for a reason. Lisa hadn't looked at it like that before, but she supposed it made sense. There had to be easier ways to pay the bills.

'You'll be pleased to know I'm here to discuss what I'll be recommending at the interim court hearing.'

Lisa fiddled with her wedding ring like she always did when she was anxious, twisting it round and round on her finger. Which reminded her – she needed to decide what she was going to do with it, because one thing was for certain – she was done with being Kevin's wife and had already reverted to the use of her maiden name: Season. Perhaps the new baby would be a Season too, just like Winter, because she and Kev had been going through a rough patch then too. 'And what will you be recommending?' She was wary.

'That all three children begin a staggered return to your full-time care, subject to the points we've already agreed upon in the case plan.'

Lisa was overwhelmed. She hadn't expected to feel so emotional, but she did.

'In a nutshell, you've made a great start on doing all we asked you to do and more. Your interaction with your children at contact has been very loving and appropriate. You've acknowledged the protective concerns on behalf of your children, and you've cooperated with Child Protection and with the services we've asked you to engage with in the relatively short timeframe allowed to you. Feedback from those services about your progress and engagement has been overwhelmingly positive. Your drug screens are now showing a clear reduction in any substance or medication use, and you haven't reunified with Kevin. Not only that, but your children have made it clear that whilst they're coping ok with their nanna, what they really want is to be back home with you.'

'They do?' Lisa hadn't expected to feel so relieved at hearing that. Especially from Autumn, whom she suspected was fast developing a new level of anger and resentment towards her – something she could recall feeling towards her own parents when she was her age, and who could blame her?

'They do,' Jenny confirmed.

'But what about Kev? Does he still want Winter?' Lisa already knew he was doing everything that had been asked of him, because he took great joy in keeping her abreast of the fact whenever she dodged his late-night booty calls and subsequent barrage of hostile texts.

Jenny nodded. 'He does, but we won't be recommending that Winter goes with him. Feedback from the Men's Insight Program hasn't been positive, and he's never been tested as Winter's primary carer. Our concerns regarding his parenting remain and have yet to be meaningfully addressed. It's no secret that the girls don't want to be separated from Winter either, which would be highly distressing for all three children.'

Lisa was surprised. Kev had been so certain this was a battle he would win. She wondered how he would take the news that that wasn't the case. If she knew Kev, it didn't bode well, and this gave her a sense of unease she hadn't experienced since he'd left. 'Does Kev know any of this?'

'Not yet,' said Jenny, 'but I have an office visit with him tomorrow and I'll have the conversation with him then. The next step, if the court agrees, is to start putting our reunification plan into action. If, by the final court date, you can demonstrate that you've continued to maintain progress and no new concerns have been raised on behalf of your children, then it's highly likely they'll be ordered to return to your care, and we would support that.' Jenny smiled.

Lisa sensed a but. 'And if not?'

'If not, then the recommendation will be that all three children remain with your parents permanently – with regular parental contact.'

'Those are the stakes?'

'They are. But do you know what?'

'What?'

Jenny fixed her in her warm gaze. 'I have the strongest feeling you can do it.'

The first thing Lisa did when Jenny had driven off was to knock on Irina next door, and together they celebrated the news over a cuppa. It was the most sedate celebration of any milestone in her life, yet to date the most poignant. She only hoped she wouldn't stuff it up.

*

**Jenny**

Jenny and Alex were at sixes and sevens. Ever since those new assessments had come in, she'd been stressed to death, and he'd warned her multiple times that the pace she was going at just wasn't healthy for either her or their unborn baby. She'd started setting her alarm extra early to beat the morning traffic creating more time to work on her reports and case notes before her hectic days of meetings, phone calls and visits began, then she was returning home late in the evenings where she continued to fight sleep so she could continue working. No matter how hard was treading water, she constantly felt that she was drowning.

'It's ok,' Jenny had reassured him. 'It's just for a couple of weeks, then it'll get better.'

'No, it won't!' said Alex, a pained expression marring his lovely face as he buttoned up his shirt. 'It'll only get worse! No sooner will you have done all those assessments than one of your cases could go into crisis, or, knowing how your place works, you'll immediately be allocated five more.'

'I won't!' said Jenny as she slipped on her ballet pumps. God forbid! 'I just need to get through these assessments, then Sue will take pity on me and give me a break. Being given five at once was a one off. And Brenda said there's a backlog – we must be making some headway into clearing it up by now. That's got to count for something.'

'Listen, Jenny,' said Alex, fixing her with his clearwater eyes that made her heart ache because she missed him so much. She knew that what he was saying was right, but she didn't know what to do about it. 'It's bad enough *you* have to go through this, but there's Flick to consider now too.' He gestured towards her stomach, where to her disappointment she still had no trace of a bump. 'You're hardly sleeping. You're racing here there and everywhere. When you *are* here, you're not present – you're too preoccupied by all the tasks you have outstanding. If we do get to keep this baby, I'm worried you'll be robbed of the chance to take care of yourself and enjoy the pregnancy!'

That hit a nerve. 'Alex, what do you want me to do? It's not like I can quit when I have nothing to move on to and we're about to start a family! I just need to survive the next few months until I start my maternity leave – then I can reconsider my options. You know I've always fancied working in fostering or adoptions and I've been keeping an eye out there for jobs. There was one, but I just missed the deadline, so I'll have to wait until next time.'

Fostering and Adoptions was a bit like a graveyard for the burnt-out frontline Child Protection staff who'd done their bit. As such, competition for posts was fierce, and Jenny suspected it wouldn't be long before Fatima abandoned ship in that direction

- maybe even Will too. The long hours had been hard for Fatima and her husband to juggle with their school-aged children.

Alex sighed. 'Look, I'm just trying to protect you. *Both* of you. Can you at least talk to Sue about how you're feeling? Tell her to cut you some slack? Maybe even tell her you're pregnant and how precarious this journey has been for us to date?'

Jenny baulked. 'I can't!' she gasped. 'Not until I'm over twelve weeks – it'll jinx it!' They were *so* close now.

'Please?' Alex begged. 'I can accept that we're going to be passing ships if I can see there's an end in sight, and if you agree to try putting yourself first for a change. Can you do that for *you*? For Flick – and us?'

Jenny sighed. 'Ok,' she promised. She could just imagine how that would go down with management. In her experience, once someone had rocked the boat, no matter how justified their reason, it was never long before they were thrown overboard.

As it turned out, Alex's predictions weren't far wrong. A crisis was never far away – but Jenny hadn't anticipated it would come from Season, or that Sue would still expect her to manage the increased workload associated with a placement breakdown alongside all her other cases and those new risk assessments. She'd given her a half-hearted promise that Shay, the new social worker, would help her out – but she'd quickly been overwhelmed with tasks too, bless her, and was probably rethinking her career choice before the ink on her degree had dried. Fatima had already found Shay crying on the phone to her boyfriend one afternoon.

'You're sure you can't be persuaded to give it another go?' said Jenny, unable to hide the desperation in her voice as she spoke to Autumn's grandmother over the phone. Just a couple of weeks would buy her some precious time.

'I'm afraid not,' said Tracy. 'If it were only up to me, I might be persuaded, but my husband is having none of it. That girl knows our rules, and she's broken them one too many times now.'

Oh, for fuck's sake, thought Jenny, who couldn't imagine willingly allowing her own flesh and blood to enter the care system – but then who knew what she might do if she'd had a similar set of life experiences? She'd seen through kids like Kai Humphries how challenging some kids' behaviours could be for anyone, even with the best of intentions, to have to manage - especially those who'd already done their time raising their own children. What made it harder to accept was that these children were already hurting so badly, and needed love, care and stability more than anything else. If push came to shove, and Jenny found herself in a similar scenario with her own child several years down the track, who could say for certain that she'd do things any differently?

Jenny knew this news would be devastating for Autumn, but most of all, it would be devastating for her siblings, who anyone could see still depended on Autumn as something of a mother figure. She hated being the one to have to go out and deliver such a terrible blow to the child, far more than she hated how much her workload would now increase in the process.

*

**Autumn**

Belinda and Gary Wright tried their best to make Autumn feel at home, but there was nothing more surreal than coming

140

to live with complete strangers and trying to make out like it was normal. They'd tried their best – the bedroom was the nicest she'd ever slept in, and it was her own - she didn't have to share it with anyone. There were clean towels laid out for her and a basket containing every toiletry she could possibly need by the bed - the good ones, as well as a selection of healthy snacks she could indulge in in her own time – the posh she could imagine someone like Jenny eating. But she missed her brother and sister, and the thought of having to live separately from them tore her apart. She closed her eyes and recalled their faces when she'd left, her few possessions packed hastily away into a suitcase and a few bin bags. She would never forget.

She just hadn't seen it coming. While she knew she'd been skating the boundaries with her increasingly late nights and poor school performance, once her nanna had come across a packet of weed in her coat pocket whilst doing the laundry, it had been game over. She was sorry of course, but her grandad had said she was only sorry about getting caught. Maybe there'd been some truth in that, because had she known her actions would have led to this, she would have been far more careful about covering her tracks. They'd known of course. Had smelled it on her for weeks. They just hadn't known for sure that *she* was doing it until then.

'Whatever you do, pet,' her grandad had said staidly just before she'd gotten into the car with Jenny, her worldly belongings crammed into the boot and spread across the back seat, 'don't turn out like your mother.'

Autumn had been surprised how much those words had hurt. She'd thought they loved her - had never imagined them giving up on her like this. She thought she'd just get grounded or

141

something – but like they'd said, they'd grounded her plenty of times before and it hadn't changed a thing.

It wouldn't be long until she'd be back home with her mum, Jenny had reassured her, but honestly – what did Jenny know? She had no idea her mum was still seeing Kev behind her back. Of all the things that had hurt Autumn, what hurt most was that her own mum didn't care enough to do the right thing to bring her home. If she *was* still seeing Kev, it was just a matter of time until things went to shit again and she lost them for good. And then where would she go?

'I'm just going out for a bit,' Autumn said to Belinda. She and Gary raised their eyebrows but said nothing. It was obvious they didn't approve, but there was nothing they could do but let her go, so long as she promised to be back by curfew. She'd promised of course, and she did feel bad, but like Blayze had said, promises were made to be broken, and it felt weird being there – like she was intruding into someone else's lives. She didn't belong there, but at least with Blayze and Starr and their friends, she had found somewhere to belong.

# 15.

**Autumn**

They were at the beach. Once Autumn had mentioned it was one of her favourite places to go – to walk and think and look out to sea imagining what distant lands lay at the opposite end of it and all the places she'd love to visit one day when she was older, as far away from Dunstonborough as it was possible to get – Jenny had made a point of taking her and Summer there during her next statutory visit, which was also doubling as a sibling contact.

They'd gone round all the amusements together, spending a small fortune in pocket money on the two pence machines and having a giggle on the roller-coaster simulator. Autumn had won a cuddly toy for Winter on the grabber much to his delight, though she knew nothing could replace his little Oaty. Afterwards, they'd shared a cone of hot, vinegary chips to warm their cool fingers as spring winds tore through their hair and sand filled their shoes. Even though it was freezing, Jenny hadn't been able to resist buying them a 99 ice cream. She told them how when she was young, they'd gotten their name because they had actually once cost 99 pence. Summer said she couldn't imagine anything so delicious being so cheap and told Jenny she should've gotten one every day.

The best thing was that for once Jenny didn't pry with all her awkward questions. She just let them be and it felt good, and Autumn realised how much she'd been missing her brother and sister and how much she regretted that things hadn't turned out differently. Her heart ached when they dropped Summer off back at their nanna's, and after a brief play with Winter, he hugged her as if he would never let her go, screaming for her when she left as he clung to his new teddy.

'I'm sorry you're going through all this,' said Jenny quietly on the drive back to placement, her eyes fixed on the road.

Autumn was silent. They were trailing the familiar coastal route, and as they did so it felt as though she was being taken away from her old life and everyone in it who meant something to her. She stifled her tears - didn't want anyone to see her cry. Crying didn't fix anything.

'During half-term, you'll be able to start having unsupervised contact with your mum out in the community or even back home in your own space, if you want to. Then after that it'll be overnight stays. Your mum said she's going to decorate your bedroom for you coming home too. That'll be nice, won't it?'

'Mmhmm,' said Autumn.

'How do you feel about that?'

Autumn hesitated. 'I don't want to go there.'

Jenny frowned. 'You don't want to go back home? How come?'

Because *he'll* be there, thought Autumn. She wondered whether to say the words aloud and what might happen if she did. The more she agonised over it however, the angrier she became towards her mum for putting her in that position in the first place, until the words somehow tumbled from her lips before she could even stop them.

'Because mum's been seeing Kev behind your back!' she said. 'I saw him there - at the house. I wanted to go see Mum without anyone knowing, but I couldn't because *he* got there first. I hoped she'd tell him to leave but she didn't, she let him in... She's been lying to you - to all of us - this whole time and I hate her for it.'

Jenny was silent as she processed this new information, her eyes never straying from the road, and all the while Autumn could have literally kicked herself for her own stupidity when she realised what this could mean for her future, and for that of her brother and sister. She was torn apart by guilt for what might now happen to her mum because of her. If only she could rewind time just a minute or two and take the words back. No matter how she felt about Kev, it just wasn't worth the consequences.

'You do understand that I'll have to speak to your mum about this?' said Jenny, her expression grave as they pulled up outside Belinda and Gary's house.

'Please don't,' Autumn pleaded. 'I'm sorry - I was just angry. I made it up!'

'I'll still have to have a conversation with your mum and Kev, but you're not in any trouble, Autumn, ok? If that *is* what happened, then it must have been a heavy secret for you to carry all this time, and it isn't your fault.'

Autumn wanted to scream because it *was* her fault. She should never have said anything. She and her brother and sister might never get to go home again because of her. When Jenny dropped her off at the door, Autumn didn't even go inside – she turned on her heel and went straight to the wasteland, where she knew Blayze and their friends would be waiting, bringing with them alcohol, a spliff, and the oblivion she craved. She just didn't care anymore. Blayze somehow seemed to sense it and sought to take advantage of the moment. It was fortunate for him then, that Autumn no longer cared what happened to her.

**Lisa**

Lisa was beside herself with terror at the prospect of what might happen next if she couldn't get the truth across to Jenny. She knew that a ball had inadvertently begun rolling and she was powerless to stop it as it threatened to destroy her whole life. It was bad enough that her parents had just given Autumn up – something she was still stewing over - and now, as if she didn't have enough to deal with, she'd had to contend with the belief that Lisa was lying to her.

It suddenly made sense why Autumn had been so frosty with her during contact lately, as the distance between them stretched wider and wider where once they'd been inseparable. No wonder, the poor girl. She longed to see her to tell her the truth and put her mind at rest – but would she even believe her? And who could blame her if she didn't? She'd heard it all before.

'It's just not true!' she tried once more, but she could see the doubt in Jenny's eyes. There was now little trace of the confidence she'd had in her during the previous week's visit, and Lisa wished there was some way she could make her see. 'Honestly, Jenny, I swear on my life - on my kid's lives - the Bible, anything! You name it and I'd swear on it!'

'So, Kev was never here?'

Lisa sighed. She didn't owe it to Kev to protect him anymore. 'Well, he *was* here, but not in the way you think.'

Jenny shook her head sorrowfully as she scribbled into her notebook.

'Wait!' Lisa held out a hand as if to stop her from writing down the words she knew would condemn her. 'He *did* come round one night to pick up some stuff. He was already at the door, and I didn't think it was unsafe for him to be there. I mean - he hadn't been drinking or anything! It just seemed more hassle than it was worth at the time to send him packing when he was going to have to collect his things sooner or later, and I could tell he wasn't in a mood to cause trouble. And I've been trying to clear up the place. I realise that's technically still a breach of the Prevention Order and he should've had a police escort with him, but I know Kev, and I can usually tell when he's about to kick off. He got his stuff and was gone within half an hour, and I haven't seen him since. Well, apart from the one time I saw him pulling up in his car as I left a meeting at your place. And he sends me text messages sometimes too - but I've never replied. Not once.'

'Have you reported any of this contact from Kev as a breach?'

'Well, no. I didn't think it was worth it for the sake of a few text messages.'

Jenny shook her head. 'If you kept that information from us, Lisa, while knowing it was against our case plan for the children and what we expected from you, how can we be sure you aren't keeping anything else from us? This one incident, you see, unfortunately undermines the confidence and trust we have developed between us. Autumn is absolutely convinced you're back together. How can I reassure her that's not the case?'

'You can't,' said Lisa. 'You can't be certain of anything. I just hope you know me well enough by now to trust me. Please, Jenny - I'm not the same woman I was when we first met. Deep down I think you know that don't you?'

Jenny was quiet. Thoughtful. She held her pen still. Lisa suspected these were lines she'd probably heard from dozens of parents before her and wondered if in the end it became hard to tell fact from fiction in her job. 'Look, with hindsight I realise I should never have let him in. I should've called police or told you about it straight away. But I was different then - I didn't see things quite the same way as I do now. Truth be told, at the time I still held a little bit of hope for us... But I don't anymore.'

'I know!' Lisa exclaimed as a thought suddenly occurred to her. 'Why don't you go speak with Irina next door? She'll tell you the truth. The night Kev came round I texted her! She probably still has the message on her phone - messaging her is part of the safety plan I agreed with my DV psych. Anyway, I texted her so she would know Kev was there just in case anything untoward *did* happen. Irina keeps an eye out for me in case he turns up here, you see. We've become good friends lately, but I know she'd snitch on me soon as look at me if she thought any harm might come to my kids. She keeps me on the straight and narrow, does Irina.'

'Oh, Lisa,' said Jenny. Lisa could see Jenny wanted to believe what she said was true.

'Just speak to Irina for me. Please? I wouldn't have made so much progress if I was still seeing Kev, would I? And if I *was* seeing him, there would've been another incident between us by now, but there's been none. I know the stakes, and I wouldn't do anything to sabotage getting my kids back now. I want that more than I want anything Kev has to offer.'

Jenny sighed. 'I'll call Irina,' she agreed, 'but I can't promise that will change anything. It'll be my manager who has the final say about what happens next.'

'But you can tell your manager what *you* think, can't you, and she'll listen?'

'She'll take my assessment on board, yes.'

'Then tell her I'm sorry. I realise I've stuffed up, and that I've hurt and confused Autumn in the process. I'm only human - I've made a mistake, but I've learned from it. Truly. Please don't let her take my kids away from me. It would kill me.'

Tears streamed down her face, and when Jenny left, this time it wasn't a celebration Lisa and Irina shared over a cuppa, but commiserations over the sheer wretchedness of the situation she now found herself in and what might happen next.

*

## Jenny

It wasn't an easy meeting. Jenny's head was full of everything that had happened with Season alongside all the balls she was frantically trying to keep in the air. It just wasn't feasible to continue working at this pace, and Jenny felt as though she was inwardly breaking. She was trying her best to hide it – from Fatima, Sue, Alex - from everyone – but she didn't know how much longer she could keep up the act. Only that morning she'd noticed during a visit that she'd somehow developed a stutter - she had so many thoughts racing around her head, mostly of tasks she needed to keep track of - it was as if her mouth could no longer keep up with her brain. She felt self-conscious about it, but thankfully it hadn't happened at the office yet. Just one more week, she told herself, then she'd get a reprieve, surely.

'I'm not sure, Jenny,' said Sue. 'My spidey senses aren't liking this one little bit. We should probably consult with Legal about it at the very least.'

'I know,' said Jenny, 'but I've gotten to know Lisa, and I *do* believe her. She knows she's stuffed up, but she didn't have the same level of insight then that she does now. Back then, she didn't quite appreciate the gravity of the situation and was probably still hopeful that Kevin could change. Now, I think she clearly understands it would be folly to pursue a relationship with him that could go either way, over a relationship with her children who need her. She does seem to be trying her best, and the feedback from services and her drug screen results support that. Let's not forget we're looking at potentially removing her children from her care permanently – I really do think she deserves another chance.'

'I dunno,' said Sue. 'You know what they say – we're damned if we do, and we're damned if we don't.' She leaned back in her chair and chewed the lid of her pen thoughtfully. 'Here's what we'll do. We'll need to dot our I's and cross our T's – let's consult with Legal, and if they're happy to proceed as planned then we will. Just make sure Mum is clear this will need to be her last slip up – she'll have to do everything by the book from now on.'

Jenny exhaled her relief and for a moment she felt lighter. She was certain this was the best decision for the children. She would need to make a time to go explain it all to Autumn. 'Absolutely,' she said, rising to leave.

'And Jenny?'

'Yeah?'

'How are you getting on with those new assessments? Brenda's asked me to do a spreadsheet keeping track of everyone's progress. They're our priority right now.'

I'm drowning, thought Jenny. 'I'm on track.' She chose her words carefully. 'But I've found doing five of them at once really heavy going, and while I'm pulling out all the stops to get them done on time, this isn't a pace I feel confident I can continue working at longer-term...'

'It's a circus in here at the moment, isn't it?' Sue nodded empathetically.

'It certainly is.'

'I'll see what I can do when the next lot of allocations comes up.'

'Thanks, Sue. A bit of breathing space before that happens would not go unappreciated.'

Now Jenny *definitely* felt lighter. She knew Sue would understand. She texted Alex to tell him as much. Just a few more days, then she'd get the reprieve she needed.

# 16.

**Jenny**

Though Jenny had somehow managed to wrap up all five assessments within the ridiculously tight timeframe she'd been given, it wasn't without its consequences. She was absolutely exhausted from a fortnight of ultra-late nights and early starts, and her anxiety had reached new peaks as she'd begun to manifest physical symptoms for the first time in her life – a stutter, chest pain, and an unceasing sense of dread and overwhelm. It couldn't be good for the baby, and she hoped and prayed that nothing would go wrong. They were so close to twelve weeks - her scan was in just a few days' time. It was the closest she'd ever got to a viable pregnancy, yet for her and Alex, the subject had become taboo and neither of them ever brought it up – they were both too scared of getting hurt again.

She'd come home late almost every day from having to cram most of her visits into after-school hours, and now she had to address all the usual tasks she'd set to one side on her other cases - she was just lucky that none of them had gone into crisis. She powered up her monitor and logged into the system, only to find to her great dismay that more tasks had been added to her list. A couple of clicks revealed another three of those bloody assessments – which meant that on top of her usual responsibilities she now had another three families to visit (one a sibling group of five), about fifteen new tasks, and three more twenty-six-page assessments to complete within the next fortnight. Tears sprang to her eyes. She couldn't believe it - she was going to cry at her desk in front of everyone and there was nothing she could do to prevent it.

Sue was laying low in her office with her Do Not Disturb sign on the door, and when Jenny heard Fatima tut and mutter aggressively in Hindi she immediately understood why. 'Can you fucking believe this?' she said. 'I'm sick of this shit - we should go on strike!'

'I... I can't do this,' said Jenny. 'I just can't.'

She sprang from her desk and dashed to the bathroom. She'd never had a panic attack before, but she was fairly sure she was having one right then. She couldn't catch her breath and she was seeing silver glitter everywhere – something that normally only happened when she stood up too fast. Her heart was beating so rapidly it felt as though it was in her throat. Maybe she was having a heart attack? Maybe she should call an ambulance? For a moment she thought she was going to die. In the privacy of the loo, she sat down on top of the lid and allowed the tears to fall. It was cathartic. It released some of the pressure that had been building up inside her body and mind. She had too much to do to risk staying in there for long, but she couldn't return to her desk until her heart rate had dropped to its usual level and her face had lost its flush.

She was just reapplying her mascara when Shay, the new girl came in, her expression something akin to a young deer trapped in headlights.

'Alright?' Jenny asked.

'Yeah,' said Shay. 'You?'

'Yeah,' said Jenny.

But it was obvious to anyone with an ounce of emotional intelligence that neither of them meant it.

What to do about it though? Jenny wondered on her return to her desk. She knew what Alex would want her to do. He'd tell her to have it out with Sue, but in the head space she was in, a face-face felt too confronting. She fired off an email instead, practically begging Sue to give her a break and free up some of her schedule. The least she could do was reallocate that bloody Barnes contact she'd been harping on about for months.

Her phone rang. 'Hello, Jenny Hurst here,' she said on autopilot.

*'Hi.'* Though it was the voice of a professional, Jenny could tell by her overly polite tone that this professional was pretty irate. 'It's Sally Smith, the assistant head from Dunston Sec. I received your closure letter for Nevaeh Martin, and I'm just wondering if you can explain *why* you're closing, when it's obvious the parents aren't coping with her severe mental health and behavioural needs and the school is now struggling to accommodate her too? I'm sure you're aware that we have fifteen-hundred other children in this school, and we simply don't have the resources to meet the intensive needs of just one.'

Join the club, thought Jenny. Social workers were usually sensitive to the fact that the police, health and education services were stretched to their limit, yet for some reason the sentiment often went unreciprocated. Stress and a lack of resources would lead to unreasonable expectations, buck passing, and losing sight of a common goal to achieve the best possible outcome for the children they represented. It was one of Jenny's bugbears that she often had to deal with hostility not just from clients, which could be expected, but from professionals too. Her heart beat uncomfortably in her chest – or was it her throat? - and when she opened her mouth, she was so anxious that at first she could barely speak.

'Because we are Child *Protection*,' she said when she could finally get her words out. 'In Nevaeh's case we have two *protective* parents who are doing everything they possibly can for their child which leaves no role for us. We're not saying there are no concerns, but they are concerns that need to be managed by the parents in collaboration with mental health and education services as opposed to *social* services. Our role is to manage cases where there is *no* protective parent.'

Sally Smith sighed, her dissatisfaction obvious, before hanging up the phone with an abrupt goodbye.

'Goodbye, have a nice day yourself,' said Jenny to the dial tone as she opened a job search tab with her free hand in a feeble attempt to make herself feel better.

'What's the matter?' Fatima asked. 'Did you forget to bring your magic wand into work again?'

Thank goodness for Fatima, thought Jenny. If she didn't have her to keep her afloat, she didn't know what she'd do.

\*

**Lisa**

'Do you like it?' Lisa asked, her face aglow with the excitement of having all three of her children back home under one roof - her *own* roof - where they belonged, without a single social worker or contact supervisor (or her mother) present to monitor her every move, and a full twenty-four hours stretching out ahead of her to spend with them.

'I love it!' said Summer, throwing herself upon the top bunk to hide herself beneath the glittery canopy and switch on the floral fairy lights. She'd always been scared of the dark, and Lisa had promised her she could leave her fairy lights on all night.

The bottom bunk was a double – something Autumn had always wanted that Lisa had scoured the whole of Dunstonborough to find at a price she could afford. And whilst space and money were still tight, Lisa had utilised some clever hacks to create low-cost storage, giving both girls a sense of their own space within the shared room. The bed and accessories had mostly been the result of Irina's keen eye for a bargain. She'd dialled down the pink a notch for Autumn's benefit, adding hues of crisp white and warm taupe, and had even managed to wedge in desk for when she started her GCSEs next year.

'What do you think, Autumn?'

Autumn shrugged, and Lisa tried not to let her lack of enthusiasm get to her. She supposed she hadn't been overly enthusiastic about much when *she* was fourteen, but it didn't stop her from hoping they could regain the common ground they had lost over the last couple of months they'd been apart. She hoped Autumn had believed her when she'd reassured her that Kev would *never* be coming back.

'Witta room,' said Winter, clutching a well-loved Oaty in his arms. 'Show Oaty!'

'Ok,' said Lisa, reluctantly pushing the status of her relationship with Autumn to the back of her mind in order to return Winter's enthusiasm. 'Let's go show Oaty your room again!'

As Winter tootled towards the next bedroom, Summer trotting behind as he hopped proudly up into his racing car bed, Lisa could scarcely believe the changes in him in such a short period of time. His speech was much clearer for a start, and the dummy that had been a permanent fixture before was now strictly used for naps and bedtimes. It was hard for her to acknowledge that her mum had obviously done something right, especially given how she'd treated Autumn - something she wasn't sure she could ever forgive her for - but she knew in her heart that Winter had progressed at a faster rate *out* of her care than he had in it. It was a painful realisation that gnawed her with guilt, another feeling to push to one side until she next met with her psychologist. Right now, she would concentrate on just enjoying her babies while she had them.

She had prepared them all a healthy dinner on a budget, and once Winter was down, the plan was for a girly night complete with face masks, nail art, and a craft activity while they watched a movie together. Winter had been far easier to settle, apparently as a result of the routine her mum insisted she maintain during her contact with the children - but whilst Summer was excited, Autumn had barely said two words all evening.

'What's it to be then, girls, Ever After or Barbie?'

'Ever After!' said Summer. It had always been one of her favourites. Earlier in their relationship, Kev had scoffed at the screen whenever anything like that was on, but later he would simply grab the remote and turn the TV over altogether, and no-one had dared argue with him from fear of his response. She wondered if the girls recalled that too. She hoped not. They'd been through so much already - she wished she could take it all back. Still, her psychologist had warned her not to torture herself by going down that road, but to focus on the road ahead of them instead - the road she had the power to change.

'Neither,' said Autumn. 'I told Starr I'd catch up with her tonight.'

As much as Lisa didn't want to engage in a confrontation with her daughter, she was hurt and starting to get annoyed. In truth, she'd been annoyed from the moment she'd come in, stinking of vape and weed yet pretending it was because she'd stood too close to Starr and not because she'd been smoking the stuff herself. She could tolerate most things but not lying. If *she'd* behaved like that at her age, her dad would have slapped her silly. Still, she was prepared to let things go to avoid compromising their night. She knew it would take time before the kids would respect her boundaries again.

'You told Starr you'd meet up with her on our first night back home together?'

Autumn did have the grace to flush slightly, however she couldn't quite meet Lisa's eye – something she'd always struggled with when she knew she was doing the wrong thing.

'Is this something to do with that Blayze kid? Because I thought we'd agreed at the last Care Team Meeting that he was bad news, and you would steer well clear of him from now on?'

Lisa was pretty sure they'd managed to get through to her about Blayze after Jenny had warned them about his behaviour, and no doubt Autumn was simply a teenager addicted to nicotine in the form of vaping instead of the roll-ups *she'd* smoked when she was young. Maybe she was just trying to find an excuse to sneak out and have a smoke? On balance, it seemed the lesser of two evils.

Autumn tutted. 'No, not him.'

Lisa sighed, unconvinced. She didn't know what to do for the best. This was all new territory for her. She was afraid of alienating Autumn even further, and afraid that any problem she was had was largely of her own making, given everything she'd been through. And the psychologist had told her to expect a bit of push back.

'Ok,' said Lisa. 'You can go out for a bit, but I want you home in an hour, ok?'

'An hour? That sucks!'

'Not when I don't want you going out at all and had hoped we'd spend the evening together,' said Lisa, and this time Autumn knew not to push it any further. 'And keep your phone on so I can reach you.'

Autumn shrugged on her jacket then left without a backwards glance. Lisa could tell that Summer was thrilled – it meant she'd get her mum all to herself for the night. But as Lisa flicked on the movie, she couldn't help but wonder what had happened to her two girls who had once been inseparable, and how could she ever fix it.

*

**Autumn**

Autumn had no intention of seeing Starr, of course. Not that she didn't want to, but because after photo-gate, Starr had been grounded and was under strict instructions to never again associate with the likes of Blayze Burns or Coby Curran – or, by association, with her either. Starr's mum had been horrified to learn that Starr had been sending nudes to Coby, whose weird, pervy uncle had somehow gotten hold of them.

Jenny had told her that Coby had sold the pictures to his uncle in exchange for alcohol and weed, but Starr and Autumn didn't believe it for a moment, because Coby and Blayze insisted they'd never do something like that and she trusted them. Coby said his uncle must've been snooping through their phones and come across the photos by accident, and that it had all been blown out of proportion by the police and social services. Autumn thought that must be true – they'd found none of Autumn' images on his uncle's phone and she'd sent Blayze a few. In most of them she hadn't included her face however, like Starr had. Autumn rolled her eyes - no wonder she'd gotten caught.

'Alright, sexy?' Blayze pulled her into his arms and began hungrily kissing and sucking her neck. She hoped she wouldn't end up with any more hickeys to hide.

'Yeah,' said Autumn. That's what she liked about Blayze. She didn't need to say much about what was going on for her at home. He got it. He handed her a spliff and within minutes she could feel her anxiety melt away as a sense of peace settled upon her.

The nights were getting lighter and warmer, and Autumn was glad that for once the wasteland was bereft of puddles and the mud beneath her feet was dry. The whole gang were there, but she missed Starr. Keira Cross had already started flirting with Coby in Starr's absence, and Autumn threw her a dirty look. Surely Coby wouldn't be so quick to ditch Starr for *her*?

'So, you wanna be part of our gang for real?' said Blayze, and Keira sniggered.

Autumn was thrown. Hadn't she already become part of their gang since the day she'd skived school to be with him, and the night she'd stolen from the supermarket, and all the nights she had spent with him since? And the nudes she'd sent and the stuff she'd let him do... The night she'd finally agreed to let

Blayze's fingers go where she hadn't been ready for them to go, and let him put her hand where she wasn't ready to put it? The night she'd taken her first drink and smoked her first spliff?

'Yeah,' said Autumn, trying her best to affect some of Starr's nonchalance to cover the fact that without Starr, she was the youngest one there.

'Great, well, you know how you stole from Penny Pinchers?' It was his slang name for the Big Savers supermarket chain. 'Well, this time you'll need to steal something from *someone*...'

The others laughed.

'You're joking, right?'

'It's no joke,' said Keira, taking a drag of the spliff they were handing round and a swig from the bottle of vodka. 'But you could always try hanging out with kids your own age if you don't want to be one of us.'

'What do you say?' said Blayze. 'Do you reckon you could do it?'

Autumn swallowed. She wished Starr was there. 'I have to go,' she said, glancing at the time on her mobile phone only to find that she was running late. Her mum would not be impressed. 'My mum's gonna kill me - I said I'd only be gone an hour.'

'Off you go home to mummy, then.' Keira smirked, and Coby grinned.

'Later,' said Blayze.

'See ya.'

Autumn dashed home without looking back, her cheeks aflame with the embarrassment and humiliation of it all. She didn't want to steal, but she was going to have to, obviously, otherwise Blayze would think she was stupid and ditch her for someone older and cooler, someone like Keira. Maybe she could steal something from someone's bag at school? That would count, wouldn't it? Because she sure didn't want to steal from someone face to face which is what they'd seemed to be getting at. Sometimes with Blayze and his friends, Autumn couldn't help but feel that she'd gotten herself into more than she'd ever bargained for. She almost envied Starr for being grounded.

# 17.

**Autumn**

Autumn was anxious. Starr thought she was crazy and had decided she wanted no part in the whole thing. Her parents had threatened to ground her forever and stop her pocket money if she continued hanging out with Autumn and the others in the evenings, and Coby had already moved on with Keira Cross, so an uncomfortable distance had settled between the previously inseparable pair, that had seemed only to widen when she'd disclosed to Starr what it was she was about to do.

'Don't do it, Autumn,' she warned. 'It's not worth it. If you get caught, you're the one who'll get into trouble – not Blayze and the others.'

'Then I'll just have to make sure I don't get caught.' Though Autumn sounded more confident than she felt. She'd seen how hurt Starr had been by Coby's betrayal, and she didn't want to go through that pain herself. She hadn't told Blayze yet, but she was falling for him.

'*D'accord,*' said Madame Blanc, their French teacher, as she walked up and down the classroom aisles holding out a large plastic Tupperware box with a missing lid. 'You know the drill people – relinquish your mobile phones into *la boîte*. I know some of you will find this a terribly painful experience, something akin to losing a *jambe*, but I promise you, you will survive the next *cinquante minutes* of your life without it.'

There were moans and groans as the sound of twenty-eight individual mobile phones were dropped into the dreaded box, which Madame Blanc proceeded to place into the lockable drawer of her desk.

'*Très bon*,' she said. 'Now. I need a helper to dish out the textbooks for me. Autumn – you will do it, *s'il vous plaît. Merci.* I will be back *dans un instant.* Turn to page *deux-cent-trois,* exercise *cinq,* and work through the questions *en silence* until I return.'

The moment Madame Blanc closed the door behind her there was uproar as the class, minus the more studious among them, quite happily disregarded her instructions. Autumn felt sick. The textbooks were piled up on Madame Blanc's desk, and it was as though the opportunity had just presented itself to her on a plate. She picked up the books and gently nudged the top of the pile, so they fell to the floor behind the desk. Just as she hoped, the key was still in the drawer where Madame Blanc kept the phones, and the others were far too distracted to pay her much heed.

As quickly as she could she turned the little silver key and took out the shiniest and newest looking mobile phone she could find before slipping it under her jumper into the waistband of her pants. Her heart was beating rapidly, but she forced herself to remain calm as she handed out the textbooks then took her seat at her desk as though nothing had happened. Starr shook her head.

'You'll never get away with it,' she whispered. 'It's too obvious. At the end of the lesson, everyone's going to know there's a missing phone and they'll also know it can only have been someone in *this* class who took it. You were at Madame Blanc's desk so you're the first person they'll think of.'

'Not necessarily,' said Autumn, who was feeling distinctly rattled but relieved the hardest part was over with. 'Look around you.'

There were several kids out of their seats – mostly boys, and several who had been in the vicinity of Madame Blanc's desk who would present as far more likely culprits than she did.

'Just put it back while you still have the chance!'

Autumn knew she was right, but the prospect of losing Blayze and the resulting social humiliation was too painful. 'I... I just can't.'

As luck would have it, she couldn't return the phone even if she'd wanted to, because Madame Blanc walked in at that exact moment, and when the door opened, an instant hush descended upon the classroom until all that could be heard was the rustling of textbooks and scribbling of pens.

'Do you think I was born yesterday?' Madame Blanc asked. 'I could hear you lot from *un mile* away! Do not do that again. Now, get to work. *Vite!*'

The lesson passed without incident until the very last moment when Madame Blanc traversed the classroom with the box of mobile phones, only to find that Lily Wright's wasn't there.

'But I just got it for my birthday,' she moaned.

Madame Blanc's face was grave. The bell went, but under her strict instructions nobody moved.

'I am extremely disappointed by this,' she said. 'No-one will leave this room without a bag search. If you do not cooperate, you will be dealt with by the head teacher, your parents, and perhaps even *la police* if necessary. If anyone has any information, you can come and see me *en confiance* at any time today.'

Autumn steeled herself for the inevitable bag search. When Madame Blanc got to her, she felt as if her guilt was written all over her face and hoped that Starr wouldn't dob her in. In that moment, her feelings towards Blayze, who had put her in this position in the first place, were shaken. Naturally the search revealed nothing, and the entire class was dismissed with a promise that the head teacher would speak to them all later.

It was now lunchtime, but Autumn couldn't settle. She knew what she did was wrong, and she could imagine how she would feel if someone did that to her. The supermarket theft was different – that had been wrong too, but it had felt impersonal. *This* was dirty.

'What are you gonna do?' Starr asked as they ate their lunch together in the canteen, where they could hear other kids from their year group speculating in frantic whispers about what had happened, embellishing the details and amping up the drama with each retelling.

Autumn took a deep breath. 'I'm going to put it back. I'll shove it to the back of the drawer and hope that Madame Blanc finds it and assumes it must've just fallen out of the box.' It wasn't entirely inconceivable - the box *had* been pretty full. Either way, she suspected Madame Blanc would be happy the culprit had had a change of heart, and Lily would just be happy to have her phone back.

Starr nodded and gave Autumn the first genuine smile she had given her in ages. For a moment it was almost as if their friendship was where it had been before they'd ever gotten mixed up with Coby and Blayze.

Autumn's plan went without a hitch. She slipped into Madame Blanc's empty classroom, returned the phone to the back of the drawer where it was just out of sight and where it could easily have been overlooked, and turned the key. She didn't know what she was going to say to Blayze, but she supposed she'd have to figure that out later. She was just a few steps from the door when it opened and in walked Madame Blanc carrying her lunch. Autumn felt herself pale. In her panic, she couldn't come up with an excuse quickly enough.

'*Autumn Season*,' said Madame Blanc, her expression accusatory as she walked over to her desk, turned the key, slipped her hand into the drawer and pulled out the missing mobile phone, nodding her head all the while as if that was the exact outcome she had expected. 'I think you have some explaining to do, don't you?'

*

**Jenny**

Alex had been livid about the whole ordeal Jenny was having at work. He'd scrutinised the email she'd sent to Sue and determined it wasn't good enough, because whilst it pointed out the difficulties she was experiencing in managing her dramatic increase in caseload, it had only implied rather than explicitly stated her desire for Sue to support her in doing something about it:

Hi Sue,

I'm just writing to advise you that I feel it is my beyond my current capacity to manage so many of these new assessments within a fortnight in addition to my usual caseload, particularly given I am unfamiliar with the processes, and we were originally advised that we would be unlikely to be allocated more than two at any one time. I'm concerned about the prospect of taking on any further tasks at the next round of allocations without some breathing space to get on top of my existing workload first, especially when I have several cases on the brink of crisis and am still managing a lot of my own family contact supervision. I hope you can understand.

Thanks,

Jenny.

The response she had received was, in Alex's opinion, disappointing to say the least:

Hi Jenny,

I received your email, thank you. We've only allocated you three new assessments this fortnight as we appreciate that five was a heavy load, however given the five cases were interlinked and a lot of the information was relevant to each case, we felt this balanced out the fact you had several more cases than originally advised. You did such a wonderful job with all five cases within the timeframe available to you, and we remain confident in your abilities to manage the challenges associated with this recent and hopefully temporary increase in workload.

We have reviewed your capacity, and given your cases are currently sitting in the green and orange zones, we have been able to allocate you these additional tasks. We will of course review your capacity at your next supervision.

Best wishes,
Sue.

Sue had copied Brenda into the email, and Jenny wondered how much of her response had come directly from her. Alex had been outraged. Jenny felt completely deflated. Whilst she had never aspired to a work ethic like Will's, she wondered if he wasn't doing something right in refusing to bend over backwards trying to meet an expectation that was completely unreasonable. He was the only one in the office who seemed nonplussed by the whole thing and carried on as before. 'I am one man, not three. I can only do what I can do,' he would often say. But then she thought of all the cases – there were real people behind the names who needed help and she didn't want to let them down. There weren't three of her, unfortunately, but she was working as if there was, and it felt as though it was slowly destroying her.

Her phone rang. 'Hi Jenny, it's Mrs O'Neil – Autumn Season's form tutor. I'm just calling in advance of the next Care Team Meeting to let you know that the police are in with her at the moment regarding her theft of another student's mobile phone. Whilst she did the right thing by returning the phone, the girl's parents still wanted to involve the police, mainly to act as a deterrent to stop her or any other student from trying anything like this in the future.'

'I see,' said Jenny, who had the uneasy sense that this case might be about to flip into the orange zone, if not the red. Mrs O'Neil had described Autumn as such a bright student, and she hated to hear of her sabotaging her potential. The sooner they could achieve some stability for her the better.

She put the phone down, but it immediately rang again. Jenny was sure she had written Urgent Calls Only on the whiteboard down in reception, but sometimes they forgot, or else there was something urgent that couldn't wait. She hoped it was the former. She also hoped it wasn't one of her talkers – she had too much to do for chitchat.

'Jenny Hurst? It's Sister Chen from Dunstonborough Hospital – we have young Kai Humphries here in Resus. He was kicked out of where he's been staying today, and it appears he's then taken an overdose. His carer is in with him at the moment, but she said she can't stay long.'

Jenny's heart was in her mouth. 'Is he ok?' she asked, picturing his warm, cheeky face and infectious grin. *Oh, Kai.* What a life he had had - he deserved so much more.

'We got in early. We've stabilised him. He might even be discharged tonight, but it's a bit too early to tell. If so, he'll obviously need somewhere to go. In the meantime, we'll need you to fax over consent for any medical treatment he might need while he's with us.'

'Of course.'

When she hung up, Jenny put her head in her hands and massaged her temples. She needed to make some phone calls, and she needed to consult with Sue. She had a full afternoon of visits planned and a whole evening allotted to her writing up, but now she would have to reschedule in order to beg the hospital to admit Kai at least socially if not medically until they could find him a suitable placement.

'Whatever you do, make sure you beg them to admit him until Monday to give us more time to find him a placement,' said Sue urgently before she left.

'I know,' said Jenny, who could feel her anxiety increasing exponentially at the prospect of all the new tasks she now had to accommodate.

'In the meantime, go speak with Placements and see what miracles they can pull out of their hat. If not, maybe Kai has a nice girlfriend waiting in the wings, or a kind grandma willing to give him another chance. We just need to get him through until the Leaving Care Team can pick him up and give him more independent living options.' Options he was unfortunately currently too young for.

'I will,' said Jenny doubtfully.

She went to the toilet on her way out and sat there wondering how on earth she was going to get through the day, let alone the next couple of weeks. Was she not good enough? The others seemed to be managing. Alex would tell her she simply wasn't advocating for herself strongly enough, but she didn't know what else to do. She was afraid that if she pushed back too much, her competency or emotional stability would be called into question just as she had seen happen to several colleagues who had gone before her. She just needed to get through to her maternity leave, then come up with a Plan B.

She was just wiping herself when she realised with a deep sense of horror that Plan B might be placed on hold indefinitely. The toilet paper was pink. She was bleeding.

\*

**Lisa**

Lisa had been warned that once Child Protection had made it clear to Kev they weren't supporting Winter being placed in his care, then the potential risk of violence he posed towards her would increase. To her surprise however, it had actually achieved the opposite. He'd been texting her none-stop, telling how much he was struggling without her and the kids, and how much he missed them and wanted to be a family again. It was the first time he'd said anything nice since they'd separated. He'd peppered her with memories of a time when things had been very different between them, promising her he had changed and that it could be like that again. Then he'd told her he was proud of the changes she had made, and she couldn't help but melt. She hadn't realised how deeply she still craved affirmation from him – in the end, it had been so rare that he'd given her any.

In all honesty, Lisa was scared to go it alone. Whilst she'd loved having the kids home for increasing amounts of contact, caring for three children without support was overwhelming. She was losing her grip on her relationship with Autumn, Winter seemed to have fared better with her mum than with her, and Summer was constantly clamouring for her attention. Not only that, but she was over three months pregnant with baby number four. She was tired, and she couldn't imagine how she would manage all four children alone. The prospect was enough to have her craving the oblivion she had given into previously. But she wouldn't go down that road. Instead, she would take the dog for a walk, just as she'd agreed in the safety plan she and her psychologist had come up with - that always helped. And she had Irina now.

But not even the balmy June air could shake off Lisa's sense that she was inadequate to the task before her. It was why when Kev asked her for the umpteenth time if he could come round and just hear him out, she said yes – but not until at least ten o'clock when she knew Irina would have gone to bed and wouldn't be able to dob her in. She knew that Jenny would say it was the wrong thing to do, but surely it couldn't hurt just to hear what he had to say, even if it was for them to simply agree to draw a line in the sand and move on. He was the father of two of her children, after all. She owed it to them to at least give him another chance.

'Hey,' he said when he quietly knocked on the door later that evening. He was smiling. He wasn't drunk. Lisa found it was surprisingly good to see his face - the familiarity was comforting. 'You look great. Can I come in?'

For a moment Lisa hesitated, but then she let him in.

# 18.

**Jenny**

Jenny closed her eyes. She didn't need to look at the screen. She didn't even need to look at the sonographer's face. His silence spoke volumes, and she already knew the outcome in her heart. This was her first twelve-week scan, and she would have given anything for a different outcome. If she'd put it off, she could've continued kidding herself that it might turn out differently this time - that she was just spotting like some women did during pregnancy, and it could all be perfectly harmless. But the fact she was spotting was what meant the scan couldn't wait – the impending miscarriage hadn't fully taken hold, and her doctor was concerned about the risk of infection and the possibility she might need a procedure to help things along.

'I'm sorry,' said the sonographer, 'but I can't find a heartbeat.'

Jenny looked at the lifeless form of her baby on the screen, so much smaller than she'd expected at twelve weeks. It turned out the baby had stopped growing two or three weeks prior. In hindsight, if she hadn't been so busy with work to pay attention, she might have realised her pregnancy symptoms had gone. She knew Alex would do the maths and blame it on her sudden increase in workload, but like her doctor had said, it was just *one of those things*. Unavoidable. Blameless. The words were meant to be reassuring but they unfortunately didn't help. She still felt responsible and incapable of doing what most people assumed should come naturally.

'Can we have a moment?' Alex asked, his face pale and defeated.

'Of course,' said the sonographer.

'I'm sorry,' said Jenny as soon as he'd gone. She could sense the gap between them widening and she felt powerless to fix it.

Alex's eyes were damp, and her heart ached. She gently touched his cheek then gripped his hand in hers. He said nothing. He simply leant down and kissed her tummy. 'Goodbye, Flick,' he said. 'We love you. We're sorry we couldn't keep you here with us.'

At last, Jenny allowed the tears to fall. To her great relief, Alex gripped her hand right back.

\*

### Autumn

As part of her reparation – the school's process for students who needed to 'make-up' for their misdeeds towards others, Autumn had agreed to meet with the school counsellor weekly for the rest of the term. Short of involving the police, it had been the only way to satisfy Lily Wright and her parents. Whilst she couldn't think of anything worse than sharing her innermost thoughts and feelings with a complete stranger, she had no choice, and Mrs O'Neil, her form tutor who she really quite liked, was particularly keen for her to do it. The only problem was that she'd warned her against Blayze all along, and Autumn didn't want to hear it. They didn't know him like she did – no-one did. He had good reason to be how he was.

Ling appeared to be somewhere between her mum and her nanna's age, her grey roots belying her age, and as Autumn took a seat opposite her in the tiny, muted room, she felt the weight of an awkward silence envelope them.

'Why don't we start with what brought you here today?' said Ling.

'I didn't want to come,' said Autumn obstinately. 'I had no choice.'

'That's a shame. We don't often appreciate having our choices taken away. My understanding is that you're here because of a choice you made?'

Autumn nodded.

'Can you tell me a bit more about that?'

'It was the wrong choice. It's not something I would normally do.' Autumn was still embarrassed about it, and she could feel her cheeks reddening.

'It sounds to me that if you knew it was the wrong choice and it wasn't something you would normally do – which is what your teacher told me too - then the choice *not* to do it must have somehow felt too risky?'

Autumn arched an eyebrow.

'While many people might see it as a choice between stealing a phone and not stealing a phone, I get the impression that for you it was a choice between stealing a phone and what you might stand to lose if you didn't?'

How could she possibly know that? Autumn wondered, and she found herself nodding.

'Do you think you might be able to tell me a little bit more about that?'

Ling was right. If she didn't steal the phone, then the others would think she was a soft touch and Blayze would dump her. It turned out that he'd probably dump her anyway, because they'd all agreed that stealing from someone's bag wasn't good enough. Stealing from a person was what they expected her to do, and

Autumn felt sick with nerves about the whole thing. It was all Keira's idea, of course. She didn't want to do it, but she couldn't see a way out. She couldn't tell Ling that though - she didn't want to get anyone into trouble. The last thing she needed was to be labelled a grass as well as a wuss.

'It's ok if you'd prefer not to share more about it today, Autumn. I do get the sense that it's something of a heavy burden for you to carry, and if it helps, we can talk about it some other time. Why don't you tell me a little more about you instead? Who's in your family?'

Autumn sighed. 'My mum, my sister and my brother - but we don't all live together right now.'

'Oh?'

'Well, Winter – that's my baby brother – he's going on two. He lives with my nanna and grandad and my sister, Summer. She's eleven. She's still in primary school. Then there's my mum – she broke up with Winter's dad recently. He wasn't very nice - we didn't like him. Then there's mine and Summer's dad, but we don't see him at all - he wasn't very nice either. And then there's me. And our dog, Rocky. Oh – and my mum is having a baby.'

'And then there's you... Where do you fit in, Autumn?'

'I'm in foster care...'

Ling smiled. 'That sounds tough, but I can see by the way your face glows when you talk about your siblings that you care about them a lot. How come you aren't placed together?'

'Because of another wrong choice,' said Autumn dryly. 'I've been making a few of those lately.'

'I see. Do you think you can tell me a bit more about that?'

Autumn hesitated. She hadn't expected to tell this woman so much already. There was just something about Ling that had caused her to let her guard down, but she knew that to do so was risky. So far, every time she'd opened her mouth about what was happening for her in her life there had been consequences, and it was her fear of those consequences that caused her to shut down and spend the rest of her time with Ling in relative silence until the school bell went and she could at last escape back to class. She didn't think she had ever been so relieved to go to double Maths.

*

## Lisa

Rocky heard the postman before Lisa did, and it was a battle between them who could get to the letters first. Thankfully, Lisa succeeded before he managed to tear any of her mail to shreds, a favourite game of his. There was a letter from Jenny telling her that the court had supported her recommendation to continue working towards reunification of the children back into her primary care. It was a hearing she hadn't had to go to, but she did have to attend the final one in three month's time. If things continued as they had been, Sophie had reassured her that she was on track to getting the outcome they all hoped for.

Jenny opened the second letter. It was a letter to say she'd been accepted onto the combined level one Hair and Beauty course she'd applied for at the local college starting in September. She smiled. The idea of going back to college with a bunch of teenagers when she had three children and a baby on the way was preposterous, but nevertheless something about the prospect still excited and energised her. She wondered what Kev would think? He'd think it was ridiculous, obviously. But then, he'd been so different that night he'd come over asking her to consider them getting back together – like the old Kev she had once known and loved - maybe he really *had* changed?

Her phone rang.

'Hi Lisa, it's just Jenny calling to check-in. How's are things going?'

'Good - I just got my acceptance letter for college this September!'

'Wow!' Lisa could hear her typing her notes from their conversation as they spoke. 'That's awesome, Lisa. Congratulations!'

'Thanks.'

'And how's your contact with the kids been going?'

Lisa had been having contact with the kids unsupervised every weekend for one night, and it had been going great. Apart from Autumn – she was still a work in progress. She'd heard about her trying to steal another kid's phone in school, and the Autumn she had known before would never have even thought of trying anything like that. It seemed to her that this period of living away from home had changed her, and Lisa was still getting to know this new version of her daughter and work out how best to manage her.

'Oh, you know – good, apart from things with Autumn being a bit strained at times. She's out a lot doing her own thing. It would be nice if she could spend more time at home with us. But she's at that age now, I suppose.'

'I'm glad it's going well overall. Your family support worker should be able to work on some strategies with you around managing your boundaries with Autumn. Once you've done a month of overnight weekend contacts, we'll look at adding in a weeknight so that you get to be part of the school and childcare routine as well.'

'Ok.'

'Look, I wanted to let you know that I've had a chat with your DV psych, and I'm aware she's upgraded your risk level because of our formal recommendation that we work towards returning the children to your care. This represents a fairly significant loss of control for Kev, so there's a concern he might retaliate towards you to try to sabotage that.'

Jenny was wrong. Kev had told her he respected the changes she'd made to achieve this outcome, and that he was simply asking her to consider him being part of it – especially now he'd completed the Men's Insight Program – a program he had never previously seen through to the end. If that didn't show he had changed, what did? He said he missed her and the kids sorely. He'd realised that life without them wasn't up to as much as he'd thought.

'Have you had any contact from him since we last caught up?'

'None,' Lisa lied.

'Great. Well, as you know, if he does make any attempts to contact you, that would be a breach of the Prevention Order - so please don't hesitate to report that to Police and to let me know as well, ok?'

'I will.'

'Great. See you at the next Care Team Meeting.'

Lisa sighed. She knew she should have been open with Jenny, but she was confused. She had thought she could go it alone, but now she wasn't so sure if that was what she really wanted, or if a life without a father in it was truly what was best for her kids.

**Jenny**

Jenny skimmed through her mail before heading upstairs to the office. Kevin's report from the Men's Insight Program was in, and a quick glance at the last page described his engagement as superficial at best and assessed his risk of perpetrating further Domestic Violence as high due to his lack of accountability or genuine desire to change. This was consistent with all their previous periods of involvement with him - the only difference was that this time he had completed the program.

Whilst he had also produced a couple of clear screens just in time for the recent court hearing, the last one had been positive for alcohol and cannabis, coinciding with when he'd found out that they wouldn't be recommending placing Winter in his care. If Winter and his unborn child couldn't motivate him to make genuine changes, she didn't know what would. Then again, he was still very much at the pointy end of his parenting journey. It wouldn't be unusual for the regrets to kick in later. Jenny shook her head. She was glad she'd had that conversation with Lisa pointing out the elevated risk he now posed to her and the children.

When Jenny got to her desk, there was a dreaded green file sitting on top of it. Fatima raised her eyebrows at her. *Nazari,* it said on the spine. Usually, this would fill her with dread, but for once Jenny embraced her work as an escape from the grief of losing another baby and the expanding distance between her and Alex, who she almost felt she was grieving just as much. She flicked through the details of the new report. Sibling sexual abuse. The parents *weren't* separated. Jenny sighed. Sibling sexual abuse was extremely difficult to safety plan – even more so when the parents weren't separated so that the children concerned might alternate between them. It was going to be messy and complicated - all things she could really do without.

'Don't worry about that one too much,' said Sue when she appeared as if from nowhere. 'I've got Shay earmarked for it, but I can't allocate it to her yet because of the newly qualified caseload restrictions. She'll work it alongside you so that it'll be yours in name only!'

Jenny plastered a smile onto her face. Great, she thought. Not only would she be dealing with this complex new case, she'd also be holding Shay's hand through it all, effectively doubling the workload. She wouldn't mind so much – she really liked the idea of supporting inexperienced staff, but it felt something akin to putting on somebody else's oxygen mask before her own.

'Could be worse,' said Will with a grin, 'Shay could be leaving us then it really would be all yours. I still have my bets she won't last six months - either that or she'll be our new team manager within the year, the way this place works!'

'Actually,' said Fatima, her kindly dark eyes crinkling at the corners, 'speaking of leaving, I have some news...'

Jenny's heart sank. If Fatima said what she thought she was going to say, she didn't think she could hold it together anymore.

'I've been offered a job in Fostering, and I've handed in my notice! But shh, I'm not ready to announce it just yet. Sue knows about it, but for now I'm only telling you two – though I do realise news tends to travel fast in this place...'

'That's awesome!' said Will. 'Congratulations! I'm really going to miss your masala chai though! And I hope you're not suggesting we would blab!'

'Congratulations,' said Jenny, the words sticking in her throat at the thought she would hardly see Fatima now, and how lucky she had been to work alongside a woman who'd become one of her closest friends. Who would she share the ups and downs of her work with now, who truly understood what she was going through? Not Alex, that's for sure, he would only get angry - and Will was off sick more than he was well. 'I'm so happy for you!'

'My leaving do will be a good excuse for us to get dolled up and dance the night away, eh? We'll finally get to go on that long overdue night out of ours, Jenny!'

'I'll be there with bells on,' said Will. 'Better get back to pretending to work.'

Oh God, thought Jenny. How on earth was she going to get through this? Fatima had been her rudder in stormy seas, and now she would be left sailing the ship without her, and she feared she might drown.

# 19.

**Lisa**

There was a knock at Lisa's door. She'd become so used to workers to-ing and fro-ing from her house that she'd considered getting them their own keys cut.

'Kev!' she said. 'What are you doing here?'

'Thought I'd surprise you,' he said with a smile, handing her a fresh apple Danish from the bakery around the corner - her favourite - and a strong latte. It was a treat they'd rarely been able to afford when they were together, and he hadn't forgotten. It was gestures like those – how he'd always noticed the little things she liked and how thoughtful he'd been in the beginning that had made her fall for him in the first place.

Lisa didn't have time to think, she simply bustled him in from the street before Irina or the other neighbours could catch sight of him. Who knew what they must make of all the comings and goings to her house – she wouldn't be surprised if they thought she was running a knocking shop. Rocky wagged his tail and yapped excitedly – he'd always been Kev's dog, but Kev's dad hadn't wanted him brought over to the place he'd been staying, so she'd been lumbered with him instead. She'd never been much of a dog person, but Rocky had endeared himself to her enough that she'd be sad if Kev ever took him away. Kev rubbed his ears and generally made a fuss of him, and Rocky embraced the attention from his favourite human.

'Kev, you know you can't be here,' said Lisa, her anxiety rising. 'The girls will be home from school soon and I've got to pick up Winter from childcare. If Autumn finds you here, she'll go spare! It'll be even worse if Jenny finds out.'

Kev was nonchalant. 'I wouldn't have come over if you'd taken the time to reply to my texts,' he said, a small hint of the old Kev in his voice. 'I was starting to worry when you didn't respond.'

Lisa sighed. 'I haven't had a chance - I've been too busy getting my act together and trying to sort my life out. I've even applied to go back to college!'

'College?' Kev exclaimed. 'At your age? You'll be the oldest one there!'

For a moment Lisa thought she saw the shadow of the other Kev cross his face, the one who still haunted her dreams, but it was gone just as fast, and he was all smiles again. 'Sounds great, love. What about the baby though? Won't that get in the way of your plans?'

He gestured at her expanding stomach. Lisa's baby bump had seemed to show earlier and earlier with each pregnancy. As self-conscious as she was about her changing body however, it was the first time Kev had properly addressed the fact she was expecting their second child.

'I'll cross that bridge when I come to it,' she said. 'At least I'll be able to make a start – that leaves me with less work to do later. Eventually I could bring a bit of money in.'

'But I thought we were getting back together? I can work hard enough for both of us.'

'I said I'd think about it – I'm still thinking...'

'Ok,' he said. 'Try not to keep me waiting too long though, eh? Men like me don't get left on the shelf for long.'

He grinned, and Lisa had to assume he was joking. 'I won't,' she promised, in her haste to get him out the door. He'd parked right across the street - he couldn't have been more obvious if he was *trying* to get caught. She hoped Irina hadn't noticed.

'I've got some news myself,' he said, as he reluctantly turned to leave.

'Oh?'

'Yeah, I've been offered an extended contract at work. Six months this time! Half a year's income and security, all cash in hand obviously, and a less laborious role for my bad back 'cause I'll be the one supervising the youngsters.'

'That's great, Kev!' Lisa genuinely meant it. He'd always been happier when he was working, and she knew how much she hated being told what to do by men half his age who were earning the same, if not more than him, even though they had something he didn't – references. Qualifications. Maybe this time things really would be different.

'You could always get the order varied to allow me to come home, you know, and of course we'd have to tell Jenny and the kids. We've got nothing to hide.' He leaned in to peck Lisa's cheek, and she thought, but couldn't be sure, that there was the slightest trace of alcohol on his breath. Then again, he and his colleagues usually took their lunch break down the pub – he wouldn't want to stand out by being the only one not joining them.

Her heart sank at the prospect of informing Jenny and what that might mean for the future for her and the kids. 'Like I said, I'm still thinking about it. If we were to get back together, Kev, things would have to be very different.' She gave a tight smile. 'Look, you really need to get going before anyone sees you here.'

The old Kev would have left on his own terms, but this Kev squeezed her hand then did as he was bid. His car had barely left the street when there was another knock on the door, and Lisa opened it up to find the stern face of old Irina glaring at her.

'Oh, spare me the lecture! I told him to leave, didn't I?' said Lisa defensively as she led her into the kitchen and put the kettle on.

'I'm glad to hear it,' said Irina. 'I wasn't sure whether to call the police! I was half expecting you to text me your safe word – you had me worried sick!'

'What can I do, Irina? He's their dad, and I'm not sure I can do this alone.'

'You can! You're better off with no-one than with someone who treats you like he does, I promise you. You're doing great!' Irina set out their teacups – she knew her way around Lisa's kitchen as well as her own by now. 'Look, while you know I don't agree with him coming round here, we're good friends, Lisa, so I'll say nothing more about it unless I think you might come to any harm. But if I catch him here when you have either one of those kids home, friend or not, I won't hesitate to report it to the authorities. I'll not stand by and watch you let him piss over your hard work then throw it all away.'

'He's not pissing over my hard work!' Lisa insisted as she tore open a packet of custard creams and dunked them in her tea.

'What's he doing then?'

'He came to see if we could get back together. Start afresh. Be a family again.'

'If that's not pissing all over your hard work, I don't know what is! A leopard never changes its spots - I hope you told him to get stuffed?'

Lisa fell silent.

'Oh, Lisa,' said Irina. 'Don't be a mug! You've come way too far to screw it up now. Think what you stand to lose! All that hard work and those beautiful children after all they've gone through. I don't know what it is Kev's up to, but I'd bet my good knee that he's up to no good. He's bad news, that one.'

What was it with everyone? Thought Lisa. No-one knew Kev like she did. He'd had a terrible time growing up, and now he was struggling with the separation and being kept away from her and the kids. Not to mention his sore back and the impact that had had on his job prospects, finances, and mental health. What was so bad about wanting her children to grow up with a father, and having some support to raise four kids instead of having to go it alone? Why couldn't everyone keep their noses in their own affairs, instead of meddling in hers?

*

## Jenny

Jenny and Alex were meeting up with Alex's parents, sister and brother-in-law at their local pub for Sunday lunch. It was a beautiful afternoon with a high sun and cornflower sky streaked with only the thinnest wisps of cloud. It was so nice out that they decided to eat in the beer garden, replete with hanging baskets bursting with colourful blooms. It should have been a perfect day – one where they could have announced their pregnancy and proudly presented a picture-perfect twelve-week scan – but instead Jenny was still cramping from her miscarriage and her back ached, though thankfully the bleeding was starting to settle, and the physical pain was nothing compared to the pain she carried in her heart.

'How have you been?' Sylvia, her mother-in-law asked as they took their seats and glanced through the menu. 'Has work settled down for you yet, Jenny? You two seem to have been passing ships lately. I can't remember the last time we all got together - it must have been at Rachel's birthday and that was weeks ago now!'

Jenny bristled. The hours she'd been working were still something of a sore point between her and Alex. In fact, they'd spent most of the morning in silence once he'd realised she couldn't be persuaded to go back to Rachel's house for coffee after lunch because she had too much to do to get a head start on the following week. In the end, they'd had to drive there in separate cars so that he could go spend time with his family and she could get back home to work. The distance between them made her heart ache, but she had no idea what to do about it. She was just trying to survive.

'It's still hectic,' she said. 'No sign of it slowing down just yet unfortunately.'

'I don't know how you do that job,' said Sylvia, though Jenny had heard it all before.

'Someone's got to do it,' said George, her father-in-law, making it obvious he lumped social workers within the same bracket as parking officers and ticket inspectors, as opposed to professionals who made a living from working their butts off to protect vulnerable children from suffering harm and abuse.

'What about you two?' Jenny asked Rachel and Matt, keen to divert the conversation onto more comfortable ground.

'We're going great!' said Rachel brightly.

'We've got some news, actually,' said Matt, looking to Rachel for approval. She nodded, her cheeks flushed and her pale eyes sparkling with happiness.

'We're pregnant!'

Jenny felt winded and Alex paled. Sylvia and George positively beamed.

'That's wonderful news!' said Sylvia. 'Isn't that wonderful?'

'Absolutely,' said Alex.

'I must admit I always thought Jenny would be first, being that bit older and having been married for longer – but then again, you've always prioritised your career, haven't you, Jenny? You young ones these days think you have all the time in the world!'

Jenny bit down the anger rising within her. She had a full-time job, just like Alex and her sister and brother-in-law, the only difference was that *their* jobs didn't consume their lives like hers did. She wanted to start a family more than she wanted anything. If she hadn't just lost her baby, then that child and Rachel's would have been cousins growing up alongside one another. Life was cruel, but she couldn't expect Sylvia to understand. They'd long since stopped announcing their pregnancies - it had been too awkward first time round when she'd failed to make it beyond a few weeks.

'Excuse me,' said Jenny, and though Alex glanced up at her, his expression was remote and unreadable.

She headed to the toilets to collect herself. She had never felt more alone and adrift in her adult life than she did that afternoon, she just didn't know what to do about it. One thing was for certain – she couldn't carry on as she was for much longer.

*

**Autumn**

It was Saturday night, and like every Saturday night, Autumn spent it at the wasteland with Blayze and their friends, drinking, smoking, and generally just having a laugh. Starr no longer joined them, and she and Autumn barely spoke to each other in school anymore – her parents didn't want them knocking around together, and Starr didn't want to get into any more trouble. Autumn missed her company, but the pull towards Blayze was too strong to resist.

'Right, are we gonna head into town then?' said Coby, his arm casually draped around Keira Cross who was pressed into his side smoking her vape and exhaling a sickly-sweet blackberry scent into the air.

'Wanna come?' Blayze asked.

'Sure,' said Autumn. 'What for?'

'Because tonight we're going to show you how it's done!' said Coby.

She knew he was referring to a theft, of course. From a real live person. 'But why do we need to go into town to do that?'

'So that no-one recognises us!' Keira rolled her eyes and looked at Autumn as if she was completely stupid. 'Everyone knows us around here. Anyway, you don't have to come. If you're too soft for us, you know where to go – back home just like your friend, Starr.' She gave a sly smile and made a show of kissing Coby deeply, who lapped it up, Starr completely forgotten.

'I'm not soft,' said Autumn, 'but I don't have any train fare.' She felt silly admitting it. She'd already spent her pocket money on vape pods in her efforts to keep up with the others.

'Neither do we!' Blayze laughed. 'It's not usually a problem if you're light on your feet and can jump over the ticket barrier. There's too many of us for the inspectors to give much chase anyway. Just stay close to me and you'll be fine.'

When the train arrived, they sat in the last carriage, the boys casually leaning back with their muddy shoes propped up on the seats. There were two girls about Autumn's age, maybe slightly younger, sitting nearby. They were mousey, studious types – the sort who would never get embroiled with the likes of Blayze and his gang. One of them was scrolling through the latest android complete with a glitzy cover. When they were about a minute or so from the next station, Coby raised his eyebrows pointedly and said to Autumn, 'Now watch and learn, kiddo, and be ready to hop off at the next stop!' Keira grinned. She'd obviously seen this before.

Coby clearly enjoyed the attention as Autumn and the others fell silent, nudging one another occasionally and grinning as he sauntered towards the two girls and asked if he could borrow the phone of the one sitting closest to him so that he could send a text to his mum to let her know he was going to be late home. Both girls looked dubious, but Autumn could see they were as intimidated as she would be in their position, and without question the phone was handed over. He made a show of fumbling with the buttons, trying to send a text message as the girls sat there anxiously awaiting the phone's return. Autumn could sense the train begin to slow, then within moments the platform came into view.

As soon as the doors were opened, Blayze yelled, 'Run!' and all ten of them, including Coby who held the stolen phone like a trophy, sprinted from the train, laughing and yelling from the excitement of it all before leaping over the barriers, relieved there wasn't a ticket inspector in sight as they ran and ran until they were swallowed by the city crowds.

'Coby hasn't even got a mum!' Blayze laughed. 'She's in a refuge! Anyway, kiddo, that's how it's done.' He clung onto Autumn's hand as promised, and they weaved in and out of the crowd until they lost sight of the others. Autumn could only picture what the poor girl's face must have been like when she realised what had happened, and a wave of guilt consumed her. 'It'll be your turn next!' Blayze grinned, oblivious to the conflict that was at that moment playing itself out in her body and mind. She smiled, but it didn't reach her eyes.

# 20.

**Lisa**

It was Kev's idea for her to let him come stay over one weekend when the kids weren't with her so that he could show her how much he'd changed to help her decide whether they should get back together. It was as though once she had opened herself up to him a chink, he had forced the chink into a wide enough crack to let him in.

She had to admit she was anxious. As much as she still missed him – the part of him that had once considered her and cared for her - she was afraid it wouldn't last, and that things would go back to how they were. She couldn't go through that again. She just couldn't. It had ruined her confidence and self-esteem and had made her feel worthless and ashamed. Worst of all, it had made her into the kind of mother she didn't want to be. The kind she had grown up with herself.

That's why she said she'd only agree to it if he came round late when she knew Irina would have already gone to bed, then left during Irina's Sunday morning walk. He was also under strict instructions to park out of sight. She had butterflies in her tummy when she heard him knocking, and Rocky went wild as though he'd picked up on his scent and knew it was Kev coming home.

'Hey,' he said with a grin when Lisa smuggled him in out of sight. As soon as he was through the door, he allowed Rocky to jump all over him as he ruffled his face and head.

'Hey,' she said awkwardly. 'How was work?'

'Great! The boys all went out for a drink afterwards, but not me - I'm a changed man now.' He raised his eyebrows pointedly and Lisa smiled. She hoped it was true. At least she knew he'd done some clean screens for Jenny, but it wouldn't be until the next Care Team Meeting that she'd find out more.

He threw his boots off and settled into his favourite armchair as though he'd never left, emptying the contents of his pockets onto her new coffee table, scratching its delicate glass. Lisa winced. That was her spot now. 'I thought I could buy us a takeaway and you could choose the movie. Even the romantic trash you love to watch if you like!'

Lisa noticed that he made no remark about the improvements she had made to the living room – not a single comment as to how clean or fresh it looked now, or how hard it had been for her to make those changes by herself. He hadn't said a thing about how she looked either, even though she'd spent the last of her benefits on a new top and having her hair styled at a salon – something she'd *never* usually splurge on. She realised she couldn't remember the last time he'd complimented her. No wonder she had felt so bad about herself - there had been too many insults and criticisms to count.

Kev didn't seem to have made any effort himself either. He was dressed in his usual t-shirt and joggers, just like it was a regular Saturday night. The thing that bothered her most, however, was that he hadn't once bothered to ask her about Winter or the girls, or enquired about her pregnancy, her health, and their ever-growing baby. Too impatient to wait, she'd booked an early private scan and found out they were having a girl. Somehow, she just knew he'd be disappointed it wasn't another boy.

'There's a new place just opened round the corner,' she said, keen to keep their topics of conversation on safe ground. 'I thought maybe we could try it?'

'Is there?' said Kev as he flicked on the TV and searched for the sports channel. It was gone. She'd stopped paying for it - she paid for the kids' channel now instead. She could see it bothered him but to his credit he said nothing. 'What kind of food is it?'

'Thai,' she said. She'd been hoping to try it. The kids weren't keen, so this seemed as good an opportunity as any.

He frowned. 'What's wrong with Chinese? You always loved Chinese.'

*No, I didn't,* thought Lisa. *You did.* If she said that though, she'd only start a fight.

'Can't we just try it?' she risked, something she would never have attempted in the past. She'd always done whatever she could to please him. 'You might find something you like?'

'I would, Lisa, but I find Thai food is a bit too rich for me, it might set my stomach off and spoil our night. Let's just get our usual, eh? My treat.'

'Ok,' she nodded reluctantly.

'What movie were you thinking?'

*Does it matter?* She thought.

He didn't wait for a response. He simply dialled the number for the Chinese on his mobile phone and ordered for both of them.

Lisa could feel herself getting irritated. Whilst Kev wasn't physically hurting her, she could feel him stifling her and she felt trapped. Pain didn't always involve fists. It had been foolish of her to think he had changed – that he could give her and the children what they needed. Having him there risked the very thing she wanted more than Kev or anything else – to have her children back home again where they belonged.

She was ready for him to go now. She should never have allowed him to come over in the first place. Part of her wanted to text Irina her safe word but she couldn't, because that would mean admitting she'd done the wrong thing. She felt vulnerable and scared. Scared of saying or doing anything that might set him off. Denying her own wants and needs to appease his. These were all the things her DV psychologist had been trying to help her recognise all along, but it was only now after weeks of having been accountable to only herself and her children (and Child Protection!) that the meaning of what she'd been taught was starting to sink in. Right now, though, doing what Kev wanted without fuss was her only tried and tested means of keeping herself safe.

'Have you decided on a movie then?'

'Why don't you choose?' said Lisa. 'I don't mind.'

'Smart girl,' he said approvingly.

When Kev smiled his first genuine smile of the evening, Lisa realised it was because in that moment she had reverted to the woman he remembered - the one who couldn't say no. She wondered how on earth she was going to get through the night. Sunday morning couldn't come quickly enough.

*

**Jenny**

Supervision. Jenny was under strict instructions from Alex to talk to Sue about how she'd been feeling lately. Ever since the miscarriage he'd become even more worried about her, and

197

he was certain the constant pressure she was under at work was affecting her health and could perhaps even have contributed to the loss of their baby. Jenny wasn't so sure – she'd lost babies before work had ever gotten this bad - but he was right insofar as she'd been struggling to sleep at night due to her racing thoughts and worries about the next day or week ahead, and she was living in a constant state of stress and anxiety that she could feel as much in her body as her mind.

The hours she spent on the clock left little time for winding down, indulging in the tasks that kept her grounded, or making space for her family, friends and marriage. She'd become snappy and sad, and whilst her work had always been something of a juggling act, it had never been as bad as it was now. Worse, if she didn't say something, for the first time since they'd met, she found herself unsure where Alex stood with their relationship and afraid of the outcome if she didn't somehow appease him. For some reason he'd taken this loss harder than the others, and it seemed her work had become as good an outlet for his anger and grief as any.

'So,' said Sue as she squinted at her notes. 'We're almost at the end of our list. Where are you at with Humphries?'

'Humphries is settled for the time being,' said Jenny gratefully. 'Kai's girlfriend's mum said he's been no bother, and his mental health has been relatively stable whilst he's been complying with his medication and laying off the drugs. The girlfriend seems to be a good influence on him.'

'Good, good.'

'The thing is, once their relationship ends, which seems pretty inevitable for a fifteen-year-old, we'll be back to square one.' Jenny desperately wished there was something better they could offer Kai, but what? He'd exhausted all their options. They were simply treading water now.

'Agreed,' said Sue. 'We'll cross that bridge when we come to it. Fingers crossed it happens after he turns sixteen – then it'll be the Leaving Care Team's issue to deal with. At least by then he'll be old enough to secure his own tenancy or live in a hybrid arrangement. It's not ideal, but it's more than we can do since he's burned all the bridges we can offer him short of placing him in secure, and we don't want to go down that road.'

A hybrid arrangement was a cross between foster care and independence – where a young person could be afforded greater autonomy but still have a carer/landlord to rely on to whom they would pay a portion of their allowance to; with the idea this would help prepare them for a life of managing on a budget and paying rent and bills. Secure meant removing Kai's freedom for the next six months, placing him in a secure residential facility where he would be intensively supported to withdraw from any substances, re-engage with his education, meet any outstanding health and mental health needs, safely reconnect with his family members, and break any unsafe habits and dodgy connections - hopefully acting as a circuit breaker in the process to help redirect him onto a healthier, safer track. It was a last resort to take away another young person's liberty and spaces were scarce, so things would have to be dire for him to end up there.

'I'm thinking of enrolling him into the Skills for Life program for the summer? That should give him something to focus on between now and starting his apprenticeship and might just get him through to sixteen without incident.' Kai was an outdoorsy, practical kid. He would enjoy their eight-week program, which included a fortnight-long residential in the countryside that would have the bonus of giving his carer a bit of a reprieve. It was run by the local police.

'Great!' said Sue. 'Go for it. And how's that new case I gave you - Nazari?'

Jenny winced. Sibling sexual abuse. 'That's a nasty one. We've got the maternal grandmother on board – Noor and Malik are spending one week with her then one week with their parents, alternating so that they're never together, except for the weekends when they usually all get together at the maternal or paternal grandparents' house – but then there are other adults around supervising the contact and making sure Malik is never left alone with Noor or their cousins.' Again, an arrangement that couldn't feasibly go on forever.

'Any disclosures from either of them yet?'

'No,' said Jenny. They strongly suspected someone within the family had sexually abused Malik and potentially Noor in the past, but since there'd been no disclosures from either of them, there was nothing they could do but hope that if they had been harmed, they could eventually tell someone about it.

'How's Shay been getting on with it in the meantime?'

'Yeah, she's doing alright.' Jenny had delegated some of the paperwork to Shay, along with some of the statutory visits and weekly check-ins. She'd been reluctant to hand over too much however – it was a complex case and Shay already had enough on her plate. She'd hate to put her off so early in her chosen career.

'And Season? Where's that at?'

'Thankfully still on track,' said Jenny, crossing her fingers that nothing would go wrong now they were so close to the final hearing.

'A success story! That's what we're all in the job for, isn't it?'

Sue smiled and Jenny nodded, though in all honesty she was no longer sure what she was in the job for. She just didn't feel she was achieving for children and their families what she'd idealistically hoped by becoming a social worker. She'd learned the hard way that they could only help people who recognised there was a problem and genuinely wanted to do something about it, otherwise they were simply throwing money for services down the drain to satisfy the courts and society at large that they'd tried. Then placements – there just weren't enough of them to go round, and sometimes for children like Kai Humphries, they were simply too damaged to have a good outcome no matter how good a fit it was.

'Well,' said Sue, putting down her paperwork. 'It looks like most of your cases are sitting on green or orange at the moment, but your caseload is full, so we won't be allocating you any more cases until you can close something off. Humphries will be transferring soon, and Season looks set to be closed off after the final hearing. That said, we still have plenty of those initial assessments to get through, so you'll continue to be allocated those in the meantime. If something pressing does come in - and fingers crossed it doesn't - we may have to allocate it to you in name, but Shay will run with it.'

Jenny couldn't help it – she burst into tears. She just couldn't hide it anymore. As though on autopilot, Sue handed her the box of tissues she always kept on her desk.

'Here,' said Sue, her expression warm and sympathetic as she patted her on the shoulder. 'Here's the contact details for the SWSP. Why don't you make yourself an appointment? You're a good worker - I hate to see you struggling.'

Not a temporary reduction in workload that would help keep Jenny in the job then, just a few counselling sessions through the Social Work Support Program, as though she was somehow at fault for failing to cope with an unrealistic workload. What would Alex say? she wondered as she headed back to her desk, where disappointment enveloped her, and a knot of anxiety settled in her stomach. She was afraid to find out.

# 21.

**Autumn**

Blayze tucked Autumn into the crook of his arm to protect her from the summer breeze. It didn't seem to matter what season it was; it was always cool out on the wasteland but especially so now the sun had finally dipped out of view. She'd been counting down the weeks until the school holidays. Not too long after that would be the final court date, then hopefully a return home to her mum so that life could go back to normal and she could be with her brother and sister again. She missed them so much that only the alcohol and weed she and Blayze shared with their friends could go any way towards numbing the pain.

'See that girl up there?' said Keira slyly. 'She looks game – look at those designer pumps she's wearing with her uniform. I can spot them a mile off. Handbag looks designer too. Her mum wants her head examined sending her out on her own at night in all that! She deserves all she gets.'

The girl Keira was referring to couldn't have been much younger than Autumn, and she walked alone along the bike track that ran parallel with the wasteland before dipping beneath an underpass towards the square with its solitary row of shops and takeaways. She looked to be around year eight – maybe she went to Summer's school. Summer had wanted those exact same pumps last year – everyone had them apparently - but their mum had put her foot down and insisted they couldn't afford any, then surprised her with a pair at Christmas after saving up for months. Kev had been pissed, and it hadn't ended well.

Autumn's hackles rose. She knew instantly what Keira was getting at, and she wasn't ready – not yet – but Coby jumped on it of course.

'Yeah!' said Coby, his eyes glazed and his countenance agitated by whatever else he had taken in addition to the spliff they'd all shared. 'Go on then, Autumn, it's about time you paid your way around here!'

Autumn hesitated. 'Go on!' Blayze grinned. 'You can do it! We'll help.'

'But I thought you said we had to do it in town so we wouldn't get recognised?' It had worked for them last time they'd pulled a stunt like this. The quality of the train's CCTV hadn't been good enough to identify Coby, according to what she'd read in her foster carer's newspaper.

'No-one'll know it's you,' Blayze reassured her. 'Anyway, it's getting dark now, and it'll be even darker in the underpass – especially since Coby smashed its lights out last week. And you can tell she doesn't go to our school. She's too young.'

Coby led them towards the underpass, egging Autumn on the whole way. 'Come on,' he said, 'then you'll *really* be one of us. That's what you want, isn't it? We've all done it – it's nothing once you get used to it and we'll even let you have your pick of the winnings! I reckon those shoes would look nice on you.'

'If *she* doesn't want them, *I'll* have them,' said Keira. 'They'd look even better on me.'

Together they congregated beneath the underpass. There was still one flickering light left aglow, and Coby picked up a stone and hurled it at it until it spluttered out. Autumn was grateful for the anonymity of shadow, and Blayze instructed her to pull her hair back from her face and cover it over with her hood so she'd be less identifiable.

The girl was about two-hundred metres away now. She had two options – to risk crossing the busy main road dividing the wasteland from the shops or use the underpass instead. *Cross the road, cross the road, cross the road,* Autumn willed, her eyes fixed on the girl as she drew ever closer, completely unaware of the trap that lay ahead. It could be Summer, she thought. This girl was someone's sister. Someone's daughter. She didn't deserve what was about to happen to her. But if she didn't do it...

She heard a sound - a sharp flick of metal – and saw something shiny in Coby's hand. Autumn paled as she looked at him, horrified.

'Don't look so worried!' He grinned. 'It's not like I'm going to use it. It's just there to offer her a little encouragement in case she needs it...' The others laughed.

The girl was only fifty metres away now, and in the distance, a group of adults had just rounded the bend from the housing estate beyond the wasteland. Autumn was relieved. The others would be less likely to give chase if they knew there were adults close by. She realised now what it was she needed to do.

'I'll handle this,' she said with a bravado she didn't feel, shooing them towards the back of the underpass. 'You guys hang towards the back ready to stop her from getting away.'

'Ooo, get you!' said Keira sarcastically. 'A pro already, eh?'

Autumn stepped out of the shadows and moved slowly towards the girl. She jumped - it was obvious she hadn't realised there was anyone in the underpass in the first place. When Autumn neared her, she realised the girl was even younger than she'd thought. Barely any older than Summer. Her face was pale with fear.

'Run,' Autumn whispered as she approached her, trying her best to convey to her the urgency of the situation with her voice and eyes. 'Whatever you do, just run. They're waiting for you *down there!*' She gestured frantically towards the underpass, just as the others, who'd cottoned on to what she had done, emerged into view.

'Wha-?' said the girl.

'RUN!' Autumn screamed again as she took flight herself. 'JUST BLOODY RUN!'

Autumn ran as fast as she could towards the foster placement she couldn't yet bring herself to call home. She hoped the girl was running too, but she was too scared to stop to find out. She knew Coby. She'd seen the pocketknife in his hand. It was *her* they'd be after now, not the girl, so she needed to put as much distance between them and her as possible.

She gained on the group of adults in seconds. Men. They were loud and brash, clearly headed for the local pub, and Autumn froze when she saw that Kev was among them, his cheeks ruddy like they always were when he'd been drinking. He looked at her, his expression unreadable and said nothing. Autumn felt a chill running through her at seeing him again.

'There's a bunch of kids down the underpass looking for trouble!' she panted, stealthily avoiding eye contact with Kev. 'They're after some girl's handbag. Do me a favour and make sure she's ok?'

She didn't wait for a response - she simply ran without stopping, all the way home. Would Blayze and the others allow her to slip from their radar like Starr had done, she wondered, or would they not rest until they'd had their revenge?

*

**Lisa**

Autumn hadn't been her usual self ever since she'd been removed by social services, and Lisa had long been at a loss as to how to reconnect with her. All Autumn ever wanted to do these days was to hang out with her friends until all hours and get up to who knew what with that wastrel of a boyfriend of hers, and even though she'd sometimes return stinking of alcohol and weed, Lisa had resisted putting her foot down in fear of losing her altogether.

This weekend though, was different. Autumn was quiet. Subdued. She made no move to go anywhere at all. 'Can we watch a movie tonight, Mum?' she asked at last, after a full afternoon laid up on the couch texting until her fingers ached and her battery went flat. Lisa assumed it must be the boyfriend, but she didn't want to pry.

'Yeah!' said Summer, her face animated and her eyes bright. 'Then will you do my nails the way you usually do them, with sparkles on the end?'

Autumn rolled her eyes. 'Sure,' she said, and Summer beamed at her. For a moment it was like it used to be. Lisa knew how much Summer still missed her big sister.

'Let me just settle Winter down then we'll put something on.' She was scared to break the spell.

Winter settled in no time, and it was still a novelty to Lisa to be able to read him a story, pop him in his cot, say goodnight, then walk away without at least an hour-long ritual to perform beforehand. Her mum had done something right, and she was still careful to stick to the routine she'd set for him and note it all in their communication book no matter how much she resented it. She stood for a moment staring at him, absorbing his beauty and innocence in a way she'd been too tired and overwhelmed to do with her first two. She longed to run her fingers through the soft nape of curls poking out of his sleeping bag, but she didn't want to disturb him. She wondered what it would be like to have him home with her every day. Soon. Hopefully soon. She'd taken it all for granted before, she realised, as she patted her stomach and made a silent promise to the new baby growing inside her that she wouldn't make the same mistake again.

Lisa had invited Irina around to join them. They were both lonely, and they found solace in the friendship that had blossomed between them. Irina had never had children of her own – had never remarried once she'd left her abusive husband - and Lisa found she now relied on her more than she did her own mother.

There was a knock at the door. Irina. Leaving the girls to choose the movie, Lisa strode to the door, just as Rocky started going wild beside her.

'Shh, Rocky,' she whispered. 'You'll wake up Winter with all your bloody carry on!'

She opened the door, and before her mind could even register that it was Kev or respond to the fact, he had pushed past her, his entire body emitting an odour of stale beer as Rocky bounded noisily in after him.

Lisa peered out into the street for signs of Irina then locked the door when she discovered the coast was clear. The last thing she needed was for Irina to walk in on him making a scene.

'*Lisa,*' he sneered.

'Kev, what the hell are you doing here?'

'Come to see my wife and kids, haven't I? Can't a man do anything, these days without a woman to answer to?'

He staggered into the living room where the girls sat frozen on the couch next to one another as they looked from Kev to Lisa then back again, both too scared to open their mouths but equally too scared to take their eyes off him for a second. They knew what he could be like in this sort of mood and had learned the hard way that the safest thing to say was nothing.

'Got the sack, didn't I? Anyway, what's this shite you're watchin'?' he said, gesturing at the telly and Lisa winced. 'Where's my son?'

'Where do you think he is?' said Lisa. 'Asleep!'

'Oh, yes - I forgot you're bloody Mary Poppins now. Well, I don't buy it for one second!' He turned towards Lisa and snarled at her, baring teeth yellowed by a lifelong nicotine addiction. The girls tensed. 'Don't know what on earth you're playing at, colludin' with social services over a cuppa like they're your best mates. Going back to college at your age, when everyone knows you've always been thick as pig shit. Too busy getting your leg over and getting yourself up the duff to do your GCSEs. Ha!' He laughed. 'You're just as useless now as you ever were! And a bloody ugly cow to boot.'

'What are you doing here then?' said Autumn, finding her voice at last. 'If she's so bad, why can't you just leave her alone? Go away, nobody wants you here! Mum, tell him!'

Lisa froze. Kev walked slowly towards Autumn, menace in his eyes. He put one hand on the arm of the couch then crouched over her until his face was centimetres from Autumn's. She wrinkled her nose when she caught a whiff of his foul breath, but she didn't look away from him, not for a moment, and Lisa admired her for it.

'I'll tell you what I'm doing here. Me and your mum are getting back together, aren't we, darlin'?'

'No. you're not! Mum would *never* get back with you. Never! Tell him, Mum!' Autumn yelled.

'Oh really?' Kev grinned. 'That's not what she said when I was round here the other night. Is it, Lisa?'

Lisa paled. She was dimly aware of Winter screaming.

'Mum,' said Autumn, 'is that true?'

Lisa shook her head. Could barely bring herself to look either of her girls in the face. Tears of guilt and regret stung her eyes. 'Get out of here,' she said to Kev. 'Get out before I call the police.'

Kev laughed, but for once she was serious. At the exact same moment, they both clocked Lisa's mobile phone where she'd left it charging on the coffee table. Just as she went to pick it up, Kev grabbed her by the wrist and squeezed so tightly her hand went numb.

'Put. It. Down,' he said, and when Lisa obliged, it clattered onto the pane of glass set into the wooden tabletop causing it to shatter. Kev shoved her backwards and the girls screamed as she fell, a shard of glass piercing her lower back followed by a surge of pain. Flashing lights illuminated the living room, then there was a sharp rapping at the door and a gruff voice demanded they open up.

'You'll never get them back now,' said Kev as Autumn sprang from the couch to open the front door and half a dozen police officers filed in. 'Now we *both* have nothing.'

He was led out in handcuffs, and soon after, Lisa's mum arrived to collect Winter and Summer, dropping Autumn back off at her foster placement on the way, their time with their mum having reached an abrupt end.

The first thing Lisa did was to walk into the bedroom and pick up the pillow from Winter's cot, which still smelled of him and the lavender bubble bath she'd started using. She held it close to her face and cried. There was a knock at the door. Lisa knew it would be Irina, but she couldn't face her. Then her phone rang. It was her mum, no doubt itching to give her a lecture. Then a missed call from her sister. All people she absolutely, most definitely did not want to speak to.

The silence of the house without her children in it was deafening. Even Rocky was subdued. Kev had once told her he would break her, and tonight he had. Lisa's grief and regret hurt more than any bruises he'd ever doled out. She went to the kitchen and opened the cupboard where she'd stored an emergency stash of medication given to her by a slightly shady friend who didn't need it anymore. She took it – lots of it - then went to bed where no-one and nothing but oblivion awaited her.

# 22.

**Lisa**

Lisa's memory was hazy as to how she'd come to be at the hospital, but she knew she was there because someone kept saying her name over and over rather than just letting her sleep, and the incessant beeping of machines had entered her consciousness and was really starting to grate on her nerves. She felt sick and desperate for a pee. She retched, flipping over just in time to vomit onto the polished floor. What on earth had happened?

'Sorry,' she mumbled, as the shadow of a nurse appeared before her. Her mouth felt dry and rank. She realised she was hooked up to IV fluids and various machinery to monitor her vital signs. 'Sorry.'

'Hi Lisa, I'm Sharon, the nurse looking after you today.' She handed Lisa a sick bag for next time she might need it. 'Don't worry, we'll get that cleaned up. You're at Dunstonborough Hospital. Do you have any idea why you're here?'

Lisa groaned. 'I took some medication,' she said, recalling the last thing she could before everything had gone all black and patchy.

'Do you know what you took and how much?'

'Cannabis. Valium. Too much. Not sure.' Lisa felt a little flutter in her tummy. 'The baby! Is my baby ok?'

'Your baby seems to be doing well, thankfully,' said Sharon. 'We'll continue to monitor though. Are you having any thoughts of harming yourself at the moment, Lisa?'

'No... I... I wasn't trying to kill myself.' But Lisa realised she hadn't exactly *not* been trying to kill herself either. When she'd taken the medication, she hadn't cared what the outcome might be either way. Without her kids, life was pointless. Anyway, they were better off without her. They deserved better. All she did was hurt them.

'You went into respiratory arrest, Lisa. You were in Resus. You had to be intubated. Some medications depress your respiratory system, and whatever you took depressed yours. Psych will be down shortly to see if you need an admission, ok? Either way, I imagine you'll be staying in at least for tonight so we can keep an eye on your baby and see to that nasty wound on your back as well. We've already cleaned out some fragments of glass - we don't want it getting infected. The hospital social worker will come down to see you soon too.'

Crap. 'But I'm fine!' said Lisa. And she'd forgotten all about the wound to her back.

Sharon raised her eyebrows. 'I'm not so sure about that, are you?'

Lisa shrugged. Nothing made sense to her anymore. Not without her kids.

Minutes later there was a knock on the door and Lisa could see her parents peering at her through the glass window opposite her bed. She hadn't seen her dad in years. He was older, greyer and frailer than she remembered. A shadow of the imposing figure they'd all spent years of their lives walking on eggshells around. She scowled and pressed her call bell, but they came in anyway.

'Get out!' she spat. 'What on earth are you playing at, Mum, bringing *him* in here?'

Tracy looked pained. 'We could've lost you, love!'

'So? If you had, whose bloody fault would it have been? Get out, Dad, I've already told you, I don't want to see you again.'

Her dad cleared his throat. 'But I'm sorry, love,' he said, his voice wispy and nothing like she recalled. 'I know what I did was wrong, and I'm sorry.'

Lisa was staggered. In all her thirty-five years, not once had he properly acknowledged what had happened or apologised for it. She'd hated all her adult years of pretence, of playing happy families with her mum and sister without anyone speaking of the elephant in the room. She'd had to stop because she just couldn't do it anymore. It had felt fake and insincere and had done her no good at all. It was easier for her sister – she couldn't remember half the shit that had happened. And now, for the very first time, her dad had *named* the elephant.

Sharon entered moments later and immediately picked up on the tension within the room. 'Everything alright?' she asked.

'They were just leaving.' Lisa glowered.

'I'll go,' said John sadly. 'I'm glad you're ok. Love you,' he whispered on his way out, so low Lisa wasn't sure she'd heard him right.

'Honestly, Lisa,' Tracy sighed when he'd gone. 'Why can't you just give him a chance?'

'No, Mum.' She shook her head, recalling all the instances she'd discussed her issues with her dad with Sophie from Happy Families and her DV worker. 'Look – I'm not trying to be difficult here. It's not that I don't agree he might have changed, but it's too late for me to get what I need for him as a parent, and that's still painful. I haven't forgotten, and what he did broke me at the time. It changed me as a person and caused me lifelong damage. While I might be able to forgive, I certainly can't forget. I mean – I still have nightmares about it even now! It's a self-preservation thing.'

'Well, said Tracy, pushing her hair behind her ears. 'Let's just hope this isn't you having the same conversation with your own kids one day, begging them to give you another chance.'

'You didn't even give your own traumatised *grandchild* another chance when she slipped up, Mum,' said Lisa, her hackles rising, 'so don't you dare stand here and have a go at me about the things that go on between me and *my* children. They're my mistakes to fix, and if I can't, who do you think I'll have to thank for it in the end? So, you can go too - you've said enough. I'm alive, as you can see. Unfortunately. So, piss off.'

Sharon was still hovering outside the door, so Lisa didn't need to ask her twice. When she'd gone, she flung herself back on her pillows and wondered if she did need a psych admission after all, because after that unexpected visit her head was in bits. Then, just when she thought things couldn't get any worse, in walked Jenny.

*

**Jenny**

'I think you can guess I probably don't have the best news,' said Jenny as she sat on a lone blue plastic chair next to Lisa's bed.

Lisa closed her eyes. She couldn't speak. A solitary tear slid out and Jenny handed her a tissue. Lisa rested her hands on the now visible mound of baby bump beneath the blankets. Did she know how lucky she was? Jenny wondered. To have not one but three children and one on the way, when some people couldn't even get one no matter how hard they tried. No matter how much love they had to offer. How had this tiny baby, who'd already been exposed to medications, alcohol, cannabis and violence still continued to grow when hers couldn't? The irony was not lost on her, and her heart still ached for the baby she'd lost. How she longed to be the one with a bump to show.

'I've spoken with my supervisor, and our recommendation for the children is unfortunately going to be for long-term out-of-home care. That means they would be looked after by someone other than a parent until they reach eighteen. We need you to start thinking about what that might look like, as we'd prefer to explore family than look at foster care as you know. Also, we're keen to avoid a plan for adoption for Winter, but we still have the issue of your sister's house being too small, and your parents' age and health. We'd probably have to look at building your sister an extension or something if she can't or won't find somewhere bigger.'

'Adoption?' Lisa gasped.

'I'm sorry,' said Jenny. 'We've been upfront with you from the start, and adoption is usually the best way we have of achieving long-term stability for very young children where there is no suitable family, or where family are unwilling or unable to help. We have a long history of concerns regarding your children, Lisa, even dating back to when the girls were little with their dad. It's time we drew a line in the sand and give them a chance at a more stable, safer future than it seems they're going to be able to get at home.'

'But...' Lisa shook her head. 'Me and Kev – we're not back together, you know? We never were! He wanted everyone to think that we were, but it was never true.'

Jenny sighed. 'What was he doing at your place, then? And not just once, according to what I've learned from my enquiries, when we'd already discussed what action you needed to take if he was ever to turn up there against the Prevention Order conditions.' She was careful not to implicate Irina.

'Look,' said Lisa. 'You don't even have kids! You're sat here judging me, yet you have no real idea how complicated these things are. My kids need a dad. I need support. It'll be bloody hard enough raising *four* kids on my own – at least one of them with additional needs and to be honest with you, I just lost confidence in my ability to do it. It's overwhelming. Kev's done everything you asked him to do. I thought maybe he really had changed...'

Not this leopard, thought Jenny, recalling the outcome of his MIP assessment. 'These are things you could have spoken to *me* about – if not me, then Sophie or your DV worker. Anyone but Kev! We're so close to the final hearing, Lisa, that you really couldn't afford to slip up now. Those kids need stability – to know who they're going to live with and that they're going to be kept safe. Based on pattern and history, I can't confidently tell the court that you have no intention of reunifying with Kevin or are any better positioned to prevent the children from being exposed to more incidents of violence. We've already had Autumn get injured in the last one, and you – pregnant – and injured in this one. The risk is simply too high. And when you leave here, Lisa, I'd strongly advise you to consider entering a refuge until the court matter is over, because I suspect this is what's triggering Kev at the moment and escalating the level of risk.'

Lisa shook her head. 'No way. I'm not going into no refuge. I'm going home. I didn't abuse anyone – *he* did! Why should I be the one to leave?'

'That's your decision,' said Jenny. 'We can only make recommendations – it's up to you what you do with them.'

'But Jenny?'

'Yes?'

Lisa was pale, her worry and distress etched into her every feature. 'Am I really going to lose my kids? I'm different now. I know it doesn't look that way because of what just happened with Kev then the fact I took the medication and ended up in here. But I really have changed. I can do it. Honestly!'

Jenny sighed. She'd held so much hope for Lisa. Could *feel* how much she loved her children. Together the Care Team had worked so hard with this family and this wasn't the outcome that either of them had hoped for. She'd advocated on behalf of Lisa at length with Sue and Brenda, but it had been no use. The evidence that Lisa could truly, sustainably care for her children and keep them safe from further harm was weighted against her. There simply wasn't enough safety. 'You'll have your day in court, Lisa, just like every parent who goes through this. Only you can convince them of that.'

Jenny hoped for the kids' sake that she would. That she could. Now more than ever she needed something positive to help keep her going in the job. Just as she was leaving Lisa's bay, Police entered to take a statement. It was terribly sad that right now Lisa was probably having one of the worst days of her life, but Jenny felt it would be even worse for those children who simply needed their mother.

*

**Autumn**

Autumn was angry. Jenny had visited and explained that she could no longer recommend she and her brother and sister return home to their mum. She said she'd revisit with her grandparents and aunt Kate the possibility of her staying with them, otherwise they'd be looking at long-term foster care. Belinda said she'd had enough of long-term foster caring after her last placement and had decided to cut back to providing only short-term care. So, either way she'd have to move house again, and would probably end up living with other strangers. Why did her mum have to let Kev come home? She wondered. Why couldn't he stay away, and worse, why couldn't she make him do it then everything would have turned out alright?

Blayze wanted nothing to do with her anymore. Starr seemed to have found a new best friend, and Autumn still missed her. She'd slipped behind at school only a couple of months out from starting her GCSEs. Nothing in her life was as it had been before, and now it never would be again. Still, at least the retribution she'd expected from Blayze and his gang had never eventuated. She'd been relieved at first, then dismayed that Blayze hadn't even bothered to see if she was ok. Keira had delighted in telling her by text that he'd already been seen kissing someone else and didn't miss her the way she missed him – her first proper boyfriend.

As she walked the lonely hallways at lunchtime, wondering if she may as well just bunk off again now she had no-one left to hang out with until she realised she had nowhere to go anyway, she became aware of some of the other kids in her year smirking at her then looking away. One group straight up pointed at her and burst into laughter. Were they laughing *at* her? She wondered. How could they be? She hardly went to school anymore – they couldn't possibly have anything to laugh at her for.

'Autumn Season, I've been looking for you.' It was Mrs O'Neil, and she gestured her inside the classroom then closed the door firmly behind them.

'What is it?' Autumn asked.

Mrs O'Neil cleared her throat. 'It seems there's a video going round. A rather *sensitive* video. Of you and Blayze Burns.'

'What?' Autumn was mortified and her cheeks burned as she tried to figure out what content the video might contain. 'But he never filmed me doing anything!'

'Then I suspect it wasn't him who filmed it...' Mrs O'Neil raised her eyebrows pointedly.

'Shit.'

'Indeed, though I'd thank you not to use such profanity in here.'

'Sorry,' Autumn mumbled.

'It's already come to the attention of Police – we take the distribution of such material *very* seriously in our school and we intend to come down as harshly as we can on whoever is responsible. I have my suspicions, do you?'

So, they had found a way to get back at her after all. No doubt Coby was behind it. Maybe even Keira Cross. If she said anything, she suspected she'd only make things worse for herself. Turned out there was worse to come anyway when the police came to visit her at the school.

'How well do you know Harry Curran?' they asked. Coby's uncle.

'I don't know him at all,' said Autumn. It was true – she'd hung out at his flat often enough with the others, but she'd never actually met him.

'Well, *he* seems to know *you* – we found images of you all over his phone and the very same video that's been circulating around your school today. When will you young people learn that it's not safe to share material like this. You never know where it'll end up, or in whose hands. We gave a talk here on it just the other week.'

It turned out the images had been found when Harry had been arrested for texting while drink-driving. Blayze and Coby had been selling him the images all along in exchange for drugs and alcohol. Drugs and alcohol she herself had partaken of. Even though they boys had gotten in trouble for it before, they hadn't stopped – the incentive was too tempting.

Autumn looked at the floor. She knew they were right. Everyone had warned her off Blayze. The idea of someone so much older than her looking at her in that way without her consent - the fact that anyone had even recorded her without her awareness in the first place - made her feel violated. She also felt stupid. Like she should have been more careful. She'd probably never find out who else's hands that material might have ended up in. What about when she got older and wanted to get a job?

Not long after that she was shipped back to the school counsellor to see if she could help her make sense of it all. She couldn't. Nothing made sense to Autumn ever since she'd been removed from her mum's care. Nothing. The best thing to do, she conceded, was to run away where nobody would ever find her.

# 23.

**Jenny**

'Hey, you,' said Fatima as Jenny took her usual seat at her desk opposite her. Gosh, she was going to miss her. Ever since she'd handed in her notice, she'd had an unmistakable glow about her.

'Hey,' said Jenny, wishing she could match Fatima's cheerful disposition.

'Did you hear about Will?' Fatima whispered conspiratorially.

'No... What happened?' She'd had a visit and had missed that morning's team meeting.

'He's gone off sick. *Long-term* sick. I texted him this morning and he told me he doesn't know if he'll bother coming back. Taken up dog walking apparently - reckons he might be able to make a business out of it. I knew those bloody assessments would tip him over the edge! That's not all – Shay's handed in her notice. Already! She's been offered a job at a not-for-profit.'

'Wow!' said Jenny as she absorbed those changes. Gosh. No Fatima and no Will. She would be all alone in the sinking ship.

'Brenda's shitting herself, obviously. They're going to have to do a bit of a recruitment drive! They're already planning a closure day so we can get rid of some cases to make way for the onslaught coming in.'

'What's the point? They'll only bounce back if they're closed prematurely anyway. You must be glad you're leaving!'

'*So* glad,' Fatima agreed. 'Sue's already started taking some of my cases off my hands. I'll be glad to get rid of Hawkins. That one's an absolute nightmare. The mum's a pathological liar - major mental health. Manipulative. Passive aggressive. Constantly in crisis. Six kids all in different placements and a new baby she's having daily supervised contact with, which as you can imagine is a major headache to organise. Baby's on a plan for adoption and the final hearing is coming up soon. Gosh, I feel sorry for whoever gets lumbered with that one. It'll be heavily contested by Mum - very stressful.'

Jenny sat at her desk, her shoulders tense. She forced herself to relax them. To breathe. But she knew that the loss of Fatima, Will and Shay could only mean one thing – another increase in workload for those who remained, and she'd probably have to resume the Barnes contact that had finally been taken off her hands by Sue as something of a peace offering.

Her phone rang. 'Hi Jenny, it's Belinda Wright, Autumn Season's Foster Carer. I'm afraid she's gone missing. I've reported it to Police, but I thought you would need to know...'

Jenny hung up the phone. She felt dizzy and sick. She couldn't catch her breath.

She switched on her computer. There was an email from Sue asking her to set aside a few minutes to catch up with her later about a new case. Hawkins. Fuck. She already had the litigious and misogynistic Cockburn on her caseload, she couldn't imagine having to deal with another parent to match his intensity and consume her working hours.

'Jenny? Jenny! Are you alright?' Fatima asked.

She couldn't breathe.

'Oh my God! Jenny! You've gone white!'

223

'I.. I'm okay...'

'You don't look okay to me!'

Jenny shook her head, gasping for air. She had to get out of there. Now. She rose from the chair and walked towards the loos as normally as she could, lest she pique the curiosity of her colleagues. When she got inside, she leaned against the locked door for support. She was practically hyperventilating. It was too hot. She loosened her shirt. There was a knock on the door.

'Jenny, are you alright?' Fatima asked. 'Do you need me to call you an ambulance?'

'No!' Jenny stiffened. Absolutely not. 'I'm fine. I'll be fine.'

'Well... Then I'm going to put the kettle on,' she said. 'I'll just be next door in the kitchen, then me and you are gonna take five, okay? And I won't take no for an answer.'

Jenny couldn't see for tears. It was though all the tension of the last few weeks and her grief had culminated in this one embarrassing outburst. She knew what she had to do. She needed to make an appointment with the Social Worker Support Service as soon as possible.

*

**Autumn**

Autumn only had five pounds left of what she'd been given by Belinda to pay for her bus fare and buy her lunch. She'd dodged the train into Dunstonborough, only narrowly avoiding the ticket inspectors, but once she'd got there, she'd realised she didn't have any idea of where she was going or what she was going to do. She didn't have a plan - she'd just needed to get away from everyone and everything. To get away from her life and all the problems in it. She'd thought she might feel better somewhere else, somewhere anonymous where she could be anyone she wanted to be, but the truth was she felt no different at all. Maybe she was just doing it wrong.

She exited the train station and found that the late afternoon sun was warm and bright. It was peak hour, and the shops were closing as workers and shoppers streamed towards the buses and train stations and the traffic was already gridlocked. She closed her denim jacket over her school blouse and tried to picture herself as one of those workers with somewhere to go. Not a girl without a mum. An ordinary life with an ordinary family. A shop assistant maybe, or a waitress.

'Got a light, love?' a man asked. He appeared to be somewhere in his late twenties or early thirties. He seemed a little edgy - he kept glancing around him as though to see who was looking at them. But no-one was. Everyone was too busy going about their own business to pay any attention to theirs.

'Sorry, I don't smoke. I vape,' said Autumn, waving her vape at him.

'Oh,' said the man. 'Didn't think you looked quite old enough to smoke.'

He was a little unkempt and a little overweight. His stubble grew in patchily and it seemed as though he needed a shave. It made him look older than he probably really was.

Autumn was affronted. 'Well, I'm eighteen, actually. I've just finished work.'

'Really?'

'Yeah!' Autumn tried to affect some of the nonchalance the girls in their group had had - girls like Keira. 'I'm a shop assistant.' She hoped that would explain her black and white uniform. She'd had no need for her jumper and her tie was in her handbag, so there was nothing about her person to identify her as a schoolgirl – not a logo in sight.

'Where are you off to?'

Autumn had no idea. 'I was er, meant to be meeting some friends after work. I think they're running late.'

The man raised his eyebrows. 'Oh. Well, do you wanna come inside and wait with me and my mates at the bar round the corner? We'll buy you a drink while you wait. Maybe they could join us?'

Autumn shrugged. She was hungry. Thirsty too. Maybe he'd get her some crisps or something. He or his mates might even know of a place she could stay. 'Okay,' she said.

'What's your name, then?'

'Shelley,' said Autumn. It sounded grown up. It also sounded ordinary, not like her real name. She didn't want anything to make her stand out.

'Hey Shelley, I'm Johnno.' He smiled, baring a mouth full of slightly yellowed teeth. 'Come with me. I'll look after ya!'

Autumn fought off the sense that maybe she shouldn't, but like Johnno said, there'd be others there with them and they'd be in a public place, so what was the worst that could happen? It certainly felt better than being by herself.

*

**Lisa**

'Missing? What do you mean, missing?' Lisa clung to her phone. She was beside herself. For a moment she wished Irina was there, but she was still too ashamed to face her. She hadn't spoken to her since the night she'd lost the kids, until in the end Irina had stopped calling round. It wasn't because she was angry at her for calling the police on her either – Irina had made it crystal clear where she'd stood in that regard - though she assumed Irina might think that was the case.

'Well,' said Jenny, her voice remote on her handsfree as she drove between appointments, 'it seems she left school sometime between lunch and last lesson. There was a bit of a carry on between Autumn and some of the other kids today apparently, and that was probably the trigger for her to take off. She usually turns up at placement to get changed and head out again but tonight she hasn't...'

Lisa tried to process this. She could feel the terror building up inside her. 'So, what's happened to her then? What's being done to find her?'

Jenny cleared her throat. 'Basically, there's a not a great deal we *can* do at this stage, unfortunately. Her phone's going straight through to voicemail, and we have no idea where she could be. Police are onto it though, Lisa. They're taking it seriously because it's not consistent with her usual pattern of behaviour. I imagine they'll start with Blayze Burns then take it from there...'

'Fuck that. I'll find her myself.'

'Lisa, I can understand you're upset and worried about Autumn, but some things are best left to the police. And you can't have unsupervised contact with her at the moment anyway, remember?'

Lisa sighed. For fuck's sake. No doubt it was those little shits that Autumn had gotten herself mixed up with. She would ring Blayze's scrawny neck! She didn't care what Jenny or any children's court thought about it - they weren't going to find her sitting on their arses.

She got up, pulled on some joggers, and knocked on Irina. Just then she needed a mum to lean on, and Irina had been as good as a mum to her, if not better. Irina took one look at her pale face and without hesitation she grabbed her phone, keys and handbag. Together they got into Irina's car, and given her knee was still in such a state, she let Lisa drive. That one gesture meant a lot to Lisa – it meant that Irina trusted her not to be affected by anything she might've taken. Irina still trusted that Lisa had what it took to get her kids back in her care, even if no-one else did.

Together they drove to the wasteland. 'You stay here,' Lisa instructed. 'There might be trouble. If you hear me scream, call the police, eh?'

'Oh, Lisa,' said Irina. 'Be careful, love. Kids these days would pull a knife on you soon as look at you. It's nothing like it was in my day where a good clip 'round the ear would've sorted them out.'

Lisa bit her lip. Only a fortnight ago she'd heard on the news about some poor man's life having been taken by a group of kids such as this for no other reason than defending himself and his family against a theft. She'd take her chances. What happened to her didn't matter - only Autumn mattered.

'Right, which one of you is Blayze Burns?' There were about ten of them hanging out under the underpass smoking vapes, their sickly-sweet fumes filling the air as they leaned casually against the wall opposite one another.

'Whose askin'?' said one of the boys indignantly. He was tall and gaunt, with dirty-blonde hair. He had something of a skater look about him that she supposed some young girls might find appealing, but Lisa thought what he needed most was a good bath. He seemed to be the ringleader. She glared at him.

'*I* am. The police will be too, if they haven't already.' Lisa refused to give into her intimidation. She was running on adrenaline, and it would carry her through.

The other kids in the group shuffled awkwardly and deferred to the older boys. '*I'm* Blayze,' said one of them. He was smaller than the other one but more solid in stature. His dark features could be quite attractive if they weren't marred by the perpetual scowl he wore. Lisa sized him up.

'Where's my daughter, Autumn Season?' she asked.

'Don't know, don't care,' said Blayze indolently, as he pulled one of the girls into his side and draped his arm about her. 'She knows she's not welcome round here. She's not one of us.'

Thank God, thought Lisa. It was the only good news she'd heard that day. She turned on her heel and returned to the car, where Irina eyed her with relief and put her phone away before they drove off to continue their search.

*

**Autumn**

Johnno draped an arm around Autumn possessively. They were in some sort of sports bar, with a bunch of screens occupying every wall as a bunch of mostly blokes sat and gawped at them over a beer. Johnno was with a couple of his mates, who barely glanced up from the screen when he introduced her to them. Thankfully, there was a packet of pork scratchings, some salt and vinegar peanuts and a bag of crisps spread out on the table, and Johnno urged her to help herself. She did so gratefully.

'What's your poison?' he asked.

'Oh, it's alright, you don't need to get me anything,' said Autumn.

He waved a hand. 'Don't worry, don't worry! My treat. Might as well make you comfortable while you wait.'

'Ok then,' she sighed. 'I'll have a beer, same as you, but just a half.'

'Do you play pool, pet?' One of the others asked. He seemed a bit younger than Johnno and was slightly more attractive.

'Yeah,' said Autumn.

'Fancy a game?'

'I suppose so,' she said. 'My friends are really late. I was meant to be staying with one of them overnight but now I'm sort of stranded...' Well, it was true. She'd only just realised her mobile phone was dead. She hadn't really thought this through. If she had, she'd have brought her charger.

The other guy smiled. 'Well, we don't usually budge from here for hours, so you can wait with us as long as you like. And if you need a place to spend the night, we might be able to help you out with that too.'

Autumn shrugged. Oh well. At least she was sorted for tonight. Johnno brought her a drink over and they started up a game of pool. They had a bit of a laugh, and Autumn found to her surprise that she was quite enjoying herself. But then she went to the toilet, and while she was there, she suddenly felt as though she was going to throw up. That was strange, she thought. She'd only had half a pint. But then she found that her limbs felt heavy, the way they did when she tried to run in her

230

dreams. It felt way too hard to stand up. She slid down to the cool tiled ground, completely aware of everything that was going on around her, but somehow completely unable to respond.

How strange, she thought. Not even the spliffs she'd shared with Blayze had made her feel like this. She wondered how she'd ever get herself up from the floor.

# 24.

**Lisa**

Lisa and Irina had been to the Dunstonborough bus and train stations, but they'd had no luck. A girl fitting Autumn's description had been seen at the train station a couple of hours earlier apparently, but she'd ran off before the inspectors could catch up with her for travelling without a ticket. That should have dismayed Lisa, but instead it energised her. If Autumn hadn't been seen at the bus station and she'd left the train station in the direction of town, then the chances were that she hadn't left Dunstonborough at all and therefore hadn't jumped on a train that could've taken her off in either direction to London, Scotland or Wales. In that case there was still hope.

They paced the high street and the shopping centre and checked every fast-food outlet, bakery and café where she might've stopped to grab a bite to eat, but there was no sign of her. The shops were closing, and it being a Friday on a humid summer's afternoon, many people who had clocked off shift were clocking straight onto a night on the town. Lisa called Starr and her parents, but it turned out they hadn't hung out together in weeks. It was just another dead end, and they'd made it obvious they didn't appreciate the call.

Irina groaned. She was starting to lag behind and her wizened face looked pained. 'Ohh,' she said. 'I should've brought my painkillers.'

'Oh, Irina, your knee!' said Lisa. 'I'm so sorry for dragging you into all of this. You must be knackered and sore. Here, why don't you stop in this café and grab a cuppa while I keep looking.'

'No, love, we can't stop. We have to find her! And besides, I'd far rather be useful than not.'

'Oh, but you *are* useful! I couldn't have covered half as much ground as I have without you. I know, why don't you hang around at the train station? There's every chance she might end up back there. There's a coffee cart and a waiting room, that way you could get yourself a drink and find somewhere comfortable to sit where you can keep an eye on the platforms.'

'Ok,' Irina conceded reluctantly. 'That does sound like a good idea.'

'And keep your phone handy.'

'I will. Good luck, love. It just doesn't bear thinking about if something bad happens to her...' Irina's eyes misted over, and Lisa shook her head. She wouldn't let anything bad happen to Autumn. Not ever.

'I'll find her, Irina. You know me - I won't stop 'til I do.

As she exited the train station back into the throng, she only hoped she was right.

'Have you seen this girl? She was last seen this afternoon at the train station. She's around five-seven, hazel eyes, pale skin, light brown hair? Wearing a Dunstonborough Sec uniform with a denim jacket?'

'No, sorry,' said the group of students standing opposite her. She'd passed them a couple of times already. They'd been sitting on the green where a lot of youth tended to congregate, and whilst it was a long shot, she thought maybe they might have seen Autumn around.

Lisa didn't know where else to try. She'd been to the local drop-in centre for teenagers, the homeless shelter, the hospital, the job centre... Everywhere she could think of. She'd asked those living rough on the streets but still nothing. It was getting dark and busy as the bars and restaurants filled up around her. Now not only was she losing hope, but she was busting for a pee. She'd tried to ignore it, but she was desperate. She glanced around to see where the nearest loo might be. The sports bar. It looked like a bit of a dump, but it would have to do.

It was one of those places where your shoes stuck to the floor, and it wasn't even ten o'clock yet, let alone midnight. It reeked of sweat and stale beer, and she couldn't wait to get out of there. It was the sort of place she imagined would be right up Kev's street. She felt self-conscious of her baby bump as she made for the Ladies and instinctively put a protective hand over it. She was just pulling her bottoms back up when she heard a commotion coming from the next loo and decided it was best not to exit her cubicle until she was sure it was safe. She could hear a man's voice yelling through the door asking if his girlfriend was in there, and a woman responded that she was, but she was shit-faced, and he laughed and said she'd always been a lightweight and he'd better get her home. It sounded as though a group of girls had helped the poor girl to the door, and then it all went quiet, so Lisa came out and washed her hands.

It was no use. She didn't want to admit defeat, but it was getting late, and she'd have to get Irina home then resume her search tomorrow. She couldn't just leave Irina in the train station at all hours at her age, and she knew she was already overdue her evening painkillers.

She passed a taxi rank. For the revellers the night was still young so it was quiet, yet she could hear a man trying to convince a taxi driver to let his girlfriend into the car, and it seemed things were starting to become quite heated between them as he refused to take no for an answer. Lisa assumed this must be the girl from the toilets and wondered what she saw in him. Then again, many might wonder – what did she see in Kev?

'Listen, mate, I've told you - I'm not taking her in here in that state, she'll wreck my car! You can report me if you want, I don't care!' The driver held firm, but the bloke was having none of it.

Lisa had passed them by a good few feet when something caused her to look back and do a double take. Though she'd only seen her from behind, something about the girl had put her in mind of Autumn – something about her cloud of light brown hair and her lace-trimmed denim jacket, but more than that, it was just her stance. It was ridiculous – all she'd thought about was Autumn all day so no wonder she was making these crazy connections. But still.

She looked behind her, and gasped. It *was* Autumn, with some bloke twice her age. Without hesitation she retraced her steps and marched towards him, her heart skipping a beat when she caught sight of Autumn's sickly pallor and wobbly gait. 'Get your filthy hands off her, right now!' she screamed, not caring whose attention she drew from those around her. 'She's only fourteen, you dirty bastard!'

The man she was with visibly paled, and his eyes darted about guiltily. 'But she said she was eighteen...' he said, as though it somehow excused everything, even though it was obvious it sounded ridiculous even to his own ears.

'And I'm bloody twenty-one again,' said Lisa. 'Do you believe *me*? You freaking *knew* she was underage. You'd have to be a total idiot not to see it - she's wearing her bloody school uniform for one! And even if she *was* eighteen, she hardly looks in any position to consent, does she? Or do you not care about that?'

Whoever he was, Lisa never got to find out because he disappeared into a crowd of people exiting the bar, and in that moment all she cared about was Autumn, who promptly threw up all over the pavement as someone else hopped into the waiting taxi. 'Autumn,' she said. 'Thank God, I found you. Autumn, are you ok? Did he hurt you?'

But Autumn said nothing. She seemed to look through Lisa and didn't respond. Then she slid down to the pavement and closed her eyes. Shit, thought Lisa, who realised she'd obviously taken something. Shit! She took out her phone and dialled 999.

*

**Autumn**

The paramedic kept asking Autumn her name, but she couldn't respond. It was so strange, she thought, as if she were trapped within her own mind. Maybe this is what being in a coma felt like? She could hear and understand everything that was happening around her, but she couldn't make her mouth up to open to speak or ger her limbs to move. She just lay there, numb. She knew they'd assume she was just another drunk, but she'd only had half a pint. It didn't matter though, because she couldn't tell them that even if she wanted to, and if she did, she knew they wouldn't believe her.

She was so relieved her mum was with her. She'd been so happy to hear her voice, to be taken care of by her once again. As Johnno had propelled her towards the taxi after an afternoon of pool and flirtatious banter, she'd definitely stopped having fun.

She'd been scared of what might happen next - had decided she would have been better off going back to Belinda's after all - but she'd been powerless to stop whatever it was he'd had in store for her. She realised now how stupid she had been and how much danger she had put herself in. It suddenly dawned on her that she must've been drugged. She'd trusted those guys, and they hadn't hesitated to take advantage of that trust. It made her feel violated and ashamed.

Autumn didn't flinch when the doctor put the cannula in and filled her vein with litres of fluids. In fact, the only time she felt physically able to stir was some time later when her sense of urgency for the loo went from mildly annoying to intolerable. In the meantime, it had been hard to tell if she was asleep or awake.

'Mum...' she croaked. 'I need a wee.'

Relief flooded her mum's face. 'Oh, love, let me get you a wheelchair or something.'

Her mum wheeled her to the loo, then they were promptly discharged. Lisa had already sent Irina off home to bed, so they had no means of getting home. They'd both assumed Autumn would get admitted overnight, but the ED was so busy they'd been keen to kick her out as soon as possible. The last thing they needed was another young drunk. Autumn knew her mum couldn't really afford a taxi, but they had no choice. She still had her five pounds on her somewhere and she resolved to give it to her mum.

She walked to the taxi rank on wobbly legs and prayed the taxi driver wouldn't turn them away. He must've taken pity on them, because against his better judgement, he let them in.

'We'd better get you back to Belinda's,' said Lisa, her face grave.

'No, Mum,' Autumn begged, cuddling into her side in the back seat of the car and closing her eyes. 'I just need to be with you tonight.'

Thankfully, Lisa acquiesced after first letting Belinda know then calling the police to tell them she'd been found. She'd had something of an argument about the whole thing with the sergeant who'd initially insisted she go back to placement, but half an hour later Autumn was curled up in bed next to her mum where she hadn't been since Summer was born. It felt nice - it felt like home.

'Mum,' she said.

'Yes, darling?'

'I'm going to be sick.'

Autumn proceeded to throw up every ten or fifteen minutes for the rest of the night until she was sure she might die – the slightest movement in the bed would immediately send her retching - but her mum was there for all of it and didn't once leave her side, topping her up with sips of water and rehydration sachets. In between, Lisa wrapped her up in her arms as though she'd never let her go again.

\*

**Lisa**

'How is she?' Irina asked as Lisa leaned over the counter to put the kettle on.

'Terrible,' said Lisa. 'Reckons the dirty bugger I found her with must've spiked her drink. She was absolutely *ill* overnight. We didn't get a wink of sleep. They should never have discharged her. I rang them this morning and told them how it's been, but they said it's already too late for them to test her urine so now we'll never know, and the prick has gotten away with it. Whatever it was he gave her, her body was having none of it, that's for sure. Doesn't bear thinking about what might've happened – heaven help the next poor girl he comes across who might not be so lucky. She's tucked up in bed finally trying to get some rest now the vomiting seems to have passed. Her face is all puffy and swollen. I'm so relieved we found her. She's had quite a scare! I really couldn't have done it without you.'

Irina face was grave as she considered the implications of what might have happened. 'What happens now then, do you have to take her back to Belinda's?'

'Huh! They wanted me to, but I'm not. The police told me to take her back, but I told them I'm keeping her here until she's better. She was in no fit state to go anywhere last night. I'll take her back to Belinda's tomorrow and face the fallout from social services on Monday.'

'I can't say I blame you,' said Irina. 'I've actually got something to tell you, though, and you probably don't want to hear it. Right now, you've got enough on your plate.'

'What?' Lisa asked, feeling her heartrate rise.

'Kev was round here last night hammering on the door looking for you. Brazen as anything. Woke up half the street! Keep your wits about you, love, especially with Autumn here. You don't want a repeat of what happened last time.'

No, she certainly did not. Bloody hell, thought Lisa, this was all she needed. 'He can hammer on the door all he likes,' she said. 'The locks were changed weeks ago, and he's been welcomed in by me for the last time.'

This time, Lisa knew with a certainty that she meant it, yet it was with some dismay that she checked her phone to find dozens of text messages from Kev telling her he would kill himself if she didn't respond. It wasn't unusual. They'd been down that road before. So far, they'd always been empty threats, but these empty threats were often a prelude to his violence.

For the second time that day, Lisa called Police and did what Jenny had wanted her to do all along – reported his contact as a breach of their Prevention Order. They said they'd do a welfare check to make sure he was alright. It was a weight off her mind that he was no longer her responsibility. She had enough responsibility already – to her children and to the new life growing inside her. They were all that mattered to her now and she was going to find a way to bring them home.

# 25.

**Autumn**

Autumn felt groggy and lethargic well into the next day. She was relieved to be home with her mum, but the prospect of having to go back to Belinda's on Sunday loomed, and in all honesty she just didn't want to go. Why couldn't she stay? Why had her mum not done all the things she'd needed to do to satisfy Jenny that they could come home for good? Now they'd never be able to go home, she'd always be separated from Summer and Winter and the new baby, and it was all her mum's fault. Didn't she want them? Didn't she love them enough? Was there something wrong with them? These questions niggled at her, and as happy as she was to be home again, all of the discontent and questions she'd been holding onto ever since Kev had first come into their lives bubbled away inside her too.

'How are you feeling, love?' Lisa asked.

'Fine,' said Autumn, who was curled up on the couch watching TV, feeling too exhausted to even bother scrolling through her phone, not that she had anyone to text anymore now that Blayze had dumped her and Starr still wasn't really speaking to her. Who could blame her? Look where her involvement with Blayze had led. She should have listened to Starr in the first place and backed right off.

'Do you think you might be able to manage something to eat?'

Autumn's stomach churned. It's been a few hours since she'd last thrown up. 'Maybe just some bread with nothing on it?'

'Ok, I'll get you some.'

'Mum?' Autumn asked.

'Yeah?'

'Nothing,' she lied. What was the point in spoiling it? They only had one more night left together.

Her mum busied herself about making her some dry toast and crackers, then she slumped onto the couch next to her. 'Gosh, I'm knackered. I think we'll both sleep well tonight. Please don't ever scare me like that again!'

They flicked on a movie. Overboard. Her mum's favourite. It was about a socialite who in the end wanted to give up her frivolous life to be a mum to four kids who weren't her own. For some reason, though they'd seen it countless times, tonight it hit a raw nerve, even if it was just make-believe.

'Mum, why couldn't you do what Jenny asked you so we could come home?' Lisa closed her eyes momentarily, as if by doing so she could make the question disappear. 'I... I tried, love. Really, I did...'

'But don't you love us? Is there something wrong with us? Do you not want us here?' Autumn could feel her eyes filling with the tears she'd fought back ever since that first night she'd been taken away from home. Something about the previous night's events with Johnno and now the fatigue, hunger and sickness all combined to make her feel vulnerable and emotional.

'No, love, you've got it all wrong.' Lisa was taken aback. 'I love you all so much, it's just that... Well, adult life is complicated. More complicated than I can explain to you right now. You'll understand better when you're grown up. I just thought you all needed a father...'

'But we were happier without him, Mum. Before he ever came along. Don't you remember? Maybe it was just *you* who needed him? Because we certainly didn't. We just needed you. We still do. And now we can't have you and it isn't fair...'

The tears fell. Autumn cried until her whole body shook. She didn't think she would ever stop. All the while, Lisa held her close.

'But... It's normal to want to love and be loved by someone, and to need help caring for three, soon to be four children. You'll understand that one day. But what Kev was offering, well, at the time I thought it was all my own fault but now I see it was never love at all, on his part at least. Or maybe it was his best attempt at love. I'm sorry, Autumn. I know I've stuffed up and I never meant to hurt the three of you. Parents make mistakes - horrible mistakes that hurt the people we love and care about most in the world. You. I wish I could fix it... I'd do anything...'

Autumn sobbed. She looked at her mum through her tears. 'But you wouldn't, Mum. That's the point.'

Lisa never got a chance to respond, because the very next moment there was a hammering at the door, and they both knew there was only one person it could be.

\*

**Lisa**

'Go out the back, over the fence and straight into Irina's!' Lisa yelled.

Autumn paled, and Lisa realised how frightened she was. 'But, Mum, I can't leave you!'

'You can!' Lisa yelled, a little more forcefully than she'd intended. 'Don't worry about me. He's not getting in here - I'm not even going to open the door. I'm calling the police. I just don't want you to have to see him like this, that's all. Go. Now!'

Autumn nodded. She grabbed her phone and was out of the back door in seconds. Rocky went wild.

Lisa picked up her own phone and noticed there were dozens of missed calls and text messages from Kev that she hadn't noticed because she'd had her phone on silent all day so as not to disturb Autumn. She dialled 999 and asked for the police, before dashing upstairs where she could keep an eye on him from her bedroom window without being seen. She could see him down there in the street and knew immediately by his gait that he was mortal drunk. His face was flushed, and she could see his belligerence in the set of his shoulders. In one hand he held a glass bottle. It didn't bode well.

'What's your emergency?' the operator asked.

'My ex is here and he's been drinking. He's violent and he's at the door - I don't want him here!'

'Sending Police. I'll stay on the line with you until they get there. Does he have a weapon?'

'No.' She heard a smash. 'Oh, wait. He does, sort of. He's just smashed a glass bottle and he's waving the neck of it in the air and yelling.'

'LISA!' he screamed. 'LISA! I know you're in there. Get down here right now you useless cow! You've got no right to lock me out of my own bloody house!'

Lisa winced. She could see that directly opposite there were people standing watching him from their windows, the same as she was doing. It would have been mortifying if it weren't for the fact she knew number that forty-two had had the police out more times than she'd had hot dinners, and number sixteen had

had her baby removed once then returned to her soon after. The son of number fifty-three had been in and out of jail...

'We have other calls coming in for your address,' said the operator.

'There's a Prevention Order,' said Lisa. 'He's not supposed to be here. Shit, he's seen me.' Kev stepped back a few paces and stared directly at her, and Lisa immediately moved away from the window.

'LISA!' he yelled. 'If you don't come out here, then I'm coming in there!'

'He's threatening me,' she said.

'LISA!' he yelled. 'I promise you, I will kill myself right now if you don't come out here. I just want to talk to you! Why do you have to be so unreasonable? Is that really too much to ask?'

'He's threatening to kill himself. He's holding a piece of broken glass up to his wrists. Oh! He's bleeding a little bit. It doesn't look deep – I'm pretty sure he's just testing me.'

'I've requested an ambulance,' said the operator. 'The police are three minutes away. Can you get out of the back of your house? Or do you have a room with a door that locks?'

'Yes,' said Lisa. 'I have a room that locks.' She couldn't risk heading back downstairs now, not when Kev was right there.

'Then go in there straight away and lock yourself in until help arrives. They're almost there.'

Lisa heard the glass panel of the front door breaking. 'Oh, no!' she cried. 'He's trying to get in!'

She ran as fast as she could to the bathroom and locked the door. She had a small shelving unit, and she blocked the door with it then crouched down with her full weight against it. She heard the front door open followed by heavy footsteps pounding up the stairs. She heard her name being called over and over, first pleading in tone, then desperate, then angry. Then Kev started punching or kicking the door, she couldn't tell which, before pushing on it with all his might.

'LISA! You're only making this worse for yourself. Get out here right now!' he screamed as he rained kicks and punches on the door causing the shelving unit to rebound against her back. She cradled her baby bump with both hands.

'Please, hurry!' she sobbed to the operator. 'Please. He'll get into the bathroom any moment! I'm pregnant...'

'The police are just around the corner,' the operator told her calmly. 'I'm right here with you. They're just pulling up into your street. I'll stay on the line.'

'LISA!' Kev yelled.

The sirens weren't on, but Lisa could see the familiar blue and red lights reflected on her ceiling as the police car flashed past her house. Moments later, more units poured into her street, followed by two ambulance crews. She heard multiple footsteps coming up the stairs. Heard Kev scream after a tussle during which he was pepper-sprayed. She heard the muffled radio voices and the slam of handcuffs and Kev being given his rights. Then she heard a sharp knock on the bathroom door.

'Lisa! It's Sergeant Fields. You can come out now - he's gone.'

Lisa moved the shelving unit, unlocked the bathroom door and sobbed. Moments later, she found herself enveloped in Irina's arms.

*

**Jenny**

*Burnout*
   *Vicarious trauma*
   *Compassion fatigue*
   *Grief and loss*
   *Stress*
   *Anxiety*
   *Depression.*

'Have you raised how you've been feeling with your manager in supervision?' The counsellor asked Jenny gently.

Huh, thought Jenny, recalling the emails she'd sent Sue asking her to ease up. 'Supervision rarely happens when it's supposed to happen - it's no-one's fault, there's just not enough hours in the day.' It was probably one of the many reasons why Shay had left.

'What about during professional debriefing?'

Jenny raised her eyebrows. No matter how distressing the case, opportunities to debrief were disappointingly rare. 'Nope! My colleague, Will, was recently assaulted by one of his clients - the only debriefing he got was a Get Well Soon card. Another had one of the teenagers on her caseload accidentally overdose - she still had to get through the rest of her week as though it was business as usual because it was more trouble than it was worth to stay off.'

The counsellor shook her head sorrowfully. 'Do you have any time-in-lieu or annual leave left that you can take?'

'Heaps. I'm not even sure they'll honour half of it.'

'Well,' she paused, 'what's the worst that can happen if you take it?'

Jenny thought about all the issues that had emerged with Season recently that had ended up with the father in jail. Of the court report she had yet to write recommending that the children be placed out of their mum's care permanently. 'If I take time off, I'm just going to have more work to do when I come back.' She could feel the anxiety envelope her again at the very thought.

'Let's say you don't take the time off then. How do you feel about that?'

Trapped, thought Jenny. Burnt out. Stressed. Exhausted.

'Jenny, the work is always going to be there. It isn't going anywhere. If a crisis happens when you're away, your team will just have to manage it the same way you all do when someone else is away. Sometimes, you do need to put yourself first. I'm sure you're familiar with the saying that you can't pour from an empty cup. In your line of work, I imagine you'll know this better than many.'

Jenny sighed. She was right. 'Alex has been saying for ages that he'd like us to get away. He's always fancied Greece. Maybe we could go there? I could make a long weekend of it, that way I wouldn't be missing so much work.'

'If that's what you feel you can manage at the moment, it's a start, but I do recommend you start making regular use of your TIL, even if it's just a day here or there to replenish yourself. Better yet, a week or two in the sun – a proper break. A real chance to give your mind and body a rest and to process your recent loss together.'

'I've been thinking of leaving altogether, actually,' said Jenny. Now she'd said it aloud, she realised that it was what she really wanted, but she couldn't leave if she had nothing to go to. Even though she'd been keeping an eye, there didn't seem to be a job out there that really appealed. And what about maternity leave? But if she stayed, the way things had gone for her and Alex, there was no guarantee of a baby at the end of it anyway. Either way, something about the changes she'd noticed in Fatima had made her realise she had to get out. Now. She wasn't coping, and it wouldn't be long before Sue and the rest of the team picked up on it too.

Then she thought of Kai Humphries. She was his *eleventh* social worker in as many years. It had taken her so long to forge a genuine connection with him. She would be letting him down, and others on her caseload like him. She thought of the idealistic youth she had been when she'd first started out in this profession, when she'd truly thought she could make a difference. She felt as though she had failed.

'There's a high turnover of staff in Child Protection for a reason,' the counsellor said as if reading her thoughts. 'This isn't a reflection of you, it's a reflection of a complex system under significant stress. Under-staffed. Under-resourced. Over-subscribed. If you choose to leave, it isn't your failure on your part. You would walk away knowing you did your very best.'

Jenny wondered what else she would do if she didn't do what she did now. It was all she knew. 'I had this idea,' she said eventually. It had actually arisen from Fatima's old case that she'd been given – Hawkins - the baby who was going up for adoption with the scary mother. It had occurred to her how little time social workers had to dedicate to life story work for children, not just those going up for adoption but those going into long-term foster care or guardianship where a family member would assume their permanent care. She recognised how important it was for children to have meaningful, in-depth life story work to refer to throughout their lives to help them truly understand the decisions that had been made on their behalf, and to support them to develop a healthier sense of identity that removal from parental care seemed to disrupt. She had the sense that done sensitively and done well, it might lead to better outcomes for those children down the track. And she would have the opportunity to work with people who actually *wanted* her around. It was the sort of work she could imagine getting a genuine sense of enjoyment and reward from - the tricky part was figuring out how to turn it into a full-time job that also paid the bills.

'Maybe some time off will give you time to explore your idea further?' the counsellor suggested.

'Maybe,' said Jenny.

When she exited the Social Work Support Program offices, instead of rushing back to the office to write up her case notes and reports like she usually would, she took out her phone and on impulse booked a bargain pair of plane tickets to Santorini, then she stopped by the supermarket and grabbed a bottle of prosecco and some nibbles. She would surprise Alex when she got home. They could worry about getting their leave approved later. Finally, she picked out a white rose from the garden section. For each baby they'd lost they always planted the same plant together, side by side. It finally felt like the right time to plant this one.

# 26.

**Lisa**

Lisa awoke that morning with a stomach full of butterflies. She hadn't felt that way since... She couldn't even recall. She'd paid extra attention to her hair and make-up until she almost didn't recognise the reflection staring back at her, it had been so long since she'd taken such care with her appearance, then dressed smartly in the prerequisite uniform of black shirt, black pants and sensible shoes. She grabbed her handbag and her satchel full of notebooks and a smart pen that Irina had bought her, then left to catch the bus to college for the first time in about twenty years.

As she entered the college, she was immediately overwhelmed by the crowds of youngsters all glued to their mobile phones, and as she navigated the long corridors in search of the training salon, she bypassed classrooms that didn't have a chalkboard or overhead projector in sight.

The training salon looked a lot like a real salon but with a classroom adjoining it, and she searched for her name badge then took a seat at the front of the class. She wasn't going to miss a thing. The immaculately groomed young teacher – at least ten years her junior - smiled at her and she smiled self-consciously back.

Minutes later a group of students fresh out of high school sauntered in and took their seats around her until the room buzzed with their constant chatter. Most seemed to have huge, spidery eyelashes, long pointed nails, even longer hair, toned tummies poking out of tiny t-shirts, and glowing bottle-tanned skin. A flustered older woman around Lisa's age bustled in last and took the last unoccupied seat beside her. Immediately, Lisa felt more at ease.

'Sorry I'm late,' she said to the teacher. 'I had to dash straight here from the school run.'

'Hi,' said Lisa, smiling with understanding.

'Hi,' said the woman, glancing at Lisa's baby bump, her face softening into a grin. 'I'm Brooke.' Somehow, Lisa had a feeling they were going to become good friends.

The day sped by, with Lisa and Brooke spending their lunch and breaktimes together in the canteen swapping stories about their kids. Brooke had come from a tough background herself, so she didn't seem to judge Lisa too much for her situation. She was a single mum determined to create a better life for herself and her children, and Lisa admired that and felt she could relate.

After college she had contact with the children, and she couldn't wait to see them and tell them all about her day. But then she remembered the children's advocate would be there again to observe them and felt worried about what she'd recommend. Jenny had already told her that the Judge would take the children's views on what they wanted to happen very seriously, and whilst all she wanted was for them to be happy, she couldn't help but hope they'd feel happiest with her.

She was just walking towards the park when her phone rang.

'Mum?' Lisa's frowned. She couldn't remember the last time her mum had called her. It had become too awkward since she'd assumed care of her children, even more so once she'd let Autumn go – her dad's idea apparently. Lisa had stopped answering, and eventually her mum had stopped calling.

'Lisa, I know you don't want to hear from me, love, but Summer told me it was your first day of college today and I... Well, I know you think I don't care but I do, and I just wanted to see how it went?'

Wow. 'Great, Mum. Thanks.' It *had* been great. They'd learned mostly about health and safety in the salon, self-presentation and rapport building with clients and put them at ease, but the teacher had hinted at all that was to come, and it sounded exciting, particularly the more hands-on subjects. They'd even had to work in pairs to do one another's hair and make-up the way they thought would look good now, then photos were taken to see how their understanding and skills progressed throughout the course. Lisa and Brooke had had a right laugh at what they'd managed to come up with.

'I just wanted to let you know that whatever happens in court, love, I was hoping that you and I can somehow find a way to keep in touch a bit more? I mean, I'll respect how you feel about it, but I thought if you wanted to, maybe we could catch up every now and again like we used to? I won't even mention your dad, not once... I know I can't change what's happened in the past, and I know I've made mistakes. In hindsight I do agree it would've been better for all of us if I'd left, but... Well, it's a bit late now, isn't it? And things are different these days. You live and learn, and the lessons are all too often painful.'

It was the closest thing to an acknowledgement of her true feelings from her mum that Lisa had ever had, and she felt completely taken aback by it.

Tracey sighed. 'I was just trying to keep us all together. A family. Trying to please everyone yet only hurting you and Kate in the process. Myself too.'

'I get it, Mum,' said Lisa, meaning it. 'Probably more now than I ever did.' Life was rarely black and white, but it was every shade of grey.

Tracey was quiet for a moment. Hesitant. 'You know, Kate would love to see you too. And the girls. They're growing up fast. Too fast.'

Lisa gave a wry smile. 'I think you're exaggerating a bit there – she might be able to tolerate me at best, but it's a start.' She knew it was what her own children needed, whatever the outcome at court – in fact, especially if the outcome at court was what she feared most - not to grow up feeling divided between the people they loved. To see the adults who cared about them managing their issues sensibly whilst prioritising them. Wasn't that what Sophie had once said - that she just needed to put the kids first? If she could do that then everything else would fall into place.

When Lisa hung up the phone, despite all that had passed over the last few months, she somehow felt lighter. She had realised you were never too old to need your mum.

*

**Autumn**

It was hot and sunny, with the slightest hint of autumn in the air, the way it always was at the start of a new school year. This was the year Autumn started her GCSEs, and it was surprisingly exciting to get her new timetable and see subjects on there that she'd chosen herself for once instead of only those that were chosen for her. It was even better to find out she'd have another two years with Mrs O'Neil and that Starr was still in her form.

Still, the mood at school was unusually sombre, and it wasn't until they were all led into a special assembly that they found out why.

It turned out that Blayze Burns, Keira Cross, Coby Curran and Neveah Martin had all been involved in a car accident in a stolen car whilst under the influence of drugs and alcohol, and Blayze had been injured most because he hadn't been wearing his seatbelt. The news made for a solemn start to the year as many dwelled on the tragic loss of Blayze's capacity to reach his full potential, whilst others wrestled with the potential real-life consequences of certain risk-taking behaviours they'd been engaging in. Everyone was quiet and subdued, but Autumn and Starr were especially so. When Autumn made eye contact with Starr across the classroom, she realised it was because they were both thinking the exact same thing.

'It could have been us,' said Starr when they found themselves side by side in the corridor on route to their next lesson. They were the first words she had spoken to Autumn in weeks.

'I was thinking the same thing.' Two of the others Blayze had been in the car with were still in hospital too, but there was no doubt that Blayze had come off worst. The accident would have a lifelong impact on his life – they said it was a wonder he hadn't been killed. The pair were quiet for a moment as the gravity of this sunk in along with the harsh reality it could have been either of them whose lives were forever changed had they continued drifting off course.

'Starr?' Autumn risked. 'I've missed you.'

Starr looked at her, then her face warmed into a smile. 'I've missed you too.'

'Did you choose art for your options?'

'I did! I've got double art next lesson.'

'Me too. Let's get there early so we can get a table together?' Autumn held her breath as she awaited her answer.

'Yeah, ok,' said Starr.

And just like that, they were inseparable again.

After school she had supervised contact, and Autumn thoroughly enjoyed the time with her mum, brother and sister - time that had become increasingly precious to her as the final court date crept closer and threatened to keep them apart for good.

The children's advocate was there, and whilst it had been hard to adjust to being in a goldfish bowl of professionals during contact, it was even harder having the advocate there because Jenny had already explained how much weight the Judge would give to her recommendation – perhaps even more weight than would be given to Jenny's or her mum's wishes. It was for this reason that she could tell her mum was on hot pins – she'd rushed there straight from college – was still in her salon uniform, and whenever she thought the advocate wasn't looking, Autumn saw her mum glancing at her uneasily as she observed them and inputted notes into her phone.

'What's *she* doing here?' Summer asked.

'She's come to watch Mum, then afterwards she's going to ask us where we want to live, remember?'

'Oh, yeah!' Summer skipped off happily to play with Winter.

Autumn and Winter were like two peas in a pod nowadays, and sometimes Autumn worried there was no room left for her in that pod. She wished things could go back to how they used to be. She would tell the advocate that.

After saying goodbye to their mum, since Autumn and her siblings were in two separate placements, on the way back the advocate stopped via a McDonald's with a play area so the support worker could occupy Winter whilst she talked to her and Summer. They managed to find a more private spot away from the other families - ordinary families who didn't need workers to accompany them on ordinary activities.

'I know Jenny has explained to you what will happen when we have to go to court – that the judge will make a decision about the safest person to care for the three of you until you grow up – so it's really important that we make sure the judge knows what you two would like to happen. I know I've asked you both before, but a lot of things have happened since then. I wanted to check-in again to make sure I'm making the right recommendation.'

'That's easy,' said Summer. 'We want to go home to Mum. Can I go play now?'

The advocate smiled. She asked a couple more questions, then Summer, who struggled to sit still at the best of times, went off to see Winter.

'What do *you* want, Autumn?'

Autumn thought about it. She remembered all the times her mum had let her down. All the times Kev had hurt or scared them – but most especially the last time. She remembered the dismay she had felt coming home from school to find her mum sleeping on the couch, and the times she'd had to care for Winter because her mum had been too out of it. Then she thought of how determined her mum was to do better. How Autumn never felt as 'at home' as she did when she was with her. She knew her mum loved her - she could feel it.

'What Summer said. I want to go home.'

The advocate smiled and tapped her notes into her phone.

'I remember you telling me that when you lived at home, you often had to look after your mum and younger siblings. How would you feel if you went home and things were like that again, only with a new baby to care for as well? And how would you feel if your stepdad came back?'

Autumn remembered the last time Kev had come home and she'd sensed the finality with which her mum had dealt with him. She couldn't know for certain, no-one could, but she felt as sure as she could possibly be that this time mum was genuinely ready to move on.

'That might happen.' Autumn sighed. 'I don't think it would - but it might. Either way though, if it were up to me and not a judge, I would still take that chance.'

*

**Jenny**

Santorini was hot, but they were lucky to have arrived just outside the school holidays when the infamous crowds had diminished but the sun and beauty hadn't. Their quaint hotel was perched on a clifftop just off the beaten track, affording them famed views of whitewashed buildings, blue-domed churches and bright, narrow streets contrasting with vibrant bougainvillea leading steeply down to meet a jewel-coloured sea. It felt a million miles away from their life in Dunstonborough as they spent their days exploring the island, lazing by the pool, and eating delicious food.

As the days went by, Jenny could feel the stress and anxiety of work slowly dissipate until she felt truly at peace for the first time in as long as she could remember. It was just what she needed, and seeing how happy Alex was, she realised it was just what their marriage needed too. It had brought them closer together than they'd been in months.

'I'm pleased you left your laptop behind.' Giselle, he'd called it. Thought he might as well name it after his favourite supermodel in the hope he might resent its presence less. 'I half expected it to accompany us. I wonder if she's lonely there at home all by herself?'

Jenny laughed. 'Giselle's company has never been a match for yours, though I did almost consider hiring a sofa bed just for her.'

Alex raised his eyebrows. 'Really?'

'Really.'

She leaned across the table towards him and pressed her lips to his, looking deeply into his clear-blue eyes, blue that was emphasised by his sun-deepened skin. Wordlessly, she took his hand and led him back to their room, where she proceeded to show him in no uncertain terms just how much she meant it. Later that evening she would tell him her news – that she was pregnant again, that her HCG levels were the highest they'd ever been, that this time it had been a struggle to hide all her pregnancy symptoms for him, and that perhaps for the very first time, she had a good feeling about what was to come.

# 27.

Jenny

**Case Plan:**
Non-reunification.

**Recommendation:**
It is the recommendation of Child Protection that Winter Season is not reunified into the primary care of either parent. There are ongoing concerns regarding his exposure to Mr Black's propensity towards aggression and violence. As discussed, he has been formally assessed by the Men's Insight Program as posing a high risk of perpetrating further Domestic Violence towards Ms Season (or subsequent intimate partners) to which the children are likely to be exposed, due to his lack of accountability for his actions, lack of meaningful engagement with the program, and his lack of commitment towards addressing the protective concerns.

During our involvement with the Season family, Mr Black has continued to produce SUDS positive for alcohol and other substances. His attendance at contact with Winter has been inconsistent, as has his level of engagement with Child Protection and with the psychologist it was recommended he engage with. His primary focus during any such encounters has been on discrediting Ms Season as opposed to maintaining his focus on the needs of his son.

Whilst a positive, reciprocal attachment has been consistently evident throughout our involvement between all three children and Ms. Season, and whilst Ms. Season has demonstrated capacity to sensitively respond to their needs and to implement positive changes with a view towards addressing the protective concerns, significant concern remains for her capacity to meaningfully sustain such changes and truly prioritise her children given the extensive history of Child Protection involvement for this family for chronic Domestic Violence and her long-term status as a victim survivor throughout her adult life in each of her intimate relationships.

The resultant trauma over a background of childhood trauma has likely compromised her protective capacity. Ms Season has at times denied, minimised or made excuses for Mr Black's use of violence and its impact upon her children, and has not consistently taken the protective action agreed upon during safety planning which has resulted in further incidences occurring. Whilst more recently, increasing insight has been demonstrated by Ms Season, this is not yet consistent.

There is a demonstrated pattern of parental separation followed by eventual reunification with subsequent relapse into further DV, alcohol, substance use, prescription medication use, mental health difficulties, environmental neglect, parentification of Autumn, and inadequate supervision of Winter; concerns which are likely to only be compounded by the additional pressures of caring for a new baby.

Given the high likelihood of these factors further compromising the children's sense of safety and stability within the family unit causing cumulative emotional, developmental as well as potential physical harm, it is respectfully recommended that a Final Care Order be granted on behalf of Autumn, Summer and Winter Season.

Sue scrolled through Jenny's court report on the screen of her monitor, 'I think you've covered the most salient points. Print it out - I'm happy to endorse it.'

Jenny hesitated. 'You don't think it reads a bit harsh on Lisa Season? I mean, she's tried her best. She really wants those kids, and they want her - you saw the advocate's report.'

The advocate had taken them all by surprise because she was recommending the return of Autumn to her mother's care, but for their maternal grandmother to retain care of the younger two children. Given Autumn was almost fifteen, had been consistently clear that she wanted to return home, and had no kinship placement options meaning she would be at the mercy of the care system (Belinda Wright was only approved as a short-term foster carer so she'd have at least one more placement move), it was assessed that on balance to keep her in the system would likely be more detrimental to her future wellbeing than taking the risk of returning her home. It was an unusual scenario, but given the complexity of the case, Jenny could appreciate how the advocate had reached her recommendation. The only trouble was, she knew Autumn would struggle without her siblings either way – and the prospects for Lisa Season's unborn still remained to be seen.

'I think if we had two or three more years, Lisa may well reach a place of meaningful, sustained change – but how long's fair to expect a child to wait for something that may never happen? I mean, anything could have happened to Winter when he was left to his own devices at only one-year-old – it's a miracle that nothing terrible *did* happen to him – imagine how much harder it'll be when Lisa has three children to care for and a newborn? Especially if she can't keep Kevin off the scene. Sounds like a recipe for disaster to me.'

As much as Jenny didn't want to admit it, she supposed Sue was probably right. She'd held a lot of hope for Lisa Season, so it was especially disappointing that things hadn't worked out. She only hoped she wouldn't be called upon to give evidence at the final hearing, because there simply weren't enough hours in the day to prepare herself for that, so it could only lead to public humiliation.

'Do you think Kevin Black is likely to contest?' she asked, biting her lip. He'd made some last-ditch effort to swing the vote in his favour by checking himself out of prison and into rehab with unexpected success, resulting in his first optimistic report.

'The MIP report is too damning, as was his most recent offence, so I very much doubt it.'

But Jenny had encountered men like him before – Mr Cockburn stood out - so Sue's words did nothing to alleviate her gnawing anxiety. She knocked off early so that she could go home to spend the evening preparing. It looked as though Giselle would be joining her and Alex for dinner once again.

*

**Lisa**

Lisa was careful to dress smartly, though barely any of her clothes fit over her straining bump anymore so she'd had to go out and buy new. She felt sick with nerves as she prepared to spend a full day in court, but her solicitor had immediately put her at ease. They'd both read Jenny's report and the advocate's report, and whilst Lisa had felt broken by Jenny's report, her solicitor had reassured her it was a great sign of confidence for a parent to reach this stage of proceedings with a recommendation for at least one of the children to be returned to her care.

Lisa was just as anxious about the prospect of seeing Kev again for the first time since he'd broken into her home, so her solicitor kindly found her an unoccupied office to sit in and wait for her case to be called.

'How long do you think I'll have to wait?' she asked.

'Oh,' the solicitor peered at the clock on the wall, 'it's impossible to say, I'm afraid. All matters are listed for ten-AM sharp, then it's a case of first-come first-served. It could be any time between now and the end of the business day.'

'Do you reckon I have time for a breath of fresh air?' The anxiety was getting to her, as was the heat and the weight of her ever-expanding bump.

'If you keep an eye on the screen so you don't miss your name being called, it should be fine.'

She stood outside the imposing old court building located in the heart of Dunstonborough's old town and wished she could be any number of the other people who sauntered past her into the throng – people who had no awareness of the significance of this day and how its stakes would shape the rest of her life and those of her three children.

'Lisa!' said a deep, familiar voice, and despite the late-summer heat her skin immediately broke out in goosebumps. She looked up and there was Kev, looking healthier and brighter than she could ever recall having seen him. He was smartly dressed in his best, and only, suit.

'Kev – you know you're not supposed to talk to me! I'll get security if you don't move away right now.' Lisa instinctively put several paces between them. Where was security when she needed them? They'd been there just a moment ago.

'Lisa, wait! Please? Hear me out. I know I don't deserve it, but please, just for a minute?'

She sighed. Kev moved closer but was careful to maintain a respectful distance.

'I'm not going to contest anything today,' he said. 'In fact, I've asked my solicitor to recommend that the children are all returned to your care. I know that's where they'll be best off.'

'What?' Lisa was thrown. She could hardly believe what she was hearing. Given their history she immediately suspected he must have a hidden agenda, presumably to be perceived as the more reasonable and gracious parent in court. She only hoped that wasn't true, because she couldn't in good faith do the same for him.

'I've been in rehab, Lisa, and I learned a lot in there. I'm not perfect by any means, and I know I'm at the very beginning of a long road, but I realise now how much I hurt you and the kids, and I've been tormented by guilt and regret ever since. I've done you all wrong and you didn't deserve it. I kept blaming each of you, but I've come to realise that the real problem was me all along.'

Lisa frowned. Was it an appeal for sympathy from her? Was he going to threaten to harm himself again? Her instinct was to dismiss everything he'd just said as manipulation, but then she'd never seen him so earnest. Usually, his manipulation would come with a barrage of text messages and abuse. She briefly glanced down at her phone, but there was nothing.

'I don't expect you to forgive me, or even to believe that I've changed, but I've resolved to spend the rest of my life proving that I have. For Winter, and for our new baby. I won't even ask for visitation rights – I'm just going to quietly disappear from your lives and leave all that up to you while I continue working on myself. The ball will always be in your court from now on - yours and our kids if they'll have me. If not, I know they'll be in safe hands. Goodbye Lisa,' he said. 'Good luck in there today.'

Then without another word he turned and entered the court building, leaving her out on the street, surrounded by people but alone with her thoughts.

*

**Autumn**

Autumn wasn't expected to attend court – it was considered too triggering or traumatic for most children - but she wanted to, and Starr's parents had even allowed her a day off school to accompany her. She knew of the advocate's recommendation that she should be returned to her mum's care without Summer and Winter, and felt she needed to be there in person to see what the outcome would be.

The courtroom was nothing like she had imagined it would be from what she'd seen on TV and in the movies. It was a far more sedate environment, containing none of the tension, drama, or passionate speeches she'd anticipated. In fact, it was hard to follow what was happening at all, as each of the solicitors spoke in a technical jargon only they understood. Whilst the court itself was in a building that dated back two hundred years, the interior had been modernised. She sat upon one of the plush green chairs and waited for the judge to make a decision that had the power to change the course of her remaining childhood – perhaps even the rest of her life.

She avoided all eye contact with Kev and focussed only on Jenny and her mum. Jenny was dressed immaculately but she looked nervous, Autumn could tell.

'Your Honour,' said her mum's solicitor. 'I would like to emphasise that my client has either met every goal identified by Child Protection at the commencement of these proceedings or is in the process of doing so. I would like to direct you to the case plan dated twentieth of April which lists each of the goals she was asked to achieve. Whilst we acknowledge there have been setbacks – setbacks which can be attributed to a trauma-response related to Ms Season's status as a chronic victim-survivor of Domestic Violence, as well as concerted efforts by Mr Black to hinder and sabotage her progress, which he has since admitted - we cannot discount that she has made considerable progress towards achieving each of these goals.

'In the most recent DV incident for instance, she acted protectively of Autumn by ensuring she was not exposed, enlisting the assistance of her identified safe person, not engaging in any interaction with Mr Black and immediately requesting the assistance of Police to report the breach of the Prevention Order. She has made a request through Housing Services for alternate accommodation which will not be disclosed to Mr Black, and she has already commenced the process of seeking a divorce. She maintains she has no intent to reunify.

'Her SUDS have been consistently negative of any alcohol or substances since her hospitalisation, she is taking steps to study towards gainful employment to enable her to provide for the children, she has maintained the home environment to an appropriate standard and has consistently attended contact with the children where reciprocal loving relationships have been observed. Feedback from her psychologist, HFSF worker, and DV support worker as you've heard has been overwhelmingly positive, and even the advocate is of the view she would be able to manage the care of both Autumn and her newborn.

'I think in this instance where we have a parent who is truly motivated towards making and sustaining positive change to address the protective concerns and prioritise the children, it would be an injustice not to seriously consider the potential reunification of all three children back to Ms Season's primary care. Mr Black himself is in support of this and as we have already heard will not be contesting matters today.'

Autumn was filled with pride when her mum's solicitor gave an account of all the positive things she had done, all the ways she had changed, and all the insights she had gained over the course of the last six months with a view towards demonstrating that she could safely manage a return of all three children to her care. It was a persuasive argument, one that she only hoped the judge would take onboard.

'Let's go outside for a moment,' whispered her solicitor, and Autumn held her breath. 'He'll need some time to make his decision, and I need to find out whether Child Protection intend to contest if he does decide upon reunification.'

The judge looked at Autumn and she looked back at him, willing with all her heart that he would understand from just that one glance how much they needed to go home to their mum. Then she rose from her chair and exited the courtroom. Minutes later they were called back in.

'I've had time to reflect upon the evidence put before me, and since I have been advised that neither Child Protection nor Mr Black will contest, I have made the decision *not* to grant the Local Authority's Application for a Final Care Order on behalf of the children today. Instead, I grant a six-month Reunification Order, effective immediately. Should no further significant concerns emerge on behalf of the children within this timeframe then Ms Season will automatically resume legal guardianship of her children, and the Local Authority will withdraw. Should any further concerns of significance emerge however, then at the end of six-month period this matter will return to court and a Final Care Order will automatically be granted on behalf of all three children.'

Autumn could hardly believe it. They were going home. They would be a family again. Across the courtroom her eyes met her mum's and at the exact same moment they both smiled widely. Outside they squeezed each other as though they would never let go, and even her nanna and Aunty Kate who had caught the tail-end of the proceedings were there, and together they spent a few minutes celebrating the outcome they had all hoped for, as Kevin Black quietly slipped out of the building and out of their lives for good.

And for once, when Autumn's mum, nanna and aunt found themselves in the same room together, there was not a shred of the usual awkwardness or tension that had been there between them before. It felt nice. It felt kind of normal. She could only take that as a good sign of things to come.

# Epilogue

**Jenny**

'It goes without saying that Fatima has been an invaluable member of our team, whose compassion, humour and spirit of generosity will be hard to match,' said Sue, as they each raised a glass towards her.

'Her compassion, generosity, *and* her masala chai and gulab jamun,' put in Will, a grin on his face. 'If not more so the masala chai and gulab jamun.'

'To Fatima,' said Jenny. 'May you find a healthy work-life balance and a lot of fulfilment in your new role. May you also get your evenings back from now on!' She grinned. 'We will miss you.'

'To Fatima!' They all clinked glasses - Fatima, Sue, Will, Jenny and their entire social work team. Even Brenda had made a rare appearance.

There was cake, then Fatima had insisted upon going dancing. Jenny was looking forward to it, even if she had had to dose herself up on antiemetics just to be there. It had been so good to give Fatima a warm send-off, and equally good to see Will again. He was looking really well. He'd handed in his notice after a few weeks of sick leave to pursue his new venture as a professional dog-walker - something the entire office had never seen coming.

'Hey, Jenny,' Fatima whispered. 'How come your champagne glass has no bubbles in it?'

Jenny flushed. She'd thought everyone would have been too preoccupied to notice.

'Aha!' said Fatima knowingly. 'You kept that one quiet, didn't you?'

'Kept what quiet?' said Will.

'This, radar ears!' said Jenny. 'But don't tell the others.'

Jenny unzipped her handbag and proudly pulled out a grainy yet unmistakable image of her healthy, developing baby.

'What on earth is that?' Will spluttered, as he struggled to make head nor tail of the image. 'Is it an alien?'

'Definitely not an alien,' Jenny smiled. 'Just a regular baby, I'm afraid.'

'Congratulations!' said Fatima. 'I'm so happy for you. I know how badly you wanted this.'

You have no idea, thought Jenny. Not really. No-one did. Just her and Alex. But she smiled anyway.

In about five months she would go on maternity leave, when she planned to apply for the grant she needed to make her dream of doing therapeutic life story work with children in long-term out-of-home care a reality. They'd only just had a team meeting that day where a restructure had been announced and they'd been told Ofsted would be coming in to inspect their service soon, so now felt as good a time as any to make the change and abandon the sinking ship as Alex would say.

Sue had already decided to use Season as a case example for the Ofsted inspectors, along with Kai Humphries, whom they'd somehow been able to get through to sixteen ready for his transfer to the Leaving Care Team. He'd just started his apprenticeship and was loving it, and Jenny hoped it would open the doors that might secure his future.

She could get through the next few months knowing there was an end in sight, especially given that towards the end, Sue would start easing up her caseload (though Alex had told her not to pin her hopes on that), even if it did mean that between now and then, Giselle would still be joining them for dinner most nights.

'Good on you,' said Will. 'That's awesome! If it doesn't work out, you could always come dog-walking with me. You could even bring your alien baby!'

'Are you still up for dancing in your condition?' Fatima asked, ignoring Will.

'Absolutely,' said Jenny. 'I thought you'd never ask!'

And she meant it. She danced until her feet hurt and laughed until her belly ached then took a taxi home in the early hours of the morning, where four pretty climbing roses framed her front door and, as always, she lightly grazed their velvet petals before kicking off her shoes and climbing into bed with Alex. She'd thought he was asleep, but he pulled her into his arms until her entire body was enveloped by his, then he cupped a hand on her expanding tummy as together they drifted off into a contented sleep, each full of thoughts of their future together as a family of three and all that might entail. A future without Giselle.

# The END

# Acknowledgements

**Dear Reader,**

Thank you for reading *Fractured*. I'd like to thank, as always, my beautiful family for their unwavering support as they continue to compete with my laptop both in my career and as a writer. I would like to thank the children, families and carers I've been privileged enough to work with throughout my years in social work, who have both challenged and enriched me and who I still think about many years later. I would also like to thank the colleagues who keep me going – you know who you are – as well as my laptop without whom my work may as well not exist (and who I'm now seriously considering naming Laptop McLaptopy Face - let me know if you have any better suggestions!). It was also a pleasure to work with Musrath Humaira Moon again on *Fractured*'s cover design.

As always, your feedback is valued, and it would be wonderful to hear from you via either my website, Facebook or Instagram. A review is one of most helpful ways to support an author and would be gratefully received.

If you require any further support regarding any of the subject matter covered in *Fractured*, please don't hesitate to reach out to someone you trust, or to contact a helpline in your local area (see below for Australia), which should be able to guide you on to other services if needed. Your GP can also be a great resource and a helpful starting point.

With very best wishes,

**Gemma Frances**

www.gemmafrances.com
@gemma_frances

# Australian Helplines:

- Lifeline (Crisis Support) – 13 11 14

- Beyond Blue (Anxiety, Depression/Mental Health) – 1300 22 46 36

- 1800 RESPECT (Family Violence) – 1800 737 732

# Ask The Author...

**What inspired *Fractured*?**

Whilst there are many books already out there drawing attention to matters such as domestic violence - my goal in writing *Fractured* was to provide an insight into the social work role. I've worked as a social worker in child protection for the past seventeen years in Australia and the UK. The role is complex and demanding, yet social workers are often misunderstood or maligned.

For example, there is a belief that social workers separate families when in my experience whilst this does occur, it's always been the last resort. Before reaching that point, parents are usually offered the opportunity to work with child protection voluntarily (without legal intervention) and referred on to support services to address factors contributing to risk such as alcohol and substance use and domestic violence, with a view to increasing safety for the child/ren.

When this is not possible or ineffective, if the risk is immediate or significant, extended family members or family friends are considered as potential carers before out-of-home-care is considered (and adoption is a last resort that rarely occurs nowadays). At this stage, reunification is often still possible. Placement out of parental care does not always need to occur via legal intervention – it can also occur via parent agreement and can be temporary in nature – for instance during a sole parents' psychiatric admission where there is a lack of suitable kinship placement options, until that parent achieves mental health stability; or to support a parent in need of respite.

I wrote *Fractured* to humanise the people behind the job title, and my hope is that it challenges negative perceptions so the true contribution of social workers can be recognised and valued.

**How realistic is Fractured?**

In just one family that comes to the attention of child protection, it is not unusual to have parents who present with their own childhood trauma histories, an ABI or cognitive difficulty, one parent with a history of perpetrating Family Violence partnered with a parent with a history of being subjected to Family Violence, complex blended families, homelessness/instability, financial stress, criminal activity, alcohol and substance use and significant mental health difficulties.

In terms of their parenting this may manifest in a myriad of ways (and over many years across multiple children) – for instance in environmental neglect, medical neglect, inadequate supervision, insufficient access to food and clothing, school absenteeism, lack of suitable housing/overcrowding and instability, inappropriate discipline, inadequate supervision, and exposure of the children to Family Violence, criminal activity, and alcohol and substance use. These parents often struggle to attend to their children's emotional, physical and other care needs.

For the children this may lead to development delays, behavioural difficulties, educational delays and place them at risk of significant emotional and physical harm and neglect. If there is a chronic pattern of exposure occurring, the harm is cumulative and can lead a child to later present with risk-taking behaviours and to repeat cyclical/intergenerational patterns of behaviour, seriously hampering their ability to reach their potential and maintain fulfilling relationships.

Though simplified, in *Fractured,* which is based on my experiences in child protection both in Australia and the UK, the parameters Jenny works within are fairly accurate – down to the unmanageable caseloads and burnout she experiences - which is why staff retention and unallocated cases remain significant challenges within child protection. The job can be all-consuming, and it takes a special kind of person to manage that and give it their all whilst also juggling the demands of their own life. In my experience, the cases referred to child protection are increasingly complex – and now often involve an increasing prevalence of children with additional needs and children who are vulnerable to sexual harm and exploitation via their peers and wider community - and though sanitised and with a relatively positive outcome, Lisa and Autumn Season's stories reflect this.


**Can you share your writing process?**

Anyone who has read my previous books would know that *Fractured* was a sidestep into a different genre for me. Initially it was uncomfortable, because I read and write for escapism and this was too close to my day job. However, once I got started, the entire novel was written within 3.5 months – a personal record. I hadn't realised how much I *needed* to write this novel. It was very cathartic. I aimed to convey just how complex, pressured and overwhelming the work can be and I hope I've done that justice. I also wanted to portray a hopeful narrative that aligns with my other books. Most importantly, I aimed to be sensitive to the perspectives of all parties – the social worker, the mother, the child, and the perpetrator. Life is complicated, no-one is perfect, and we all make mistakes – it's what we choose to do about it that matters.

**Why do you think there is a negative public perception of child protection social workers?**

I think it stems from a lack of understanding. When things go wrong, which is inevitable in an over-stretched and under-resourced system, it's social workers who are often scapegoated, and we're just people with good intentions doing the best we can with the resources we have available. Our job isn't black and white, and we don't always get it right - we operate within shades of grey, where the answer isn't always obvious and we have to make decisions based on our best risk assessment of the information we have available at the time.

Robust and fluid risk assessment is crucial, as is the gathering of credible sources of evidence. Significant decisions are not made in isolation – the social worker and their line of management in collaboration with the child and family, professionals and services involved with the family, and the legal representatives for all parties contribute their views and are each integral to the decision-making process affecting a child. If we make the wrong choice, we feel it acutely and we learn from it.

In an ideal world, protecting children would be a shared responsibility that starts at home and expands outwards into the community surrounding that child. My hope is that we can move away from a scapegoating culture and demonstrate compassion as we work out how we can best work together to do better for the children whose safety depends on us.

**What advice would you give an aspiring social worker?**

Social work can be an incredibly rewarding and humbling career, but it's important to go into it with your eyes open and take very good care of yourself. Protect your time and regularly (daily!) do the things that are meaningful to you – whether it's spending time with family and friends, hitting the gym, reading, movies, walking, art... Whether you're a social worker or in management, contribute to the morale of the team – that's essential to play your part in staff retention and wellness. And wherever possible, carve a boundary between work and home and maintain it.

Join the union, insist upon regular supervision, and if you need to, make use of the support systems your workplace has in place. If you aren't deriving sufficient sense of reward either from your work or from the workplace culture to sustain you in the role (and especially if both areas are lacking) – you may need to consider moving into a role that fulfills one or both areas. The good thing about social work is that it's broad and you can move around until you find your best fit – whether that's in statutory services, the voluntary sector, or overseas.

**What message do you hope readers will take away from *Fractured*?**

I hope readers will feel compassion and empathy towards all involved in the child protection system – from children to their parents, carers, adoptive parents, and the many professionals and services doing their very best to make a meaningful difference to the lives of those they work with. That beneath it all, where systems fail, our good intentions are recognised.

# Book Club Questions

- Did you empathise with the Season family's social worker, Jenny Hurst? Why?

- Did you empathise with the children's mother, Lisa Season? Why?

- Did you empathise with the children's stepfather, Kevin Black? Why?

- What factors could have contributed to Lisa Season's parenting challenges?

- What factors could have contributed to Kevin Black's aggression?

- How did Autumn Season's experiences impact her emotionally and influence her behaviours?

- Could you work as a social worker in child protection? Why?

- If you were allocated the Season case, what final recommendation would you make to the court and why?

- What changes could be made to better support families in need?

- Looking 10 years ahead, what outcomes do you foresee for Jenny, Lisa and Autumn?

- After reading *Fractured*, have your original perceptions of social workers and families managed by child protection altered? If so, how?

# Also by Gemma Frances

**The Melbourne Community Cafe**
Meet Me at The Melbourne

**Worthington Manor**
The Debutante

**Standalone**
Fractured

Watch for more at www.gemmafrances.com.

## About the Author

Gemma Frances is a married mum from Newcastle upon Tyne, UK currently living in Melbourne, Australia. She's a writer by day, and a social worker with children and families by night. Her childhood dream of travelling the world as cabin crew was never quite realised, as her interview with a major airline was cancelled during the Global Financial Crisis, and she was left with an approved career break but nothing to do (which is probably for the best, as she now has a fear of flying!). Armed with a round-the-world flight and a suitcase (never a backpack), she travelled to Australia on a gap year, fell in love with her husband, and the rest is history.

Gemma's is the author of Meet Me At the Melbourne and The Debutante. *Meet Me At The Melbourne*, her debut novel, won Dick and Angel Strawbridge of the TV show Escape to the

Chateau's Literature Competition in 2020 and was published through The Chateau Publishing Limited in 2021.

Read more at www.gemmafrances.com.